Francis James Child

English and Scottish Ballads

Vol. II.

Francis James Child

English and Scottish Ballads
Vol. II.

ISBN/EAN: 9783744784382

Printed in Europe, USA, Canada, Australia, Japan

Cover: Foto ©Andreas Hilbeck / pixelio.de

More available books at **www.hansebooks.com**

ENGLISH AND SCOTTISH

BALLADS.

EDITED BY

FRANCIS JAMES CHILD.

VOL. II.

BOSTON:

JAMES R. OSGOOD AND COMPANY,

LATE TICKNOR & FIELDS, AND FIELDS, OSGOOD, & CO.

1877.

UNIVERSITY PRESS:
WELCH, BIGELOW, AND COMPANY,
CAMBRIDGE.

CONTENTS OF VOLUME SECOND.

BOOK II.

iv CONTENTS.

BOOK III.

APPENDIX.

BOOK II.

GLASGERION.

THE two following ballads have the same subject, and perhaps had a common original. The " Briton GLASKYRION " is honourably mentioned as a harper by Chaucer, in company with Chiron, Orion, and Orpheus, (*House of Fame*, B. iii. v. 118,) and with the last he is also associated, as Mr. Finlay has pointed out, by Bishop Douglas, in the *Palice of Honour.* " The Scottish writers," says Jamieson, " adapting the name to their own meridian, call him GLENKINDY, GLENSKEENIE, &c."

Glasgerion is reprinted from Percy's *Reliques*, iii. 83.

GLASGERION was a kings owne sonne,
    And a harper he was goode;
He harped in the kings chambere,
    Where cuppe and caudle stoode,

And soe did hee in the queens chambere,
   Till ladies waxed wood,

And then bespake the kinges daughter,
   And these wordes thus shee sayd :—

" Strike on, strike on, Glasgerion,
   Of thy striking doe not blinne ;
Theres never a stroke comes oer thy harpe,
   But it glads my hart withinne."

" Faire might him fall, [1] ladye," quoth hee,
   " Who taught you nowe to speake !
I have loved you, ladye, seven longe yeere,
   My harte I neere durst breake."

" But come to my bower, my Glasgerion,
   When all men are att rest :
As I am a ladie true of my promise,
   Thou shalt bee a welcome guest."

Home then came Glasgerion,
   A glad man, lord ! was hee :
" And, come thou hither, Jacke my boy,
   Come hither unto mee.

" For the kinges daughter of Normandye
   Hath granted mee my boone ;
And att her chambere must I bee
   Beffore the cocke have crowen."

---

1 him fall

"O master, master," then quoth hee,
  "Lay your head downe on this stone;
For I will waken you, master deere,
  Afore it be time to gone."

But up then rose that lither ladd,
  And hose and shoone did on;
A coller he cast upon his necke,
  Hee seemed a gentleman.

And when he came to the ladyes chambei,
  He thrild upon a pinn:
The lady was true of her promise,
  And rose and lett him inn.

He did not take the lady gaye
  To boulster nor to bed:
[Nor thoughe hee had his wicked wille,
  A single word he sed.]

He did not kisse that ladyes mouthe,
  Nor when he came, nor yode:
And sore that ladye did mistrust,
  He was of some churls bloud.

But home then came that lither ladd,
  And did off his hose and shoone;
And cast the coller from off his necke:
  He was but a churlès sonne.

"Awake, awake, my deere master,
  The cock hath well-nigh crowen ;
Awake, awake, my master deere,
  I hold it time to be gone.

"For I have saddled your horsse, master,
  Well bridled I have your steede,
And I have served you a good breakfast,
  For thereof ye have need."

Up then rose good Glasgerion,
  And did on hose and shoone,
And cast a coller about his necke :
  For he was a kinge his sonne.

And when he came to the ladyes chambere,
  He thrilled upon the pinne ;
The ladye was more than true of promise,
  And rose and let him inn.

"O whether have you left with me
  Your bracelet or your glove?
Or are you returned back againe
  To know more of my love?"

Glasgerion swore a full great othe,
  By oake, and ashe, and thorne ;
"Ladye, I was never in your chambere,
  Sith the time that I was borne."

" O then it was your lither [1] foot-page,
    He hath beguiled mee : "
Then shee pulled forth a little pen-kniffe,
    That hanged by her knee.

Sayes, " there shall never noe churlès blood
    Within my bodye spring :
No churlès blood shall e'er defile
    The daughter of a kinge."

Home then went Glasgerion,
    And woe, good lord! was hee .
Sayes, " come thou hither, Jacke my boy,
    Come hither unto mee.

" If I had killed a man to-night,
    Jack, I would tell it thee :
But if I have not killed a man to-night,
    Jacke, thou hast killed three."

And he puld out his bright browne sword,
    And dryed it on his sleeve,
And he smote off that lither ladds head,
    Who did his ladye grieve.

He sett the swords poynt till his brest,
    The pummil untill a stone :
Throw the falsenesse of that lither ladd,
    These three lives werne all gone.

---

1 MS. litle.

GLENKINDIE.

From Jamieson's *Popular Ballads and Songs*, i. 91. The copy in the *Thistle of Scotland*, p. 31, is the same.

GLENKINDIE was ance a harper gude,
　　He harped to the king;
And Glenkindie was ance the best harper
　　That ever harp'd on a string.

He'd harpit[1] a fish out o' saut water,
　　Or water out o' a stane;
Or milk out o' a maiden's breast,
　　That bairn had never nane.

He's taen his harp intil his hand,
　　He harpit and he sang;
And ay as he harpit to the king,
　　To haud him unthought lang.

[1] These feats are all but equalled by the musician in the Swedish and Danish *Harpans Kraft*.

"He harped the bark from every tree,
　　And he harped the young from folk and from fee.

"He harped the hind from the wild-wood home,
　　He harped the bairn from its mother's womb."
　　　　　　　　　　　　　　ARWIDSSON, No. 149.

"Villemand takes his harp in his hand,
　　He goes down by the water to stand.

"He struck the harp with his hand,
　　And the fish leapt out upon the strand."
　　　　　　　　　　　　　　GRUNDTVIG, No. 40.

" I'll gie you a robe, Glenkindie,
    A robe o' the royal pa',
Gin ye will harp i' the winter's night
    Afore my nobles a'."

And the king but and his nobles a'
    Sat birling at the wine ;
And he wad hae but his ae dochter,
    To wait on them at dine. [1]

He's taen his harp intill his hand,
    He's harpit them a' asleep,
Except it was the young countess,
    That love did waukin keep.

And first he has harpit a grave tune,
    And syne he has harpit a gay ;

[1] This stanza is found in the opening of *Brown Robin*, which commences thus : —

> " The king but and his nobles a'
>   Sat birling at the wine, [*bis*]
> He would hae nane but his ae daughter
>   To wait on them at dine.

> " She served them but, she served them ben,
>   Intill a gown o' green ;
> But her e'e was ay on Brown Robin,
>   That stood low under the rain," &c.   **J.**

And mony a sich atween hands
   I wat the lady gae. [1]

Says, "Whan day is dawen, and cocks hae
     crawen,
   And wappit their wings sae wide,
It's ye may come to my bower door,
   And streek you by my side.

But look that ye tell na Gib your man,
   For naething that ye dee;
For, an ye tell him, Gib your man,
   He'll beguile baith you and me."

He's taen his harp intill his hand;
   He harpit and he sang;
And he is hame to Gib his man,
   As fast as he could gang.

" O mith I tell you, Gib, my man,
   Gin I a man had slain?"
" O that ye micht, my gude master,
   Altho' ye had slain ten."

---

[1] The following stanza occurs in one of the editor's copies
of *The Gay Gosshawk* : —

    " O first he sang a merry song,
      And then he sang a grave;
    And then he pecked his feathers gray,
      To her the letter gave."   J.

" Then tak ye tent now, Gib, my man,
    My bidden for to dee ;
And, but an ye wauken me in time,
    Ye sall be hangit hie.

" Whan day has dawen, and cocks hae crawen,
    And wappit their wings sae wide,
I'm bidden gang till yon lady's bower,
    And streek me by her side."

" Gae hame to your bed, my good master ;
    Ye've waukit, I fear, o'er lang ;
For I'll wauken you in as good time,
    As ony cock i' the land."

He's taen his harp intill his hand,
    He harpit and he sang,
Until he harpit his master asleep,
    Syne fast awa did gang.

And he is till that lady's bower,
    As fast as he could rin ;
When he cam till that lady's bower,
    He chappit at the chin.[1].

" O wha is this," says that lady,
    " That opens nae and comes in ? "
" It's I, Glenkindie, your ain true love,
    O open and lat me in ! "

---

[1] at the chin.   Sic.

She kent he was nae gentle knicht
  That she had latten in ;
For neither whan he gaed nor cam,
  Kist he her cheek or chin.

He neither kist her whan he cam,
  Nor clappit her when he gaed;
And in and at her bower window,
  The moon shone like the gleed.

" O, ragged is your hose, Glenkindie,
  And riven is your sheen,
And reavel'd is your yellow hair
  That I saw late yestreen."

" The stockings they are Gib my man's,
  They came first to my hand;
And this is Gib my man's shoon;
  At my bed feet they stand.
I've reavell'd a' my yellow hair
  Coming against the wind."

He's taen the harp intill his hand,
  He harpit and he sang,
Until he cam to his master,
  As fast as he could gang.

" Won up, won up, my good master;
  I fear ye sleep o'er lang ;

There's nae a cock in a' the land
 But has wappit his wings and crawn."

Glenkindie's tane his harp in hand,
 He harpit and he sang,
And he has reach'd the lady's bower,
 Afore that e'er he blan.

When he cam to the lady's bower,
 He chappit at the chin ;
" O, wha is that at my bower door,
 That opens na and comes in ? "
" It's I, Glenkindie, your ain true love,
 And in I canna win."

* * * * *

" Forbid it, forbid it," says that lady,
 " That ever sic shame betide ;
That I should first be a wild loon's lass,
 And than a young knight's bride."

There was nae pity for that lady,
 For she lay cald and dead ;
But a' was for him, Glenkindie,
 In bower he must go mad.

He'd harpit a fish out o' saut water ;
 The water out o' a stane ;

The milk out o' a maiden's breast,
　　That bairn had never nane.

He's taen his harp intill his hand;
　　Sae sweetly as it rang,
And wae and weary was to hear
　　Glenkindie's dowie sang. [1]

But cald and dead was that lady,
　　Nor heeds for a' his maen;
An he wad harpit till domisday,
　　She'll never speak again.

He's taen his harp intill his hand;
　　He harpit and he sang;
And he is hame to Gib his man
　　As fast as he could gang.

" Come forth, come forth, now, Gib, my man,
　　Till I pay you your fee;
Come forth, come forth, now, Gib, my man;
　　Weel payit sall ye be!"

And he has taen him, Gib, his man,
　　And he has hang'd him hie;
And he's hangit him o'er his ain yate,
　　As high as high could be.

---

[1] This stanza has been altered, to introduce a little variety, and prevent the monotonous tiresomeness of repeti-
tion. J.

THE OLD BALLAD OF LITTLE MUSGRAVE
AND THE LADY BARNARD.

THE popularity of this ancient ballad is evinced by its being frequently quoted in old plays. In Beaumont and Fletcher's *Knight of the Burning Pestle*, (produced in 1611,) the fourteenth stanza is cited, thus:

" And some they whistled and some they sung,
Hey, down, down !
And some did loudly say,
Ever as the lord Barnet's horn blew,
Away, Musgrave, away."

Act V. Scene 3.

The oldest known copy of this piece is found in *Wit Restor'd*, (1658,) p. 174, and from the reprint of that publication we have taken it, (p. 293.) Dryden seems to have adopted it from the same source into his *Miscellanies*, and Ritson has inserted Dryden's version in *Ancient Songs and Ballads*, ii. 116. Percy's copy (*Reliques*, iii. 106,) was inferior to the one here used, and was besides somewhat altered by the editor.

A Scottish version, furnished by Jamieson, is given in the Appendix to this volume, and another, extending to forty-eight stanzas, in *Scottish Traditional Versions of Ancient Ballads*, Percy Society, vol. xvii. p. 21.

Similar incidents, with a verbal coincidence in one stanza, occur in the ballad immediately succeeding the present.

As it fell one holy-day, *hay downe*,
　　As manybe in the yeare,
When young men and maids together did goe,
　　Their mattins and masse to heare,

Little Musgrave came to the church dore,
　　The preist was at private masse ;
But he had more minde of the faire women,
　　Then he had of our ladys grace. [1]

The one of them was clad in green,
　　Another was clad in pall [2];
And then came in my lord Barnards [3] wife,
　　The fairest amonst them all.

She cast an eye on little Musgrave,
　　As bright as the summer sun,
And then bethought this little Musgrave,
　　" This ladys heart have I woonn."

[1] lady.　　　　[2] pale.　　　　[3] Bernards.

Quoth she, " I have loved thee, little Musgrave,
   Full long and many a day : "
" So have I loved you, fair lady,
   Yet never word durst I say."

" I have a bower at Buckelsfordbery,
   Full daintyly it is deight[1] ;
If thou wilt wend[2] thither, thou little Musgrave,
   Thou's lig in mine armes all night."

Quoth he, " I thank yee, faire lady,
   This kindnes thou showest to me ;
But whether it be to my weal or woe,
   This night I will lig with thee."

All that heard a little tinny page,[3]
   By his ladyes coach as he ran :
[Quoth he,] " allthough I am my ladyes foot-
     page,
   Yet I am lord Barnards man.

" My lord Barnard shall knowe of this,
   Whether I sink[4] or swim : "
And ever where the bridges were broake,
   He laid him downe to swimme.

" Asleepe, awake[5] ! thou lord Barnard,
   As thou art a man of life ;

---

1 geight   2 wed.   3 With that he heard: tyne.
        4 sinn.   5 or wake.

For little Musgrave is at Bucklesfordbery,
    Abed with thy own wedded wife."

" If this be true, thou little tinny page,
    This thing thou tellest to mee,
Then all the land in Bucklesfordbery
    I freely will give to thee.

" But if it be a ly, thou little tinny page,
    This thing thou tellest to me,
On the hyest tree in Bucklesfordbery
    There hanged shalt thou be."

He called up his merry men all : —
    " Come saddle me my steed;
This night must I to Buckellsfordbery,
    For I never had greater need."

And some of them whistl'd, and some of them
        sung,
    And some these words did say,
Ever[1] when my lord Barnards horn blew,
    " Away, Musgrave, away ! "

" Methinks I hear the thresel-cock,
    Methinks I hear the jaye ;
Methinks I hear my Lord Barnard,—
    And I would I were away."

[1] And ever.

" Lye still, lye still, thou little Musgrave,
   And huggell me from the cold ;
Tis nothing but a shephards boy,
   A driving his sheep to the fold.

" Is not thy hawke upon a perch ?
   Thy steed eats oats and hay,
And thou [a] fair lady in thine armes,—
   And wouldst thou bee away ? "

With that my lord Barnard came to the dore,
   And lit a stone upon ;
He plucked out three silver keys,
   And he open'd the dores each one.

He lifted up the coverlett,
   He lifted up the sheet ;
" How now, how now, thou little Musgrave,
   Doest thou find my lady sweet ? "

" I find her sweet," quoth little Musgrave,
   " The more 'tis to my paine ;
I would gladly give three hundred pounds
   That I were on yonder plaine."

" Arise, arise, thou littell Musgrave,
   And put thy clothés on ;
It shal ne'er be said in my country,
   I have killed a naked man.

"I have two swords in one scabberd,
    Full deere they cost my purse;
And thou shalt have the best of them,
    And I will have the worse."

The first stroke that little Musgrave stroke,
    He hurt Lord Barnard sore;
The next stroke that Lord Barnard stroke,
    Little Musgrave ne're struck more.

With that bespake this faire lady,
    In bed whereas she lay;
"Although thou'rt dead, thou little Musgrave,
    Yet I for thee will pray;

"And wish well to thy soule will I,
    So long as I have life;
So will I not for thee, Barnard,
    Although I am thy wedded wife."

He cut her paps from off her brest,
    (Great pity it was to see,)
That some drops of this ladies heart's blood
    Ran trickling downe her knee.

"Woe worth you, woe worth [you], my mery
        men all,
    You were ne're borne for my good;
Why did you not offer to stay my hand,
    When ye saw [1] me wax so wood!

1 see.

" For I have slaine the bravest sir knight
   That ever rode on steed ;
So have I done the fairest lady
   That ever did womans deed.

" A grave, a grave," Lord Barnard cryd,
   To put these lovers in ;
But lay my lady on [the] upper hand,
   For she came of the better kin."

LORD RANDAL (A).

From Jamieson's *Popular Ballads and Songs*, i. 162.

" THE story of this ballad very much resembles that
of *Little Musgrave and Lord Barnard*. The common
title is, *The Bonny Birdy*. The first stanza is sung
thus :—

> 'There was a knight, on a summer's night,
>   Was riding o'er the lee, *diddle* ;
> And there he saw a bonny birdy
>   Was singing on a tree, *diddle* :
> O wow for day, *diddle* !
>   And dear gin it were day !
> Gin it were day, and I were away,
>   For I ha'ena lang time to stay.'

In the text, the burden of *diddle* has been omitted;
and the name of Lord Randal introduced, for the sake
of distinction, and to prevent the ambiguity arising
from 'the knight,' which is equally applicable to both."
    The lines supplied by Jamieson have been omitted.
    Allan Cunningham's "improved" version of the
Bonny Birdy may be seen in his *Songs of Scotland*, ii.
130.

Lord Randal wight, on a summer's night,
    Was riding o'er the lee,
And there he saw a bonny birdie
    Was singin' on a tree :

" O wow for day!
    And dear gin it were day !
Gin it were day, and I were away,
    For I ha'ena lang time to stay !

" Mak haste, mak haste, ye wicht baron ;
    What keeps ye here sae late ?
Gin ye kent what was doing at hame,
    I trow ye wad look blate.

" And O wow for day!
    And dear gin it were day .
Gin it were day, and ye were away ;
    For ye ha'ena lang time to stay ! "

" O what needs I toil day and night,
    My fair body to spill,
When I ha'e knichts at my command,
    And ladies at my will ? "

" O weel is he, ye wight baron,
    Has the blear drawn o'er his e'e ;
But your lady has a knight in her arms twa,
    That she lo'es far better nor thee.

" And O wow for day !
   And dear gin it were day !
Gin it were day, and ye were away ,
   For ye ha'ena lang time to stay ! "

" Ye lie, ye lie, ye bonny birdie ;
   How you lie upon my sweet ;
I will tak out my bonny bow,
   And in troth I will you sheet."

" But afore ye ha'e your bow weel bent,
   And a' your arrows yare,
I will flee till anither tree,
   Whare I can better fare.

" And O wow for day
   And dear gin it were day !
Gin it were day, and I were away ;
   For I ha'ena lang time to stay ! "

" O whare was ye gotten, and where was ye
     clecked,
   My bonny birdie, tell me ? "
" O, I was clecked in good green wood,
   Intill a holly tree ;
A baron sae bald my nest herried,
   And ga'e me to his ladie.

" Wi' good white bread, and farrow-cow milk,
   He bade her feed me aft ;

And ga'e her a little wee summer-dale wandie,
   To ding me sindle and saft.

" Wi' good white bread, and farrow-cow milk,
   I wat she fed me nought ;
But wi' a little wee summer-dale wandie,
   She dang me sair and oft :—
Gin she had done as ye her bade,
   I wadna tell how she has wrought.

" And O wow for day !
   And dear gin it were day !
Gin it were day, and ye were away ;
   For ye ha'ena lang time to stay."

Lord Randal rade, and the birdie flew,
   The live-lang summer's night,
Till he cam till his lady's bower-door,
   Then even down he did light.
The birdie sat on the crap o' a tree,
   And I wat it sang fu' dight :

" O wow for day !
   And dear gin it were day !
Gin it were day, and I were away ;
   For I ha'ena lang time to stay !"

*   *   *   *   *   *   *

"O wow for day!
    And dear gin it were day!
Gin it were day, and ye were away;
    For ye ha'ena lang time to stay!"

"Now Christ assoile me o' my sin,"
    The fause knight he could say;
"It's nae for nought that the hawk whistles[1];
    And I wish that I were away!

"And O wow for day!
    And dear gin it were day!
Gin it were day, and I were away;
    For I ha'ena lang time to stay!"

"What needs ye lang for day,
    And wish that ye were away?
Is na your hounds in my cellar
    Eating white meal and gray?"

"Yet, O wow for day!
    And dear gin it were day!
Gin it were day, and I were away,
    For I ha'ena lang time to stay!"

"Is na your horse in my stable,
    Eating good corn and hay?

---

[1] This is a proverbial saying in Scotland.   **J.**

Is na your hawk on my perch tree,
  Just perching for his prey ?
And isna yoursel in my arms twa ;
  Then how can ye lang for day ?"

" Yet, O wow for day !
  And dear gin it were day !
Gin it were day, and I were away,
  For I ha'ena lang time to stay.

" Yet, O wow for day !
  And dear gin it were day !
For he that's in bed wi' anither man's **wife,**
  Has never lang time to stay."

*   *   *   *   *   *   *

Then out Lord Randal drew his brand,
  And straiked it o'er a strae ;
And through and through the fause knight's
    waste
  He gar'd cald iron gae ;
And I hope ilk ane sall sae be serv'd,
  That treats an honest man sae !

GIL MORRICE.

" OF the many ancient ballads which have been preserved by tradition among the peasantry of Scotland, none has excited more interest in the world of letters than the beautiful and pathetic tale of *Gil Morice*; and this, no less on account of its own intrinsic merits as a piece of exquisite poetry, than of its having furnished the plot of the justly celebrated tragedy of *Douglas*. It has likewise supplied Mr. Langhorne with the principal materials from which he has woven the fabric of his sweet, though prolix poem of *Owen of Carron*. Perhaps the list could be easily increased of those who have drawn their inspiration from this affecting strain of Olden Minstrelsy.

" If any reliance is to be placed on the traditions of that part of the country where the scene of the ballad is laid, we will be enforced to believe that it is founded on facts which occurred at some remote period of Scottish History. The 'grene wode' of the ballad was the ancient forest of Dundaff, in Stirlingshire, and Lord Barnard's Castle is said to have occupied a precipitous cliff, overhanging the water of Carron, on the lands of Halbertshire. A small burn, which joins the Carron

about five miles above these lands, is named the Earls-
burn, and the hill near the source of that stream is
called the Earlshill, both deriving their appellations,
according to the unvarying traditions of the country,
from the unfortunate Erle's son who is the hero of the
ballad. He, also, according to the same respectable
authority, was 'beautiful exceedingly,' and especially
remarkable for the extreme length and loveliness of
his yellow hair, which shrouded him as it were a gold-
en mist. To these floating traditions we are, probably,
indebted for the attempts which have been made to
improve and embellish the ballad, by the introduction
of various new stanzas since its first appearance in a
printed form.

" In Percy's *Reliques*, it is mentioned that it had run
through two editions in Scotland, the second of which
appeared at Glasgow in 1755, 8vo.; and that to both
there was prefixed an advertisement, setting forth that
the preservation of the poem was owing ' to a lady, who
favoured the printers with a copy, as it was carefully collected from the mouths of old women and nurses,' and
requesting that ' any reader, who could render it more
correct or complete, would oblige the public with such
'improvements.' This was holding out too tempting a
bait not to be greedily snapped at by some of those ' Ingenious Hands' who have corrupted the purity of legen-
dary song in Scotland by manifest forgeries and gross im-
positions. Accordingly, sixteen additional verses soon
appeared in manuscript, which the Editor of the *Reliques* has inserted in their proper places, though he
rightly views them in no better light than that of an
ingenious interpolation. Indeed, the whole ballad of
Gil Morice, as the writer of the present notice has been
politely informed by the learned and elegant Editor of

the *Border Minstrelsy*, underwent a total revisal about
the period when the tragedy of *Douglas* was in the ze-
nith of its popularity, and this improved copy, it seems,
embraced the ingenious interpolation above referred
to. Independent altogether of this positive informa-
tion, any one, familiar with the state in which traditionary poetry has been transmitted to the present
times, can be at no loss to detect many more 'ingenious interpolations,' as well as paraphrastic additions,
in the ballad as now printed. But, though it has been
grievously corrupted in this way, the most scrupulous
inquirer into the authenticity of ancient song can have
no hesitation in admitting that many of its verses, even
as they now stand, are purely traditionary, and fair,
and genuine parcels of antiquity, unalloyed with any
base admixture of modern invention, and in nowise
altered, save in those changes of language to which all
oral poetry is unavoidably subjected, in its progress
from one age to another." MOTHERWELL.

We have given *Gil Morrice* as it stands in the *Reliques*, (iii. 132,) degrading to the margin those stanzas which are undoubtedly spurious, and we have
added an ancient traditionary version, obtained by
Motherwell, which, if it appear short and crude, is at
least comparatively incorrupt. *Chield Morice*, taken
down from recitation, and printed in Motherwell's
Minstrelsy, (p. 269,) nearly resembles *Gil Morrice*, as
here exhibited. We have also inserted in the Appendix *Childe Maurice*, "the very old imperfect copy,"
mentioned in the *Reliques*, and first published from
the Percy MS. by Jamieson.

The sets of *Gil Morrice* in the collections of Herd,
Pinkerton, Ritson, &c., are all taken from Percy.

GIL MORRICE was an erles son,
   His name it waxed wide:
It was nae for his great riches,
   Nor zet his mickle pride;
Bot it was for a lady gay
   That liv'd on Carron side. [1]

" Quhair sall I get a bonny boy,
   That will win hose and shoen;
That will gae to Lord Barnard's ha',
   And bid his lady cum?

" And ze maun rin my errand, Willie,
   And ze may rin wi' pride;
Quhen other boys gae on their foot,
   On horseback ze sall ride."

"O no! O no! my master dear!
   I dare nae for my life;
I 'll no gae to the bauld barons,
   For to triest furth his wife."

[1] The stall copies of the ballad complete the stanza thus:

> *His face was fair, lang was his hair,*
>   *In the wild woods he staid;*
> But his fame was for a fair lady
>   That lived on Carronside.

Which is no injudicious interpolation, inasmuch as it is founded upon the traditions current among the vulgar, regarding
Gil Morice's comely face and long yellow hair. MOTHERWELL.

" My bird Willie, my boy Willie,
 My dear Willie," he sayd :
" How can ze strive against the stream ?
 For I sall be obeyd."

 : Bot, O my master dear !" he cry'd,
 " In grene wod ze 're zour lain ;
Gi owre sic thochts, I walde ze rede,
 For fear ze should be tain."

" Haste, haste, I say, gae to the ha',
 Bid hir cum here wi' speid :
If ze refuse my heigh command,
 I 'll gar zour body bleid.

" Gae bid hir take this gay mantel,
 'T is a' gowd bot the hem ;
Bid hir cum to the gude grene wode,
 And bring nane bot hir lain :

" And there it is, a silken sarke,
 Hir ain hand sewd the sleive ;
And bid hir cum to Gill Morice,
 Speir nae bauld barons leave."

" Yes, I will gae zour black errand,
 Though it be to zour cost ;
Sen ze by me will nae be warn'd,
 In it ze sall find frost.

" The baron he is a man of might,
    He neir could bide to taunt ;
As ze will see, before it 's nicht,
    How sma' ze hae to vaunt.

" And sen I maun zour errand rin
    Sae sair against my will,
I 'se mak a vow and keip it trow,
    It sall be done for ill."

And quhen he came to broken brigue,
    He bent his bow and swam ;
And quhen he came to grass growing,
    Set down his feet and ran. [1]

And quhen he came to Barnard's ha',
    Would neither chap nor ca' ;
Bot set his bent bow to his breist,
    And lichtly lap the wa'. [2]

He wauld nae tell the man his errand,
    Though he stude at the gait ;
Bot straiht into the ha' he cam,
    Quhair they were set at meit.

" Hail ! hail ! my gentle sire and dame !
    My message winna waite ;

[1] [2] A familiar commonplace in ballad poetry. See *Childe
Vyet, Lady Maisry, Lord Barnaby*, &c.

Dame, ze maun to the gude grene wod,
    Before that it be late.

" Ze 're bidden tak this gay mantel,
    'T is a' gowd bot the hem :
Zou maun gae to the gude grene wode,
    Ev'n by your sel alane.

" And there it is, a silken sarke,
    Your ain hand sewd the sleive :
Ze maun gae speik to Gill Morice ;
    Speir nae bauld barons leave."

The lady stamped wi' hir foot,
    And winked wi' hir ee ;
But a' that she could say or do,
    Forbidden he wad nae bee.

" It 's surely to my bow'r-woman ;
    It neir could be to me."
" I brocht it to Lord Barnard's lady ;
    I trow that ze be she."

Then up and spack the wylie nurse,
    (The bairn upon hir knee) :
" If it be cum frae Gill Morice,
    It 's deir welcum to mee."

" Ze leid, ze leid, ze filthy nurse,
    Sae loud I heird ze lee ;
I brocht it to Lord Barnard's lady :
    I trow ze be nae shee."

Then up and spack the bauld baron,
   An angry man was hee;
He 's tain the table wi' his foot,
   Sae has he wi' his knee,
Till siller cup and ezer dish [1]
   In flinders he gard flee.

" Gae bring a robe of zour cliding,
   That hings upon the pin;
And I 'il gae to the gude grene wode,
   And speik wi' zour lemman."

" O bide at hame, now, Lord Barnard
   I warde ze bide at hame;
Neir wyte a man for violence,
   That neir wate ze wi' nane."

Gil Morice sate in gude grene wode,
   He whistled and he sang :
" O what mean a' the folk coming?
   My mother tarries lang."

The baron came to the grene wode,
   Wi' mickle dule and care;
And there he first spied Gill Morice
   Kameing his zellow hair. [2]

---

[1] mazer.

[2] His hair was like the threeds of gold
   Drawne frae Minerva's loome;
  His lipps like roses drapping dew;
   His breath was a' perfume.

" Nae wonder, nae wonder, **Gill Moric**
　　My lady loed thee weel ;
The fairest part of my bodie
　　Is blacker than thy heel.

" Zet neir the less now, Gill Morice,
　　For a' thy great beautie,
Ze 's rew the day ze eir was born ;
　　That head sall gae wi' me."

Now he has drawn his trusty brand,
　　And slait[1] it on the strae ;
And thro' Gill Morice' fair body
　　He 's gar cauld iron gae.

And he has tain Gill Morice' head, -
　　And set it on a speir :
The meanest man in a' his train
　　Has gotten that head to bear.

　　His brow was like the mountain snae
　　　Gilt by the morning beam ;
　　His cheeks like living roses glow;
　　　His een like azure stream.

　　The boy was clad in robes of grene,
　　　Sweete as the infant spring;
　　And like the mavis on the bush,
　　　He gart the vallies ring.

　　That sweetly wavd around his face,
　　　That face beyond compare;
　　He sang sae sweet, it might dispel
　　　A' rage but fell dispair.

　　　　1 slaited.

And he has tain Gill Morice up,
  Laid him across his steid,
And brocht him to his painted bowr,
  And laid him on a bed.

The lady sat on castil wa',
  Beheld baith dale and doun ;
And there she saw Gill Morice' head
  Cum trailing to the toun.

" Far better I loe that bluidy head,
  Bot and that zellow hair,
Than Lord Barnard, and a' his lands,
  As they lig here and thair."

And she has tain her Gill Morice,
  And kissd baith mouth and chin :
" I was once as fow of Gill Morice,
  As the hip is o' the stean.

" I got ze in my father's house,
  Wi' mickle sin and shame ;
I brocht thee up in gude green wode,
  Under the heavy rain.

" Oft have I by thy cradle sitten,
  And fondly seen thee sleip ;
Bot now I gae about thy grave,
  The saut tears for to weip."

And syne she kissd[1] his bluidy cheik,
 And syne his bluidy chin:
" O better I loe my Gill Morice
 Than a' my kith and kin ! "

" Away, away, ze il woman,
 And an ill deith mait ze dee :
Gin I had ken'd he 'd bin zour son,
 He 'd neir bin slain for mee."

177 " Obraid me not, my Lord Barnard!
 Obraid me not for shame!
  Wi' that saim speir, O pierce my heart!
  And put me out o' pain.

 " Since nothing bot Gill Morice' head
  Thy jelous rage could quell,
 Let that saim hand now tak hir life
  That neir to thee did ill.

 " To me nae after days nor nichts
  Will eir be saft or kind;
 I 'll fill the air with heavy sighs,
  And greet till I am blind."

 " Enouch of blood by me 's bin spilt,
  Seek not zour death frae me;
 I rather lourd it had been my sel
  Than eather him or thee.

 " With waefo wae I hear zour plaint;
  Sair, sair I rew the deid,
 That eir this cursed hand of mine
  Had gard his body bleid.

  [1] Stall copy, And *first* she kissed.

" Dry up zour tears, my winsome dame,
   Ze neir can heal the wound;
Ze see his head upon the speir,
   His heart's blude on the ground.

" I curse the hand that did the deid,
   The heart that thocht the ill;
The feet that bore me wi' sik speid,
   The comely zouth to kill.

" I 'll ay lament for Gill Morice,
   As gin he were mine ain;
I 'll neir forget the dreiry day
   On which the zouth was slain."

CHILD NORYCE.

From Motherwell's *Minstrelsy*, p. 282.

" By testimony of a most unexceptionable description,—but which it would be tedious here to detail,—the Editor can distinctly trace this ballad as existing in its present shape at least a century ago, which carries it decidedly beyond the date of the first printed copy of *Gil Morice;* and this with a poem which has been preserved but by oral tradition, is no mean *positive* antiquity."

In the Introduction to his collection, Motherwell ntions his having found a more complete copy of this lad under the title of *Babe Nourice.*

CHILD NORYCE is a clever young man,
  He wavers wi' the wind;
His horse was silver shod before,
  With the beaten gold behind.

He called to his little man John,
  Saying, " You don't see what I see ;
For O yonder I see the very first woman
  That ever loved me.

" Here is a glove, a glove," he said,
  " Lined with the silver gris ;
You may tell her to come to the merry green
    wood,
  To speak to Child Nory.

" Here is a ring, a ring," he says,
  " It 's all gold but the stane ;
You may tell her to come to the merry green
    wood,
  And ask the leave o' nane."

" So well do I love your errand, my master,
  But far better do I love my life ;
O would ye have me go to Lord Barnard's castel,
  To betray away his wife ? "

" O don't I give you meat," he says,
  " And don't I pay you fee ?
How dare you stop my errand ? " he says ;
  " My orders you must obey."

O when he came to Lord Barnard's castel,
  He tinkled at the ring ;

Who was as ready as Lord Barnard[1] himself
   To let this little boy in?

" Here is a glove, a glove," he says,
   " Lined with the silver gris ;
You are bidden to come to the merry green
     wood,
   To speak to Child Nory.

" Here is a ring, a ring," he says,
   " It 's all gold but the stane :
You are bidden to come to the merry green
     wood,
   And ask the leave o' nane."

Lord Barnard he was standing by,
   And an angry man was he :
" O little did I think there was a lord in this
     world
   My lady loved but me !"

O he dressed himself in the Holland smocks,
   And garments that was gay ;
And he is away to the merry green wood,
   To speak to Child Nory.

---

[1] This unquestionably should be Lady Barnard, instead of
her lord. See third stanza under. M.

.iild Noryce sits on yonder tree,
  He whistles and he sings :
O wae be to me," says Child Noryce,
  " Yonder my mother comes ! "

'hild Noryce he came off the tree,
  His mother to take off the horse :
Och alace, alace," says Child Noryce,
  " My mother was ne'er so gross."

.ord Barnard he had a little small sword,
  That hung low down by his knee ;
He cut the head off Child Noryce,
  And put the body on a tree.

And when he came to his castel,
  And to his lady's hall,
He threw the head into her lap,
  Saying, " Lady, there is a ball ! "

;he turned up the bloody head,
  She kissed it frae cheek to chin :
 Far better do I love this bloody head
  Than all my royal kin.

 When I was in my father's castell,
  In my virginitie,
There came a lord into the North,
  Gat Child Noryce with me."

" O wae be to thee, Lady Margaret,' he said,
   " And an ill death may you die ;
For if you had told me he was your son,
   He had ne'er been slain by me."

CLERK SAUNDERS

From the *Minstrelsy of the Scottish Border*, (iii. 175,) where it was first published. It was " taken from Mr. Herd's MSS., with several corrections from a shorter and more imperfect copy in the same volume, and one or two conjectural emendations in the arrangement of the stanzas."

That that part of the ballad which follows the death of the lovers is an independent story, is obvious both from internal evidence, and from the separate existence of those concluding stanzas in a variety of forms: as, *Sweet William's Ghost*, (*Tea-Table Miscellany*, ii. 142,) *Sweet William and May Margaret*, (Kinloch, p. 241,) *William and Marjorie*, (Motherwell, p. 186.) Of this second part, Motherwell observes, that it is often made the tail-piece to other ballads where a deceased lover appears to his mistress. The two were, however, combined by Sir Walter Scott, and the present Editor has contented himself with indicating distinctly the close of the proper story.

An inferior copy of *Clerk Saunders*, published by Jamieson, is inserted in the Appendix, for the sake of a few valuable stanzas. It resembles the Swedish ballad of *The Cruel Brother*, (*Svenska Folk-Visor*, iii. 107,) which, however, is much shorter. The edition of Buchan, (i. 160,) is entirely worthless. A North-Country version of the First Part is given by Kinloch *Ancient Scottish Ballads*, 233.

PART FIRST.

CLERK SAUNDERS and may Margaret,
   Walked ower yon garden green;
And sad and heavy was the love
   That fell thir twa between.

"A bed, a bed," Clerk Saunders said,
   " A bed for you and me ! "—
" Fye na, fye na," said may Margaret,
   " Till anes we married be ;

" For in may come my seven bauld brothers
   Wi' torches burning bright ;
They'll say—' We hae but ae sister,
   And behold she's wi' a knight !' "—

" Then take the sword from my scabbard
   And slowly lift the pin ;
And you may swear, and safe your aith,
   Ye never let Clerk Saunders in.

" And take a napkin in your hand,
   And tie up baith your bonny een ;

And you may swear, and safe your aith,
    Ye saw me na since late yestreen."[1]

It was about the midnight hour,
    When they asleep were laid,
When in and came her seven brothers,
    Wi' torches burning red.

When in and came her seven brothers,
    Wi' torches burning bright;
They said, " We hae but ae sister,
    And behold her lying with a knight!"

Then out and spake the first o' them,
    " I bear the sword shall gar him die!"
And out and spake the second o' them,
    " His father has nae mair than he!"

And out and spake the third o' them,
    " I wot that they are lovers dear!"
And out and spake the fourth o' them,
    "They hae been in love this mony a year!"

[1] In Kinloch's version of this ballad we have an additional
stanza here:—

    —— " Ye'll take me in your arms twa,
    Ye'll carry me into your bed,
    And ye may swear, and save your aith,
    That in your bour floor I ne'er gae'd."

Then out and spake the fifth o' them,
   " It were great sin true love to twain ! "
And out and spake the sixth of them,
   " It were shame to slay a sleeping man !

Then up and gat the seventh o' them,
   And never a word spake he ;
But he has striped his bright brown brand
   Out through Clerk Saunders' fair bodye.

Clerk Saunders he started, and Margaret she
      turn'd
   Into his arms as asleep she lay ;
And sad and silent was the night
   That was atween thir twae.

And they lay still and sleeped sound,
   Until the day began to daw ;
And kindly to him she did say,
   " It is time, true love, you were awa.

But he lay still, and sleeped sound,
   Albeit the sun began to sheen ;
She looked atween her and the wa',
   And dull and drowsie were his een.

Then in and came her father dear,
   Said—" Let a' your mourning be :
I'll carry the dead corpse to the clay,
   And I'll come back and comfort thee."—

" Comfort weel your seven sons,
　　For comforted will I never be :
I ween 'twas neither knave nor loon
　　Was in the bower last night wi' me."—

PART SECOND.

The clinking bell gaed through the town, [1]
　　To carry the dead corse to the clay ;
And Clerk Saunders stood at may Margaret's
　　　　window,
　　I wot, an hour before the day.

" Are ye sleeping, Margaret ? " he says,
　　" Or are ye waking presentlie?
Give me my faith and troth again,
　　I wot, true love, I gied to thee."—

" Your faith and troth ye sall never get,
　　Nor our true love sall never twin,
Until ye come within my bower,
　　And kiss me cheik and chin."—

" My mouth it is full cold, Margaret,
　　It has the smell, now, of the ground ;

[1] The custom of the passing bell is still kept up in many villages in Scotland. The sexton goes through the town, ringing a small bell, and announcing the death of the de parted, and the time of the funeral. SCOTT.

And if I kiss thy comely mouth,
    Thy days of life will not be lang.

"O cocks are crowing a merry midnight,
    I wot the wild fowls are boding day;
Give me my faith and troth again,
    And let me fare me on my way."—

"Thy faith and troth thou sall na get,
    And our true love shall never twin,
Until ye tell what comes of women,
    I wot, who die in strong traiveling."

"Their beds are made in the heavens high,
    Down at the foot of our good Lord's knee,
Weel set about wi' gillyflowers;
    I wot sweet company for to see.

"O cocks are crowing a merry midnight,
    I wot the wild fowl are boding day;
The psalms of heaven will soon be sung,
    And I, ere now, will be miss'd away."—

Then she has ta'en a crystal wand,[1]
    And she has stroken her troth thereon;
She has given it him out at the shot-windo'
    Wi' mony a sad sigh, and heavy groan.

"I thank ye, Marg'ret; I thank ye, Marg'ret;
    And aye I thank ye heartilie;

Gin ever the dead come for the quick,
    Be sure, Marg'ret, I'll come for thee."—

It's hosen and shoon and gown alone,
    She climb'd the wall, and follow'd him,
Until she came to the green forest,
    And there she lost the sight o' him.

" Is there ony room at your head, Saunders?
    Is there ony room at your feet?
Or ony room at your side, Saunders,
    Where fain, fain, I wad sleep?"—

" There's nae room at my head, Marg'ret,
    There's nae room at my feet;
My bed it is full lowly now:
    Amang the hungry worms I sleep.

" Cauld mould is my covering now,
    But and my winding-sheet;
The dew it falls nae sooner down,
    Than my resting place is weet.

" But plait a wand o' bonny birk,
    And lay it on my breast[1];

[1] The custom of binding the new-laid sod of the churcn-yard with osiers, or other saplings, prevailed both in England and Scotland, and served to protect the turf from injury by cattle, or otherwise. SCOTT.

And shed a tear upon my grave,
    And wish my saul gude rest.

"And fair Marg'ret, and rare Marg'ret,
    And Marg'ret o' veritie,
Gin e'er ye love another man,
    Ne'er love him as ye did me."—

Then up and crew the milk-white cock,
    And up and crew the grey;
Her lover vanish'd in the air,
    And she gaed weeping away.

SWEET WILLIE AND LADY MARGERIE

From Motherwell's *Minstrelsy*, p. 370.

" THIS Ballad, which possesses considerable beauty
and pathos, is given from the recitation of a lady,
now far advanced in years, with whose grandmother
it was a deserved favourite. It is now for the first
time printed. It bears some resemblance to *Clerk
Saunders.*"

Subjoined is a different copy from Buchan's *Ballads
of the North of Scotland.*

SWEET WILLIE was a widow's son,
  And he wore a milk-white weed O ;
And weel could Willie read and write,
  Far better ride on steed O.

Lady Margerie was the first ladye
  That drank to him the wine O ;
And aye as the healths gaed round and round,
  " Laddy, your love is mine O."

Lady Margerie was the first ladye
    That drank to him the beer O ;
 And aye as the healths gaed round and round,
    Laddy, ye 're welcome here O.

· You must come intill my bower,
    When the evening bells do ring O ;
And you must come intill my bower,
    When the evening mass doth sing O."

He 's taen four-and-twenty braid arrows,
    And laced them in a whang O ;
And he 's awa to Lady Margerie's bower,
    As fast as he can gang O.

He set his ae foot on the wa',
    And the other on a stane O ;
And he 's kill'd a' the king's life guards,
    He 's kill'd them every man O.

" O open, open, Lady Margerie,
    Open and let me in O ;
The weet weets a' my yellow hair,
    And the dew draps on my chin O."

With her feet as white as sleet,
    She strode her bower within O ;
And with her fingers lang and sma',
    She 's looten sweet Willie in O.

She 's louted down unto his foot,
    To lowze sweet Willie's shoon O ;
The buckles were sae stiff they wadna lowze,
    The blood had frozen in O.

" O Willie, O Willie, I fear that thou
    Hast bred me dule and sorrow ;
The deed that thou hast done this nicht
    Will kythe upon the morrow."

  then came her father dear,
    And a braid sword by his gare O ;
And he 's gien Willie, the widow's son,
    A deep wound and a sair O.

" Lye yont, lye yont, Willie," she says,
    " Your sweat weets a' my side O;
Lye yont, lye yont, Willie, she says,
    For your sweat I downa bide O."

She turned her back unto the wa',
    Her face unto the room O ;
And there she saw her auld father,
    Fast walking up and doun O.

" Woe be to you, father," she said,
    " And an ill deid may you die O ;
For ye 've kill'd Willie, the widow's son,
    And he would have married me O."

She turned her back unto the room,
   Her face unto the wa' O ;
And with a deep and heavy sich,
   Her heart it brak in twa O.

,m Buchan's *Ballads of the North of Scotland*, i. 155.

The Bent sae Brown, in the same volume, p. 30,
resembles both *Clerk Saunders* and the present ballad,
but has a different catastrophe.

SWEET WILLIE was a widow's son,
   And milk-white was his weed ;
It sets him weel to bridle a horse,
   And better to saddle a steed, my dear,
   And better to saddle a steed.

But he is on to Maisry's bower door,
   And tirled at the pin ;
" Ye sleep ye, wake ye, Lady Maisry,
   Ye'll open, let me come in, my dear,
   Ye'll open, let me come in."

" O who is this at my bower door,
   Sae well that knows my name ? "
' It is your ain true love, Willie,
   If ye love me, lat me in, my dear,
   If ye love me, lat me in."

Then huly, huly raise she up,
    For fear o' making din ;
Then in her arms lang and bent,
    She caught sweet Willie in, my dear,
    She caught sweet Willie in.

She lean'd her low down to her toe,
    To loose her true love's sheen ;
But cauld, cauld were the draps o' bleed,
    Fell fae his trusty brand, my dear,
    Fell fae his trusty brand.

" What frightfu' sight is that, my love ?
    A frightfu' sight to see ;
What bluid is this on your sharp brand,
    O may ye not tell me, my dear?
    O may ye not tell me ? "

" As I came thro' the woods this night,
    The wolf maist worried me ;
O shou'd I slain the wolf, Maisry ?
    Or shou'd the wolf slain me, my dear?
    Or shou'd the wolf slain me ? "

They hadna kiss'd nor love clapped,
    As lovers when they meet,
Till up it starts her auld father,
    Out o' his drowsy sleep, my dear,
    Out o' his drowsy sleep.

" O what's become o' my house cock
　　Sae crouse at ane did craw ?
I wonder as much at my bold watch,
　　That's nae shootin ower the wa,' my dear,
　　That's nae shooting ower the wa.

' My gude house cock, my only son,
　　Heir ower my land sae free ;
f ony ruffian hae him slain,
　　High hanged shall he be, my dear,
　　High hanged shall he be."

Then he's on to Maisry's bower door,
　　And tirled at the pin ;
" Ye sleep ye, wake ye, daughter Maisry,
　　Ye'll open, lat me come in, my dear,
　　Ye'll open, lat me come in."

Between the curtains and the wa',
　　She row'd her true love then ;
And huly went she to the door,
　　And let her father in, my dear,
　　And let her father in.

" What's become o' your maries, Maisry,
　　Your bower it looks sae teem ?
What's become o' your green claithing?
　　Your beds they are sae thin, my dear,
　　Your beds they are sae thin."

" Gude forgie you, father," she said,
  " I wish ye be't for sin ;
Sae aft as ye hae dreaded me,
    But never found me wrang, my dear,
    But never found me wrang."

He turn'd him right and round about,
  As he'd been gaun awa' ;
But sae nimbly as he slippet in,
    Behind a screen sae sma', my dear,
    Behind a screen sae sma.'

Maisry thinking a' dangers past,
  She to her love did say ;
" Come, love, and take your silent rest,
    My auld father's away, my dear,
    My auld father's away ! "

Then baith lock'd in each other's arms,
  They fell full fast asleep ;
When up it starts her auld father,
    And stood at their bed feet, my dear,
    And stood at their bed feet.

" I think I hae the villain now,
  That my dear son did slay ;
But I shall be reveng'd on him,
    Before I see the day, my dear,
    Before I see the day."

Then he's drawn out a trusty brand,
   And stroak'd it o'er a stray ;
And thro' and thro' sweet Willie's midd·
   He's gart cauld iron gae, my dear,
   He's gart cauld iron gae.

Then up it waken'd Lady Maisry,
   Out o' her drowsy sleep ;
And when she saw her true love slain,
   She straight began to weep, my dear,
   She straight began to weep.

" O gude forgie you now, father," she said,
   " I wish ye be't for sin ;
For I never lov'd a love but ane,
   In my arms ye've him slain, my dear,
   In my arms ye've him slain."

" This night he's slain my gude bold watch,
   Thirty stout men and twa;
Likewise he's slain your ae brother,
   To me was worth them a', my dear,
   To me was worth them a'."

" If he has slain my ae brither,
   Himsell had a' the blame ;
For mony a day he plots contriv'd,
   To hae sweet Willie slain, my dear
   To hae sweet Willie slain.

" And tho' he's slain your gude bold watch,
  He might hae been forgien ;
They came on him in armour bright,
  When he was but alane, my dear,
  When he was but alane."

Nae meen was made for this young knight,
  In bower where he lay slain ;
But a' was for sweet Maisry bright,
  In fields where she ran brain, my dear,
  In fields where she ran brain.

THE CLERK'S TWA SONS O' OWSENFORD

"This singularly wild and beautiful old ballad," says
Chambers, (*Scottish Ballads*, p. 345,) "is chiefly taken
from the recitation of the editor's grandmother, who
learned it, when a girl, nearly seventy years ago, from a
Miss Anne Gray, resident at Neidpath Castle, Peeblesshire; some additional stanzas, and a few various
readings, being adopted from a less perfect, and far
less poetical copy, published in Mr. Buchan's [*Ancient
Ballads and Songs of the North of Scotland*, i. 281,]
and from a fragment in the *Border Minstrelsy*, entitled
The Wife of Usher's Well, [vol. i. p. 214, of this collection,] but which is evidently the same narrative."*

"The editor has been induced to divide this ballad
into two parts, on account of the *great superiority of
what follows over what goes before, and because the latter portion is in a great measure independent of the
other*, so far as sense is concerned. The first part is
composed of the Peeblesshire version, mingled with
that of the northern editor: the second is formed of
the Peeblesshire version, mingled with the fragment
called *The Wife of Usher's Well*."

* There is to a certain extent a resemblance between this
ballad and the German ballad *Das Schloss in Oesterreich*
found in most of the German collections, and in Swedish
and Danish: also to the Italian and Catalan ballad, *The Stu-
dents of Tolosa*, Nigra, *Canzoni Popolari del Piemonte, Rivist.
Cn.*, xx. 62, and (from Milá y Fontanals) p 74.

The natural desire of men to hear more of characters in whom they have become strongly interested, has frequently stimulated the attempt to continue successful fictions, and such supplements are proverbially unfortunate. A ballad-singer would have powerful inducements to gratify this passion of his audience, and he could most economically effect the object by stringing two ballads together. When a tale ended tragically, the sequel must of necessity be a ghost-story, and we have already had, in *Clerk Saunders*, an instance of this combination. Mr. Chambers has furnished the best possible reasons for believing that the same process has taken place in the case of the present ballad, and that the two parts, (which occur separately,) having originally had no connection, were arbitrarily united, to suit the purposes of some unscrupulous rhapsodist.

PART FIRST.

O I will sing to you a sang,
   Will grieve your heart full sair;
How the Clerk's twa sons o' Owsenford
   Have to learn some unco lear.

They hadna been in fair Parish
   A twelvemonth and a day,
Till the Clerk's twa sons fell deep in love
   Wi' the Mayor's dauchters twae.

And aye as the twa clerks sat and wrote
   The ladies sewed and sang;

There was mair mirth in that chamber,
    Than in a' fair Ferrol's land.

But word's gane to the michty Mayor,
    As he sailed on the sea,
That the Clerk's twa sons made licht lemans
    O' his fair dauchters twae.

" If they hae wranged my twa dauchters,
    Janet and Marjorie,
The morn, ere I taste meat or drink,
    Hie hangit they shall be."

And word 's gane to the clerk himsell,
    As he was drinking wine,
That his twa sons at fair Parish
    Were bound in prison strang.

Then up and spak the Clerk's ladye,
    And she spak tenderlie :
" O tak wi' ye a purse o' gowd,
    Or even tak ye three;
And if ye canna get William,
    Bring Henry hame to me."

O sweetly sang the nightingale,
    As she sat on the wand ;
But sair, sair mourned Owsenford,
    As he gaed in the strand.

When he came to their prison strang,
   He rade it round about,
And at a little shot-window,
   His sons were looking out.

" O lie ye there, my sons," he said,
   " For owsen or for kye ?
Or what is it that ye lie for,
   Sae sair bound as ye lie ? "

" We lie not here for owsen, father;
   Nor yet do we for kye ;
But it's for a little o' dear-boucht love,
   Sae sair bound as we lie.

" O borrow us, borrow us, father," they said,
   " For the luve we bear to thee ! "
" O never fear, my pretty sons,
   Weel borrowed ye sall be."

Then he's gane to the michty Mayor,
   And he spak courteouslie :
" Will ye grant my twa sons' lives,
   Either for gold or fee ?
Or will ye be sae gude a man,
   As grant them baith to me ? "

" I'll no grant ye your twa sons' lives,
   Neither for gold nor fee ;

Nor will I be sae gude a man,
  As gie them baith to thee;
But before the morn at twal o'clock,
  Ye'll see them hangit hie!"

Ben it came the Mayor's dauchters,
  Wi' kirtle coat alone;
Their eyes did sparkle like the gold,
  As they tripped on the stone.

" Will ye gie us our loves, father,
  For gold, or yet for fee?
Or will ye take our own sweet lives,
  And let our true loves be? "

He's taen a whip into his hand,
  And lashed them wondrous sair;
" Gae to your bowers, ye vile limmers;
  Ye'se never see them mair."

Then out it speaks auld Owsenford;
  A sorry man was he:
" Gang to your bouirs, ye lilye flouirs;
  For a' this maunna be."

Then out it speaks him Hynde Henry:
  " Come here, Janet, to me;
Will ye gie me my faith and troth,
  And love, as I gae thee? "

"Ye sall hae your faith and troth,
  Wi' God's blessing and mine : "
And twenty times she kissed his mouth,
  Her father looking on.

Then out it speaks him gay William :
  " Come here, sweet Marjorie ;
Will ye gie me my faith and troth,
  And love, as I gae thee ? "

" Yes, ye sall hae your faith and troth,
  Wi' God's blessing and mine : "
And twenty times she kissed his mouth,
  Her father looking on.

*   *   *   *   *

' O ye'll tak aff your twa black hats,
  Lay them down on a stone,
That nane may ken that ye are clerks,
  Till ye are putten doun."

The bonnie clerks they died that morn ;
  Their loves died lang ere noon ;
And the waefu' Clerk o' Owsenford
  To his lady has gane hame.

PART SECOND.

His lady sat on her castle wa',
   Beholding dale and doun ;
And there she saw her ain gude lord
   Come walking to the toun.

" Ye're welcome, ye're welcome, my ain gude
     lord,
   Ye're welcome hame to me ;
But where-away are my twa sons ?
   Ye suld hae brought them wi' ye."

" O they are putten to a deeper lear,
   And to a higher scule :
Your ain twa sons will no be hame
   Till the hallow days o' Yule."

" O sorrow, sorrow, come mak my bed ;
   And, dule, come lay me doun ;
For I will neither eat nor drink,
   Nor set a fit on groun' ! "

The hallow days o' Yule were come,
   And the nights were lang and mirk,
When in and cam her ain twa sons,
   And their hats made o' the birk.

It neither grew in syke nor ditch,
    Nor yet in ony sheuch ;
But at the gates o' Paradise
    That birk grew fair eneuch.

" Blow up the fire, now, maidens mine,
    Bring water from the well ;
For a' my house shall feast this night,
    Since my twa sons are well.

" O eat and drink, my merry-men a',
    The better shall ye fare ;
For my two sons they are come hame
    To me for evermair."

And she has gane and made their bed,
    She's made it saft and fine ;
And she's happit them wi' her gay mantil,
    Because they were her ain.

But the young cock crew in the merry Linkum,
    And the wild fowl chirped for day ;
And the aulder to the younger said,
    " Brother, we maun away.

" The cock doth craw, the day doth daw,
    The channerin worm doth chide ;
Gin we be missed out o' our place,
    A sair pain we maun bide."

" Lie still, lie still a little wee while,
    Lie still but if we may ;
Gin my mother should miss us when she wakes,
    She'll gae mad ere it be day."

    *   *   *   *   *   *

O it's they've taen up their mother's mantil,
    And they've hung it on a pin :
" O lang may ye hing, my mother's mantil,
    Ere ye hap us again."

CHILDE VYET.

First printed in a complete form in Maidment's *North Countrie Garland*, p. 24. The same editor contributed a slightly different copy to Motherwell's *Minstrelsy*, (p. 173.) An inferior version is furnished by Buchan, i. 234, and Jamieson has published a fragment on the same story, here given in the Appendix.

Lord Ingram and Childe Vyet,
　Were both born in ane bower,
Had both their loves on one Lady,
　The less was their honour. [1]

Childe Vyet and Lord Ingram,
　Were both born in one hall,
Had both their loves on one Lady
　The worse did them befall.

[1] The less was their bonheur. Motherwell

Lord Ingram woo'd the Lady Maiserey,
 From father and from mother ;
Lord Ingram woo'd the Lady Maiserey,
 From sister and from brother.

Lord Ingram wooed the Lady Maiserey,
 With leave of all her kin ;
And every one gave full consent,
 But she said no, to him.

Lord Ingram wooed the Lady Maiserey,
 Into her father's ha' ;
Childe Vyet wooed the Lady Maiserey,
 Among the sheets so sma'.

Now it fell out upon a day,
 She was dressing her head,
That ben did come her father dear,
 Wearing the gold so red.

" Get up now, Lady Maiserey,
 Put on your wedding gown,
For Lord Ingram will be here,
 Your wedding must be done ! "

" I'd rather be Childe Vyet's wife,
 The white fish for to sell,
Before I were Lord Ingram's wife,
 To wear the silk so well !

" I'd rather be Childe Vyet's wife,
      With him to beg my bread,
Before I'd be Lord Ingram's wife,
      To wear the gold so red.

" Where will I get a bonny boy,
      Will win gold to his fee,
Will run unto Childe Vyet's ha',
      With this letter from me ? "

" O here, I am the boy," says one,
      " Will win gold to my fee,
And carry away any letter,
      To Childe Vyet from thee."

And when he found the bridges broke,
      He bent his bow and swam ;
And when he found the grass growing
      He hasten'd and he ran.

And when he came to Vyet's castle,
      He did not knock nor call,
But set his bent bow to his breast,
      And lightly leaped the wall;
And ere the porter open'd the gate,
      The boy was in the hall.

The first line that Childe Vyet read,
      A grieved man was he;

The next line that he looked on,
   A tear blinded his e'e.

" What ails my own brother," he says,
   " He'll not let my love be ;
But I'll send to my brother's bridal;
   The woman shall be free.

" Take four and twenty bucks and ewes,
   And ten tun of the wine,
And bid my love be blythe and glad,
   And I will follow syne."

There was not a groom about that castle,
   But got a gown of green ;
And a' was blythe, and a' was glad,
   But Lady Maiserey was wi' wean. [1]

There was no cook about the kitchen,
   But got a gown of gray ;
And a' was blythe, and a' was glad,
   But Lady Maiserey was wae.

'Tween Mary Kirk and that castle,
   Was all spread o'er with garl, [2]
To keep the lady and her maidens,
   From tramping on the marl. [3]

---

[1] she was neen. Motherwell.   [2] gold, [3] mould. **N. C. G.**

From Mary Kirk to that castle,
  Was spread a cloth of gold,
To keep the lady and her maidens,
  From treading on the mould.

When mass was sung, and bells were rung,
  And all men bound for bed,
Then Lord Ingram and Lady Maiserey,
  In one bed they were laid.

When they were laid upon their bed,
  It was baith soft and warm,
He laid his hand over her side,
  Says he, " you are with bairn."

" I told you once, so did I twice,
  When ye came as my wooer,
That Childe Vyet, your one brother,
  One night lay in my bower.

" I told you twice, so did I thrice,
  Ere ye came me to wed,
That Childe Vyet, your one brother,
  One night lay in my bed ! "

" O will you father your bairn on me,
  And on no other man ?
And I'll gie him to his dowry,
  Full fifty ploughs of land."

" I will not father my bairn on you,
   Nor on no wrongous man,
Tho' you'd gie him to his dowry,
   Five thousand ploughs of land."

Then up did start him Childe Vyet,
   Shed by his yellow hair,
And gave Lord Ingram to the heart,
   A deep wound and a sair.

Then up did start him Lord Ingram,
   Shed by his yellow hair,
And gave Childe Vyet to the heart,
   A deep wound and a sair.

There was no pity for the two lords,
   Where they were lying slain,
All was for Lady Maiserey :
   In that bower she gaed brain!

There was no pity for the two lords,
   When they were lying dead,
All was for Lady Maiserey :
   In that bower she went mad !

"O get to me a cloak of cloth,
   A staff of good hard tree ;
If I have been an evil woman,
   I shall beg till I die.

" For ae.bit I'll beg for Childe Vyet,
     For Lord Ingram I'll beg three,
All for the honourable marriage, that
     At Mary Kirk he gave me ! "

LADY MAISRY.

This ballad, said to be very popular in Scotland,
was taken down from recitation by Jamieson, and is
extracted from his collection, vol. i. p. 73. A different
copy, from Motherwell's *Minstrelsy*, p. 234, is given in
the Appendix. Another, styled *Young Prince James*,
may be seen in Buchan's *Ballads*, vol. i. 103. *Bonnie
Susie Cleland*, Motherwell, p. 221, is still another version.

In *Lady Maisry* we seem to have the English form
of a tragic story which, starting from Denmark, has
spread over almost all the north of Europe, that of
King Waldemar and his Sister. Grundtvig's collection
gives seven copies of the Danish ballad upon this subject (*Kong Valdemar og hans Söster*, No. 126), the
oldest from a manuscript of the beginning of the 17th
century. Five Icelandic versions are known, one
Norse, one Faroish, five Swedish (four of them in Arwidsson, No. 53, *Liten Kerstin och Fru Sofia*), and
several in German, as *Graf Hans von Holstein und
seine Schwester Annchristine*, Erk, *Liederhort*, p. 155

Der Grausame Bruder, Erk, p. 153, and Hoffmann, *Schlesische Volkslieder*, No. 27 ; *Der Grobe Bruder*, *Wunderhorn*, ii. 272 ; *Der Pfalzgraf am Rhein*, *id.* i. 259, etc.; also a fragment in Wendish. The relationship of the English ballad to the rest of the cycle can perhaps be easiest shown by comparison with the simplified and corrupted German versions.

The story appears to be founded on facts which occurred during the reign and in the family of the Danish king, Waldemar the First, sometime between 1157 and 1167. Waldemar is described as being, with all his greatness, of a relentless and cruel disposition (*in ira pertinax ; in suos tantum plus justo crudelior*). Tradition, however, has imputed to him a brutal ferocity beyond belief. In the ballad before us, Lady Maisry suffers for her weakness by being burned at the stake, but in the Danish, Swedish, and German ballads, the king's sister is beaten to death with leathern whips, by her brother's own hand.

> " Er schlug sie so sehre, er schlug sie so lang,
> Bis Lung und Leber aus dem Leib ihr sprang! "

The Icelandic and Faroe ballads have nothing of this horrible ferocity, but contain a story which is much nearer to probability, if not to historical truth. While King Waldemar is absent on an expedition against the Wends, his sister Kristín is drawn into a *liaison* with her second-cousin, the result of which is the birth of two children. Sofía, the Queen, maliciously makes the state of things known to the king the moment he returns (which is on the very day of Kristín's lying in, according to the Danish ballad), but he will not believe the story, — all the more because the accused parties are within prohibited degrees of

consanguinity. Kristín is summoned to come instantly
to her brother, and obeys the message, though she is
weak with childbirth, and knows that the journey will
cost her her life.   She goes to the court on horseback
(in the Danish ballads falling from the saddle once or
twice on the way), and on her arrival is put to various
tests to ascertain her condition, concluding with a long
dance with the king, to which, having held out for a
considerable time, she at last succumbs, and falls dead
in her brother's arms.

The incidents of the journey on horseback, and the
cruel probation by the dance, are found in the ballad
which follows the present (*Fair Janet*), and these coin-
cidences Grundtvig considers sufficient to establish its
derivation from the Danish.   The *general* similarity of
Lady Maisry to *King Waldemar and his Sister* is,
however, much more striking.   For our part, we are
inclined to believe that *both* the English ballads had
this origin, but the difference in their actual form is so
great, that, notwithstanding this conviction, we have
not felt warranted in putting them together.

THE young lords o' the north country
    Have all a-wooing gane,
To win the love of lady Maisry,
    But o' them she wou'd hae nane.

O thae hae sought her, lady Maisry,
    Wi' broaches, and wi' rings ;
And they hae courted her, lady Maisry,
    Wi' a' kin kind of things.

And they hae sought her, lady Maisry,
    Frae father and frae mither ;
And they hae sought her, lady Maisry,
    Frae sister and frae brither.

And they hae follow'd her, lady Maisry,
    Thro' chamber, and through ha' ;
But a' that they could say to her,
    Her answer still was " Na."

" O haud your tongues, young men," she said,
    " And think nae mair on me ;
For I've gi'en my love to an English lord,
    Sae think nae mair on me."

Her father's kitchey-boy heard that,
    (An ill death mot he die !)
And he is in to her brother,
    As fast as gang cou'd he.

" O is my father and my mother weel,
    But and my brothers three ?
Gin my sister lady Maisry be weel,
    There's naething can ail me."

" Your father and your mother is weel,
    But and your brothers three ;
Your sister, lady Maisry's, weel,
    Sae big wi' bairn is she."

" A malison light on the tongue,
 Sic tidings tells to me !—
But gin it be a lie you tell,
 You shall be hanged hie."

He's doen him to his sister's bower,
 Wi' mickle dool and care ;
And there he saw her, lady Maisry,
 Kembing her yellow hair.

" O wha is aucht that bairn," he says,
 " That ye sae big are wi' ?
And gin ye winna own the truth,
 This moment ye sall die." [1]

She's turned her richt and round about,
 And the kembe fell frae her han' ;
A trembling seized her fair bodie,
 And her rosy cheek grew wan.

" O pardon me, my brother dear,
 And the truth I'll tell to thee ;
My bairn it is to Lord William,
 And he is betrothed to me."

" O cou'dna ye gotten dukes, or lords,
 Intill your ain countrie,
That ye drew up wi' an English dog,
 To bring this shame on me ?

[1] See preface to *Clerk Saunders*, p. 319.

" But ye maun gi'e up your English lord,
    Whan your young babe is born ;
For, gin ye keep by him an hour langer,
    Your life shall be forlorn."

" I will gi'e up this English lord,
    Till my young babe be born ;
But the never a day nor hour langer,
    Though my life should be forlorn."

" O whare is a' my merry young men,
    Wham I gi'e meat and fee,
To pu' the bracken and the thorn,
    To burn this vile whore wi'? "

" O whare will I get a bonny boy,
    To help me in my need,
To rin wi' haste to Lord William,
    And bid him come wi' speed? "

O out it spak a bonny boy,
    Stood by her brother's side ;
" It's I wad rin your errand, lady,
    O'er a' the warld wide.

" Aft ha'e I run your errands, lady,
    When blawin baith wind and weet ;
But now I'll rin your errand, lady,
    With saut tears on my cheek."

O whan he came to broken briggs,
   He bent his bow and swam ;
And whan he came to the green grass growin',
   He slack'd his shoon and ran.

And when he came to Lord William's yeats,
   He badena to chap or ca' ;
But set his bent bow to his breast,
   And lightly lap the wa' ;
And, or the porter was at the yeat,
   The boy was in the ha'.

" O is my biggins broken, boy ?
   Or is my towers won ?
Or is my lady lighter yet,
   O' a dear daughter or son ? "

" Your biggin isna broken, sir,
   Nor is your towers won ;
But the fairest lady in a' the land
   This day for you maun burn."

" O saddle to me the black, the black,
   Or saddle to me the brown ;
Or saddle to me the swiftest steed
   That ever rade frae a town."

Or he was near a mile awa',
   She heard his weir-horse sneeze ;

" Mend up the fire, my fause brother,
　　It's nae come to my knees."

O whan he lighted at the yeat,
　　She heard his bridle ring :
" Mend up the fire, my fause brother ;
　　It's far yet frae my chin.

" Mend up the fire to me, brother,
　　Mend up the fire to me ;
For I see him comin' hard and fast,
　　Will soon men't up for thee.

" O gin my hands had been loose, Willy,
　　Sae hard as they are boun',
I wadd hae turn'd me frae the gleed,
　　And casten out your young son."

" O I'll gar burn for you, Maisry,
　　Your father and your mother ;
And I'll gar burn for you, Maisry,
　　Your sister and your brother ;

" And I'll gar burn for you, Maisry
　　The chief o' a' your kin ;
And the last bonfire that I come to,
　　Mysell I will cast in."

FAIR JANET.

From Sharpe's *Ballad Book*, p. 1.

" This ballad, the subject of which appears to have been very popular, is printed as it was sung by an old woman in Perthshire. The air is extremely beautiful."

Herd gave an imperfect version of this ballad under the title of *Willie and Annet*, in his *Scottish Songs*, i. 219 ; repeated after him in Ritson's *Scottish Songs*, and in Johnson's *Museum*. Finlay's copy, improved, but made up of fragments, follows the present, and in the Appendix is *Sweet Willie and Fair Maisry*, from Buchan's collection. We have followed Motherwell by inserting (in brackets) three stanzas from *Willie and Annet* and *Sweet Willie*, which contribute slightly to complete Sharpe's copy. None of these ballads is satisfactory, though Sharpe's is the best. Touching the relation of *Fair Janet* to the Danish ballad of *King Waldemar and his Sister*, the reader will please look at the preface to the preceding ballad.

" Ye maun gang to your father, Janet,
  Ye maun gang to him soon ;
Ye maun gang to your father, Janet,
  In case that his days are dune ! "

Janet 's awa' to her father,
  As fast as she could hie ;
" O what 's your will wi' me, father?
  O what 's your will wi' me ? "

" My will wi' you, Fair Janet," he said,
  " It is both bed and board ;
Some say that ye lo'e Sweet Willie,
  But ye maun wed a French lord."

" A French lord maun I wed, father ?
  A French lord maun I wed?
Then, by my sooth," quo' Fair Janet,
  " He 's ne'er enter my bed."

Janet 's awa' to her chamber,
  As fast as she could go ;
Wha 's the first ane that tapped there,
  But Sweet Willie her jo !

" O we maun part this love, Willie,
  That has been lang between;
There 's a French lord coming o'er the sea
  To wed me wi' a ring;

There 's a French lord coming o'er the sea,
   To wed and tak me hame."

"If we maun part this love, Janet,
   It causeth mickle woe ;
If we maun part this love, Janet,
   It makes me into mourning go."

"But ye maun gang to your three sisters,
   Meg, Marion, and Jean ;
Tell them to come to Fair Janet,
   In case that her days are dune."

Willie 's awa' to his three sisters,
   Meg, Marion, and Jean ;
"O haste, and gang to Fair Janet,
   I fear that her days are dune."

Some drew to them their silken hose,
   Some drew to them their shoon,
Some drew to them their silk manteils,
   Their coverings to put on ;
And they 're awa' to Fair Janet,
   By the hie light o' the moon.

    *   *   *   *   *   *   *

"O I have born this babe, Willie,
   Wi' mickle toil and pain ;
Take hame, take hame, your babe, Willie,
   For nurse I dare be nane."

He 's tane his young son in his arms,
   And kist him cheek and chin,—
And he 's awa' to his mother's bower,
   By the hie light o' the moon.

"O open, open, mother," he says,
   "O open, and let me in ;
The rain rains on my yellow hair,
   And the dew drops o'er my chin,—
And I hae my young son in my arms,
   I fear that his days are dune."

With her fingers lang and sma'
   She lifted up the pin ;
And with her arms lang and sma'
   Received the baby in.

"Gae back, gae back now, Sweet Willie,
   And comfort your fair lady ;
For where ye had but ae nourice,
   Your young son shall hae three."

Willie he was scarce awa',
   And the lady put to bed,
When in and came her father dear :
   "Make haste, and busk the bride."

"There 's a sair pain in my head, father,
   There 's a sair pain in my side ;

And ill, O ill, am I, father,
    This day for to be a bride."

"O ye maun busk this bonny bride,
    And put a gay mantle on;
For she shall wed this auld French lord,
    Gin she should die the morn."

Some put on the gay green robes,
    And some put on the brown;
But Janet put on the scarlet robes,
    To shine foremost through the town.

And some they mounted the black steed,
    And some mounted the brown;
But Janet mounted the milk-white steed,
    To ride foremost through the town.

"O wha will guide your horse, Janet?
    O wha will guide him best?"
"O wha but Willie, my true love,
    He kens I lo'e him best!"

And when they cam to Marie's kirk,
    To tye the haly ban,
Fair Janet's cheek looked pale and wan,
    And her colour gaed and cam.

When dinner it was past and done,
    And dancing to begin,

"O we 'll go take the bride's maidens,
  And we 'll go fill the ring."

O ben than cam the auld French lord,
  Saying, " Bride, will ye dance with me ? "
" Awa', awa', ye auld French Lord,
  Your face I downa see."

O ben than cam now Sweet Willie,
  He cam with ane advance :
" O I 'll go tak the bride's maidens,
  And we 'll go tak a dance."

" I 've seen ither days wi' you, Willie,
  And so has mony mae ;
Ye would hae danced wi' me mysel',
  Let a' my maidens gae."

O ben than cam now Sweet Willie,
  Saying, " Bride, will ye dance wi' me ? "
" Aye, by my sooth, and that I will,
  Gin my back should break in three."

[And she 's ta'en Willie by the hand,
  The tear blinded her e'e ;
" O I wad dance wi' my true love,
  Tho' bursts my heart in three !"] ·

She hadna turned her throw the dance,
  Throw the dance but thrice,

Whan she fell doun at Willie's feet,
    And up did never rise!

[She 's ta'en her bracelet frae her arm,
    Her garter frae her knee:
" Gie that, gie that, to my young son;
    He 'll ne'er his mother see."]

Willie 's ta'en the key of his coffer,
    And gi'en it to his man;
" Gae hame, and tell my mother dear,
    My horse he has me slain;
Bid her be kind to my young son,
    For father he has nane."

[" Gar deal, gar deal the bread," he cried,
    " Gar deal, gar deal the wine;
This day has seen my true love's death,
    This night shall witness mine."]

The tane was buried in Marie's kirk,
    And the tither in Marie's quire:
Out of the tane there grew a birk,
    And the tither a bonny brier.

SWEET WILLIE.

" This ballad has had the misfortune, in common
with many others, of being much mutilated by reciters.
I have endeavoured, by the assistance of some fragments, to make it as complete as possible ; and have
even taken the liberty of altering the arrangement of
some of the stanzas of a lately-procured copy, that they
might the better cohere with those already printed."
Finlay's *Scottish Ballads*, ii. 61.

" Will you marry the southland lord,
    A queen o' fair England to be ?
Or will you mourn for sweet Willie,
    The morn upon yon lea ? "

"I will marry the southland lord,
    Father, sen it is your will ;
But I'd rather it were my burial day,
    For my grave I'm going till.

" O go, O go now my bower wife,
    O go now hastilie,
O go now to sweet Willie's bower,
    And bid him cum speak to me.—

" Now, Willie, gif ye love me weel,
    As sae it seems to me,
Gar build, gar build a bonny ship,
    Gar build it speedilie !

"And we will sail the sea sae green
   Unto some far countrie ;
Or we'll sail to some bonny isle,
   Stands lanely midst the sea."

But lang or e'er the ship was built,
   Or deck'd or rigged out,
Cam sic a pain in Annet's back,
   That down she cou'dna lout.

" Now, Willie, gin ye love me weel,
   As sae it seems to me,
O haste, haste, bring me to my bower,
   And my bower maidens three."

He's ta'en her in his arms twa,
   And kiss'd her cheek and chin,
He's brocht her to her ain sweet bower,
   But nae bower maid was in.

"Now leave my bower, Willie," she said,
   " Now leave me to my lane ;
Was never man in a lady's bower
   When she was travailing."

He's stepped three steps down the stair,
   Upon the marble stane,
Sae loud's he heard his young son greet,
   But and his lady mane.

"Now come, now come, Willie," she said,
  "Tak your young son frae me,
And hie him to your mother's bower,
  With speed and privacie."

And he is to his mother's bower,
  As fast as he could rin ;
"Open, open, my mother dear,
  Open, and let me in ;

"For the rain rains on my yellow hair,
  The dew stands on my chin,
And I have something in my lap,
  And I wad fain be in."

"O go, O go now, sweet Willie,
  And make your lady blithe,
For wherever you had ae nourice,
  Your young son shall hae five."—

Out spak Annet's mother dear,
  An' she spak a word o' pride ;
Says, "Whare is a' our bride's maidens,
  They're no busking the bride ?"

"O haud your tongue, my mother dear,
  Your speaking let it be,
For I'm sae fair and full o' flesh,
  Little busking will serve me."

Out an' spak the bride's maidens,
 They spak a word o' pride ;
Says, " Whare is a' the fine cleiding?
 Its we maun busk the bride."

" Deal hooly wi' my head, maidens,
 Deal hooly wi' my hair,
For it was washen late yestreen,
 And it is wonder sair.

" My maidens, easy wi' my back,
 And easy wi' my side ;
O set my saddle saft, Willie,
 I am a tender bride."

O up then spak the southland lord,
 And blinkit wi' his ee ;
" I trow this lady's born a bairn,"
 Then laucht loud lauchters three.

" Ye hae gi'en me the gowk, Annet,
 But I'll gie you the scorn ;
For there's no a bell in a' the town
 Shall ring for you the morn."

Out and spak then sweet Willie,
 " Sae loud's I hear you lie,
There's no a bell in a' the town
 But shall ring for Annet and me."

And Willie swore a great great oath,
  And he swore by the thorn,
That she was as free o' a child that night,
  As the night that she was born.

O up an' spak the brisk bridegroom,[1]
  And he spak up wi' pride,
" Gin I should lay my gloves in pawn,
  I will dance wi' the bride."

" Now haud your tongue, my lord," she said[2]
  " Wi' dancing let me be,
I am sae thin in flesh and blude,
  Sma' dancing will serve me."

But she's ta'en Willie by the hand,
  The tear blinded her ee ;
" But I wad dance wi' my true love,
  But bursts my heart in three."

She's ta'en her bracelet frae her arm,
  Her garter frae her knee,
" Gie that, gie that, to my young son ;
  He'll ne'er his mother see."

----

[1] *Sic* Herd. Finlay, then sweet Willie.
[2] *Sic* Herd. Finlay, Willie, she said.

OF this beautiful piece a complete copy was **first** published by Scott, another afterwards by Jamieson. Both are here given, the latter, as in some respects preferable, having the precedence. The ballad is found almost entire in Herd's *Scottish Songs*, i. 206, a short fragment in Johnson's *Museum*, p. 5, and a more considerable one, called *Love Gregory*, in Buchan's collection, ii. 199. This last has been unnecessarily repeated in a very indifferent publication of the Percy Society, vol. xvii. Dr. Wolcot, Burns, and Jamieson have written songs on the story of Fair Annie, and Cunningham has modernized Sir Walter Scott's version, after his fashion, in the *Songs of Scotland*, i. 298.

Of his text, Jamieson remarks, " it is given *verbatim* from the large MS. collection, transmitted from Aberdeen, by my zealous and industrious friend, Professor Robert Scott of that university. I have every reason to believe, that no liberty whatever has been taken with the text, which is certainly more uniform than

any copy heretofore published. It was first written
down many years ago, with no view towards being
committed to the press; and is now given from the
copy then taken, with the addition only of stanzas
twenty-two and twenty-three, which the editor has inserted from memory." *Popular Ballads,* i. 36.

" Lochryan is a beautiful, though somewhat wild and
secluded bay, which projects from the Irish Channel
into Wigtonshire, having the little seaport of Stran-
raer situated at its bottom. Along its coast, which is
in some places high and rocky, there are many ruins
of such castles as that described in the ballad." CHAM-
BERS.

" O WHA will shoe my fair foot,
 And wha will glove my han' ?
And wha will lace my middle jimp
 Wi' a new-made London ban' ?

" Or wha will kemb my yellow hair
 Wi' a new-made silver kemb ?
Or wha'll be father to my young bairn,
 Till love Gregor come hame ? "

" Your father'll shoe your fair foot,
 Your mother glove your han' ;
Your sister lace your middle jimp
 Wi' a new-made London ban' ;

" Your brethren will kemb your yellow hair
   Wi' a new-made silver kemb ;
And the king o' Heaven will father your
     bairn,
   Till love Gregor come hame."

"O gin I had a bonny ship,
   And men to sail wi' me,
It's I wad gang to my true love,
   Sin he winna come to me ! "

Her father's gien her a bonny ship,
   And sent her to the stran' ;
She's taen her young son in her arms,
   And turn'd her back to the lan'.

She hadna been o' the sea sailin'
   About a month or more,
Till landed has she her bonny ship
   Near her true-love's door.

The nicht was dark, and the wind blew cald,
   And her love was fast asleep,
And the bairn that was in her twa arms
   Fu' sair began to greet.

Lang stood she at her true love's door,
   And lang tirl'd at the pin ;
At length up gat his fause mother,
   Says, " Wha's that wad be in ?"

"O it is Annie of Lochroyan,
    Your love, come o'er the sea,
But and your young son in her arms ;
    So open the door to me."

" Awa, awa, ye ill woman,
    You're nae come here for gude ;
You're but a witch, or a vile warlock,
    Or mermaid o' the flude."

"I'm nae a witch or vile warlock,
    Or mermaiden," said she ;—
"I'm but your Annie of Lochroyan ;—
    O open the door to me ! "

" O gin ye be Annie of Lochroyan,
    As I trust not ye be,
What taiken can ye gie that e'er
    I kept your companie ? "

" O dinna ye mind, love Gregor," she says,
    " Whan we sat at the wine,
How we changed the napkins frae our
        necks ?
    It's nae sae lang sinsyne.

" And yours was gude, and gude enough,
    But nae sae gude as mine ;
For yours was o' the cambrick clear,
    But mine o' the silk sae fine.

" And dinna ye mind, love Gregor," she says,
　　" As we twa sat at dine,
How we chang'd the rings frae our fingers,
　　And I can shew thee thine:

" And yours was gude, and gude enough,
　　Yet nae sae gude as mine;
For yours was o' the gude red gold,
　　But mine o' the diamonds fine.

" Sae open the door, now, love Gregor,
　　And open it wi' speed ;
Or your young son, that is in my arms,
　　For cald will soon be dead."

" Awa, awa, ye ill woman,
　　Gae frae my door for shame ;
For I hae gotten anither fair love,
　　Sae ye may hie you hame."

" O hae ye gotten anither fair love,
　　For a' the oaths ye sware?
Then fare ye weel, now, fause Gregor ;
　　For me ye's never see mair ! "

O hooly, hooly gaed she back,
　　As the day began to peep ;
She set her foot on good ship board,
　　And sair, sair did she weep.

"Tak down, tak down the mast o' goud ;
  Set up the mast o' tree ;
Ill sets it a forsaken lady
  To sail sae gallantlie.

!

"Tak down, tak down the sails o' silk ;
  Set up the sails o' skin ;
Ill sets the outside to be gay,
  Whan there's sic grief within!"

Love Gregor started frae his sleep,
  And to his mother did say,
"I dreamt a dream this night, mither,
  That maks my heart richt wae ;

"I dreamt that Annie of Lochroyan,
  The flower o' a' her kin,
Was standin' mournin' at my door,
  But nane wad lat her in."

"O there was a woman stood at the door,
  Wi' a bairn intill her arms ;
But I wadna let her within the bower,
  For fear she had done you harm."

O quickly, quickly raise he up,
  And fast ran to the strand ;
And there he saw her, fair Annie,
  Was sailing frae the land.

And "heigh, Annie !" and "how, Annie !
  O, Annie, winna ye bide ?"
But ay the louder that he cried " Annie,"
  The higher rair'd the tide.

And "heigh, Annie ! " and " how, Annie !
  O, Annie, speak to me ! "
But ay the louder that he cried " Annie,"
  The louder rair'd the sea.

The wind grew loud, and the sea grew rough,
  And the ship was rent in twain ;
And soon he saw her, fair Annie,
  Come floating o'er the main.

He saw his young son in her arms,
  Baith toss'd aboon the tide ;
He wrang his hands, and fast he ran,
  And plunged in the sea sae wide.

He catch'd her by the yellow hair,
  And drew her to the strand ;
But cald and stiff was every limb,
  Before he reach'd the land.

O first he kist her cherry cheek,
  And syne he kist her chin ;
And sair he kist her ruby lips,
  But there was nae breath within.

O he has mourn'd o'er fair Annie,
   Till the sun was ganging down ;
Syne wi' a sich his heart it brast,
   And his saul to heaven has flown.

THE LASS OF LOCHROYAN.

Minstrelsy of the Scottish Border, iii. 199.

" This edition of the ballad is composed of verses selected from three MS. copies, and two obtained from recitation. Two of the copies are in Herd's MS.; the third in that of Mrs. Brown of Falkland."

Lord Gregory is represented in Scott's version, " as confined by fairy charms in an enchanted castle situated in the sea." But Jamieson assures us that when a boy he had frequently heard this ballad chanted in Morayshire, and no mention was ever made of enchantment, or " fairy charms." " Indeed," he very justly adds, " the two stanzas on that subject [v. 41–52,] are in a style of composition very peculiar, and different from the rest of the piece, and strongly remind us of the interpolations in the ballad of *Gil Morris*."

" O WHA will shoe my bonny foot?
    And wha will glove my hand?
And wha will lace my middle jimp
    Wi' a lang, lang linen band ?

" O wha will kame my yellow hair,
    With a new-made silver kame?
And wha will father my young son,
    Till Lord Gregory come hame ? "—

" Thy father will shoe thy bonny foot,
    Thy mother will glove thy hand,
Thy sister will lace thy middle jimp,
    Till Lord Gregory come to land.

" Thy brother will kame thy yellow **hair**
    With a new-made silver kame,
And God will be thy bairn's father
    Till Lord Gregory come hame."—

" But I will get a bonny boat,
    And I will sail the sea;
And I will gang to Lord Gregory,
    Since he canna come hame to me."

Syne she's gar'd build a bonny boat,
    To sail the salt, salt sea;
The sails were o' the light green silk,
    The tows o' taffety.

She hadna sailed but twenty leagues,
   But twenty leagues and three,
When she met wi' a rank robber,
   And a' his company.

" Now whether are ye the queen hersell,
   (For so ye weel might be,)
Or are ye the Lass of Lochroyan,
   Seekin' Lord Gregory? "—

" O I am neither the queen," she said,
   " Nor sic I seem to be ;
But I am the Lass of Lochroyan,
   Seekin' Lord Gregory."—

" O see na thou yon bonny bower,
   It's a' cover'd o'er wi' tin?
When thou hast sail'd it round about,
   Lord Gregory is within."

And when she saw the stately tower
   Shining sae clear and bright,
Whilk stood aboon the jawing wave,
   Built on a rock of height ;

Says—" Row the boat, my mariners,
   And bring me to the land !
For yonder I see my love's castle
   Close by the salt-sea strand."

She sail'd it round, and sail'd it round,
    And loud, loud cried she—
"Now break, now break, ye fairy charms,
    And set my true love free!"

She's ta'en her young son in her arms,
    And to the door she's gane;
And long she knock'd, and sair she ca'd,
    But answer got she nane.

"O open the door, Lord Gregory!
    O open and let me in!
For the wind blaws through my yellow hair,
    And the rain draps o'er my chin."—

"Awa, awa, ye ill woman!
    Ye're no come here for good!
Ye're but some witch or wil warlock,
    Or mermaid o' the flood."—

"I am neither witch, nor wil warlock,
    Nor mermaid o' the sea;
But I am Annie of Lochroyan;
    O open the door to me!"—

"Gin thou be Annie of Lochroyan,
    (As I trow thou binna she,)
Now tell me some o' the love tokens
    That past between thee and me."—

"O dinna ye mind, Lord Gregory,
  As we sat at the wine,
We changed the rings frae our fingers?
  And I can show thee thine.

"O yours was gude, and gude enough,
  But aye the best was mine;
For yours was o' the gude red gowd,
  But mine o' the diamond fine.

"And has na thou mind, Lord Gregory,
  As we sat on the hill,
Thou twin'd me o' my maidenheid
  Right sair against my will?   .

"Now open the door, Lord Gregory!
  Open the door, I pray!
For thy young son is in my arms,
  And will be dead ere day."—

"If thou be the lass of Lochroyan,
  (As I kenna thou be,)
Tell me some mair o' the love tokens
  Past between me and thee."

Fair Annie turn'd her round about—
  "Weel! since that it be sae,
May never a woman that has borne a son,
  Hae a heart sae fou o' wae!

"Take down, take down, that mast o' gowd !
  Set up a mast o' tree !
It disna become a forsaken lady
  To sail sae royallie."

When the cock had crawn, and the day did
    dawn,
  And the sun began to peep,
Then up and raise him Lord Gregory,
  And sair, sair did he weep.

" Oh I hae dream'd a dream, mother,
  I wish it may prove true !
That the bonny Lass of Lochroyan
  Was at the yate e'en now.

" O I hae dream'd a dream, mother,
  The thought o't gars me greet !
That fair Annie o' Lochroyan
  Lay cauld dead at my feet."—

" Gin it be for Annie of Lochroyan
  That ye make a' this din,
She stood a' last night at your door,
  But I true she wan na in."—

" O wae betide ye, ill woman !
  An ill deid may ye die !
That wadna open the door to her,
  Nor yet wad waken me."

O he's gane down to yon shore side
　　As fast as he could fare ;
He saw fair Annie in the boat,
　　But the wind it toss'd her sair.

" And hey, Annie, and how, Annie !
　　O Annie, winna ye bide ! "
But aye the mair he cried Annie,
　　The braider grew the tide.

" And hey, Annie, and how, Annie !
　　Dear Annie, speak to me ! "
But aye the louder he cried Annie,
　　The louder roar'd the sea.

The wind blew loud, the sea grew rough,
　　And dash'd the boat on shore ;
Fair Annie floated through the faem,
　　But the babie rose no more.

Lord Gregory tore his yellow hair,
　　And made a heavy moan ;
Fair Annie's corpse lay at his feet,
　　Her bonny young son was gone.

O cherry, cherry was her cheek,
　　And gowden was her hair ;
But clay-cold were her rosy lips—
　　Nae spark o' life was there.

And first he kiss'd her cherry cheek,
  And syne he kiss'd her chin,
And syne he kiss'd her rosy lips—
  There was nae breath within.

" O wae betide my cruel mother!
  An ill death may she die!
She turn'd my true love frae my door,
  Wha came sae far to me.

" O wae betide my cruel mother!
  An ill death may she die!
She turn'd fair Annie frae my door,
  Wha died for love o' me."

THE DOUGLAS TRAGEDY.

Minstrelsy of the Scottish Border, iii. 3.

This ballad, of which more than thirty versions have been published in the Northern languages, is preserved in English in several forms, all of them more or less unsatisfactory. Of these the present copy comes nearest to the pure original, as it is found in Danish. The next best is *The Brave Earl Brand and The King of England's Daughter*, recently printed for the first time in Bell's *Ballads of the Peasantry*, and given at the end of this volume. *Erlinton* (vol. iii. 220) is much mutilated, and has a perverted conclusion, but retains a faint trace of one characteristic trait of the ancient ballad, which really constitutes the turning point of the story, but which all the others lack. (See *Erlinton*.) A fragment exists in the Percy MS., of which we can only say that if it much resembled Percy's *Child of Elle* (which it cannot), it might without loss be left undisturbed forever. In the only remaining copy Robin Hood appears as the hero. (See vol. v. p. 334.) It is of slight value, but considerably less insipid than the *Child of Elle*. Motherwell (*Minstrelsy*, p. 180) has given a few variations to Scott's ballad, but they are of no importance. — Of the corresponding Danish ballad, *Ribolt og Guldborg*, Grundtvig has collected more than twenty versions, some of them ancient, many obtained from recitation, and eight of the kindred *Hildebrand og Hilde.* There have also been printed of the latter, three versions in Swedish, and of the former, three in Icelandic, two in Norse, and seven in Swedish. (*Danmarks Gamle Folkeviser,* ii. 308-403, 674-81.) Jamieson has translated an inferior copy of the Danish ballad in *Illustrations of North. Antiq.,* p. 317.

" The ballad of *The Douglas Tragedy,*" says Scott, " is one of the few (?) to which popular tradition has ascribed complete locality.

" The farm of Blackhouse, in Selkirkshire, is said to have been the scene of this melancholy event. There are the remains of a very ancient tower, adjacent to the farm-house, in a wild and solitary glen, upon a torrent named Douglas burn, which joins the Yarrow, after passing a craggy rock, called the Douglas craig. . . . From this ancient tower Lady Margaret is said to have been carried by her lover. Seven large stones, erected upon the neighboring heights of Blackhouse, are shown, as marking the spot where the seven brethren were slain ; and the Douglas burn is averred to have been the stream at which the lovers stopped to drink : so minute is tradition in ascertaining the scene of a tragical tale, which, considering the rude state of former times, had probably foundation in some real event."

Were it not for Scott's concluding remark, and the obstinate credulity of most of the English and Scotch editors, we should hardly think it necessary to say that the locality of some of the incidents in *Ribolt and Guldborg,* is equally well ascertained (Grundtvig, 342, 343). " Popular tales and anecdotes of every kind," as Jamieson well remarks, " soon obtain locality wherever they are told ; and the intelligent and attentive

traveller will not be surprised to find the same story
which he had learnt when a child, with every appro-
priate circumstance of names, time, and place, in a
Glen of Morven, Lochaber, or Rannoch, equally do-
mesticated among the mountains of Norway, Caucasus,
or Thibet." *Ill. North. Ant.* p. 317.

"RISE up, rise up, now, Lord Douglas," she says,
  "And put on your armour so bright;
Let it never be said that a daughter of thine
  Was married to a lord under night.

"Rise up, rise up, my seven bold sons,
  And put on your armour so bright,
And take better care of your youngest sister,
  For your eldest's awa' the last night."—

He's mounted her on a milk-white steed,
  And himself on a dapple grey,
With a bugelet horn hung down by his side,
  And lightly they rode away.

Lord William lookit o'er his left shoulder,
  To see what he could see,
And there he spy'd her seven brethren bold,
  Come riding o'er the lee.

"Light down, light down, Lady Marg'ret," he said,
  "And hold my steed in your hand,

Until that against your seven brethren bold,
   And your father, I make a stand."—

She held his steed in her milk-white hand,
   And never shed one tear,
Until that she saw her seven brethren fa',
   And her father hard fighting, who loved her so
     dear.

" O hold your hand, Lord William ! " she said,
   " For your strokes they are wondrous sair ;
True lovers I can get many a ane,
   But a father I can never get mair."—

O she's ta'en out her handkerchief,
   It was o' the holland sae fine,
And aye she dighted her father's bloody wounds,
   That were redder than the wine.

"O chuse, O chuse, Lady Marg'ret," he said,
   " O whether will ye gang or bide ? "—
" I'll gang, I'll gang, Lord William," she said,
   " For you have left me no other guide."—

He's lifted her on a milk-white steed,
   And himself on a dapple grey,
With a bugelet horn hung down by his side,
   And slowly they baith rade away.

O they rade on, and on they rade,
   And a' by the light of the moon,
Until they came to yon wan water,
   And there they lighted down.

They lighted down to tak a drink
   Of the spring that ran sae clear ;
And down the stream ran his gude heart's blood,
   And sair she 'gan to fear.

" Hold up, hold up, Lord William," she says,
   " For I fear that you are slain !"—
" 'Tis naething but the shadow of my scarlet cloak,
   That shines in the water sae plain."—

O they rade on, and on they rade,
   And a' by the light of the moon,
Until they cam to his mother's ha' door,
   And there they lighted down.

" Get up, get up, lady mother," he says,
   " Get up, and let me in !"—
Get up, get up, lady mother," he says,
   " For this night my fair lady I've win.

" O mak my bed, lady mother," he says,
   " O mak it braid and deep !
And lay Lady Marg'ret close at my back,
   And the sounder I will sleep."—

Lord William was dead lang ere midnight,
　Lady Marg'ret lang ere day—
And all true lovers that go thegither,
　May they have mair luck than they!

Lord William was buried in St. Marie's kirk,
　Lady Marg'ret in Marie's quire;
Out o' the the lady's grave grew a bonny red
　rose,
And out o' the knight's a brier.

And they twa met, and they twa plat,
　And fain they wad be near;
And a' the warld might ken right weel,
　They were twa lovers dear.[1]

But bye and rade the Black Douglas,
　And wow but he was rough!
For he pull'd up the bonny brier,
　And flang't in St Marie's Loch.

[1] This miracle is frequently witnessed over the graves of faithful lovers.—King Mark, according to the German romance, planted a rose on Tristan's grave, and a vine on that of Isold. The roots struck down into the very hearts of the dead lovers, and the stems twined lovingly together. The French account is somewhat different. An eglantine sprung from the tomb of Tristan, and twisted itself round the monument of Isold. It was cut down three times, but grew up every morning fresher than before, so that it was allowed to stand. Other examples are, in this volume,

Fair Janet, Lord Thomas and Fair Annet; in the third volume, *Prince Robert,* &c. The same phenomenon is exhibited in the Swedish ballads of *Hertig Fröjdenborg och Fröken Adelin, Lilla Rosa, Hilla Lilla, Hertig Nils,* (*Svenska Folk-Visor,* i. 95, 116, Arwidsson, ii. 8, 21, 24,) in the Danish ballad of *Herr Sallemand,* (*Danske Viser,* iii. 348,) in the Breton ballad of *Lord Nann and the Korrigan,* translated in Keightley's *Fairy Mythology,* p. 433, in the Romansch ballad, *Ring und Schnupftuch,* translated by Schuller, *Romänische Volkslieder,* p. 36, in a Servian tale cited by Talvi, *Versuch,* &c., p. 139, in the Roumanian ballad of *Ring and Handkerchief,* Stanley's *Rouman Anthology,* p. 193, Schuller's Romänische Volkslieder, p. 36, and in the Afghan poem of *Audam and Doorkhaunee,* described by Elphinstone, *Account of the Kingdom of Caubul,* i. 295, — which last reference we owe to Talvi. — In the case of the Danish ballad it is certain, and in some of the other cases probable, that the idea was derived from the romance of *Tristan.*

The four pieces which follow have all the same subject. *Lord Thomas and Fair Ellinor*, is given from the *Collection of Old Ballads*, 1723, vol. i. p. 249, where it is entitled, *A Tragical Ballad on the unfortunate Love of Lord Thomas and Fair Ellinor, together with the Downfal of the Brown Girl*. The text differs but slightly from that of Percy, (iii. 121,) and Ritson, *Ancient Songs*, ii. 89.

Lord Thomas he was a bold forrester,
　And a chaser of the king's deer;
Fair Ellinor was a fine woman,
　And Lord Thomas he loved her dear

" Come riddle my riddle, dear mother," he said,
　" And riddle us both as one ;
Whether I shall marry with fair Ellinor,
　And let the brown girl alone ? "

"The brown girl she has got houses and land,
  And fair Ellinor she has got none ;
Therefore I charge you on my blessing,
  Bring me the brown girl home."

As it befell on a high holiday,
  As many more did beside,
Lord Thomas he went to fair Ellinor,
  That should have been his bride.

But when he came to fair Ellinors bower,
  He knocked there at the ring ;
But who was so ready as fair Ellinor,
  For to let Lord Thomas in.

"What news, what news, Lord Thomas?" she
    said,
  "What news hast thou brought unto me?"
"I am come to bid thee to my wedding,
  And that is bad news for thee."

"O God forbid, Lord Thomas," she said,
  "That such a thing should be done ;
I thought to have been thy bride my own self,
  And you to have been the bridegrom."

"Come riddle my riddle, dear mother," she
    said,
  "And riddle it all in one ;

Whether I shall go to Lord Thomas's wedding,
   Or whether I shall tarry at home ? "

" There are many that are your friends, daugh·
      ter,
   And many that are your foe ;
Therefore I charge you on my blessing,
   To Lord Thomas's wedding don't go."

" There's many that are my friends, mother ;
   And if a thousand more were my foe,
Betide my life, betide my death,
   To Lord Thomas's wedding I'll go.

She cloathed herself in gallant attire,
   And her merry men all in green ;
And as they rid through every town,
   They took her to be some queen.

But when she came to Lord Thomas's gate,
   She knocked there at the ring ;
But who was so ready as Lord Thomas,
   To let fair Ellinor in.

" Is this your bride ? " fair Ellinor said ;
   " Methinks she looks wonderful brown ;
Thou might'st have had as fair a woman,
   As ever trod on the ground."

"Despise her not, fair Ellin," he said,
  "Despise her not unto me ;
For better I love thy little finger,
  Than all her whole body.

This brown bride had a little penknife,
  That was both long and sharp,
And betwixt the short ribs and the long,
  Prick'd fair Ellinor to the heart.

" O Christ now save thee," Lord Thomas he said,
  "Methinks thou look'st wondrous wan ;
Thou us'd to look with as fresh a colour,
  As ever the sun shin'd on."

"O art thou blind, Lord Thomas ?" she said,
  "Or canst thou not very well see ?
O dost thou not see my own heart's blood
  Run trickling down my knee ?"

Lord Thomas he had a sword by his side ;
  As he walk'd about the hall,
He cut off his bride's head from her shoulders,
  And threw it against the wall.

He set the hilt against the ground,
  And the point against his heart ;
There never were three lovers met,
  That sooner did depart.

LORD THOMAS AND FAIR ANNET.

FROM Percy's *Reliques*, iii. 290, where it was " given,
with some corrections, from a MS. copy transmitted
from Scotland." There is a corresponding Swedish
Ballad, *Herr Peder och Liten Kerstin*, in the *Svenska
Folk-Visor*, i. 49. It is translated in *Literature and
Romance of Northern Europe*, by William and Mary
Howitt, i. 258.

LORD Thomas and fair Annet
 Sate a' day on a hill ;
Whan night was cum, and sun was sett,
 They had not talkt their fill.

Lord Thomas said a word in jest,
 Fair Annet took it ill :
" A' I will nevir wed a wife
 Against my ain friends will."

" Gif ye wull nevir wed a wife,
   A wife wull neir wed yee : "
Sae he is hame to tell his mither,
   And knelt upon his knee.

" O rede, O rede, mither," he says,
   " A gude rede gie to mee :
O sall I tak the nut-browne bride,
   And let faire Annet bee ? "

" The nut-browne bride haes gowd and gear,
   Fair Annet she has gat nane ;
And the little beauty fair Annet has,
   O it wull soon be gane."

And he has till his brother gane :
   " Now, brother, rede ye mee ;
A', sall I marrie the nut-browne bride,
   And let fair Annet bee ? "

" The nut-browne bride has oxen, brother,
   The nut-browne bride has kye :
I wad hae ye marrie the nut-browne bride,
   And cast fair Annet bye."

" Her oxen may dye i' the house, billie,
   And her kye into the byre,
And I sall hae nothing to mysell,
   Bot a fat fadge by the fyre."

And he has till his sister gane :
  " Now sister, rede ye mee ;
O sall I marrie the nut-browne bride,
  And set fair Annet free ? "

" Ise rede ye tak fair Annet, Thomas,
  And let the browne bride alane ;
Lest ye sould sigh, and say, Alace,
  What is this we brought hame ! "

" No, I will tak my mithers counsel,
  And marrie me owt o' hand ;
And I will tak the nut-browne bride ;
  Fair Annet may leive the land."

Up then rose fair Annets father,
  Twa hours or it wer day,
And he is gane into the bower
  Wherein fair Annet lay.

" Rise up, rise up, fair Annet," he says,
  " Put on your silken sheene ;
Let us gae to St. Maries kirke,
  And see that rich weddeen."

" My maides, gae to my dressing-roome,
  And dress to me my hair ;
Whair-eir yee laid a plait before,
  See yee lay ten times mair.

"My maids, gae to my dressing-room,
  And dress to me my smock;
The one half is o' the holland fine,
  The other o' needle-work."

The horse fair Annet rade upon,
  He amblit like the wind;
Wi' siller he was shod before,
  Wi' burning gowd behind.

Four and twanty siller bells
  Wer a' tyed till his mane,
And yae tift o' the norland wind,
  They tinkled ane by ane.

Four and twanty gay gude knichts
  Rade by fair Annets side,
And four and twanty fair ladies,
  As gin she had bin a bride.

And whan she cam to Maries kirk,
  She sat on Maries stean :
The cleading that fair Annet had on
  It skinkled in their een.

And whan she cam into the kirk,
  She shimmer'd like the sun ;
The belt that was about her waist,
  Was a' wi' pearles bedone.

She sat her by the nut-browne bride,
    And her een they wer sae clear,
Lord Thomas he clean forgat the bride,
    Whan fair Annet she drew near.

He had a rose into his hand,
    And he gave it kisses three,
And reaching by the nut-browne bride,
    Laid it on fair Annets knee.

Up than spak the nut-browne bride,
    She spak wi' meikle spite ;
"And whair gat ye that rose-water,
    That does mak yee sae white ? "

" O I did get the rose-water
    Whair ye wull neir get nane,
For I did get that very rose-water
    Into my mithers wame."

The bride she drew a long bodkin
    Frae out her gay head-gear,
And strake fair Annet unto the heart,
    That word she nevir spak mair.

Lord Thomas he saw fair Annet wex pale,
    And marvelit what mote bee :
But whan he saw her dear hearts blude,
    A' wood-wroth wexed hee.

He drew his dagger, that was sae sharp,
  That was sae sharp and meet,
And drave into the nut-browne bride,
  That fell deid at his feit.

"Now stay for me, dear Annet," he sed,
  " Now stay, my dear," he cry'd ;
Then strake the dagger untill his heart,
  And fell deid by her side.

Lord Thomas was buried without kirk-wa',
  Fair Annet within the quiere ;
And o' the tane thair grew a birk,
  The other a bonny briere.

And ay they grew, and ay they threw,
  As they wad faine be neare ;
And by this ye may ken right weil,
  They were twa luvers deare.

SWEET WILLIE AND FAIR ANNIE

Is another version of the foregoing piece, furnished
by Jamieson, *Popular Ballads*, i. 22.

"The text of *Lord Thomas and Fair Annet*," remarks Jamieson, "seems to have been adjusted, pre-
vious to its leaving Scotland, by some one who was
more of a scholar than the reciters of ballads generally
are ; and, in attempting to give it an antique cast, it
has been deprived of somewhat of that easy facility
which is the distinguished characteristic of the traditionary ballad narrative. With the text of the following ditty, no such experiment has been made. It is
here given pure and entire, as it was taken down by
the editor, from the recitation of a lady in Aberbrothick, (Mrs. W. Arrot.) As she had, when a child,
learnt the ballad from an elderly maid-servant, and
probably had not repeated it for a dozen years before
I had the good fortune to be introduced to her, it may
be depended upon, that every line was recited to me
as nearly as possible in the exact form in which she
learnt it."

Mr. Chambers, in conformity with the plan of his work, presents us with an edition composed out of Percy's and Jamieson's, with some amended readings and additional verses from a manuscript copy, (*Scottish Ballads*, p. 269.)

Sweet Willie and fair Annie
    Sat a' day on a hill;
And though they had sitten seven year,
    They ne'er wad had their fill.

Sweet Willie said a word in haste,
    And Annie took it ill:
" I winna wed a tocherless maid,
    Against my parent's will."

" Ye're come o' the rich, Willie,
    And I'm come o' the poor ;
I'm o'er laigh to be your bride,
    And I winna be your whore."

O Annie she's gane till her bower,
    And Willie down the den ;
And he's come till his mither's bower,
    By the lei light o' the moon.

" O sleep ye, wake ye, mither ?" he says,
    " Or are ye the bower within ? "

"I sleep richt aft, I wake richt aft[1];
    What want ye wi' me, son?

" Whare hae ye been a' night, Willie?
    O wow! ye've tarried lang!"
"I have been courtin' fair Annie,
    And she is frae me gane.

" There is twa maidens in a bower;
    Which o' them sall I bring hame?
The nut-brown maid has sheep and cows,
    And fair Annie has nane."

" It's an ye wed the nut-brown maid,
    I'll heap gold wi' my hand;
But an ye wed her, fair Annie,
    I'll straik it wi' a wand.

" The nut-brown maid has sheep and cows,
    And fair Annie has nane;
And Willie, for my benison,
    The nut-brown maid bring hame."

" O I sall wed the nut-brown maid,
    And I sall bring her hame;
But peace nor rest between us twa,
    Till death sinder's again.

[1] That is, my slumbers are short, broken, and interrupted. J.

" But, alas, alas ! " says sweet Willie,
  " O fair is Annie's face ! "
" But what's the matter, my son Willie,
  She has nae ither grace."

" Alas, alas ! " says sweet Willie,
  " But white is Annie's hand ! "
" But what's the matter, my son Willie,
  She hasna a fur o' land."

" Sheep will die in cots, mither,
  And owsen die in byre ;
And what's this warld's wealth to me,
  An I get na my heart's desire ?

" Whare will I get a bonny boy,
  That wad fain win hose and shoon,
That will rin to fair Annie's bower,
  Wi' the lei light o' the moon ?

" Ye'll tell her to come to Willie's weddin',
  The morn at twal at noon ;
Ye'll tell her to come to Willie's weddin',
  The heir o' Duplin town. [1]

 Duplin town. Duplin is the seat of the earl of Kinnoul,
from which he derives his title of viscount. It is in the
neighborhood of Perth. It is observable, that ballads are
very frequently adapted to the meridian of the place where
they are found. J.

" She manna put on the black, the black,
   Nor yet the dowie brown ;
But the scarlet sae red, and the kerches sae
      white,
And her bonny locks hangin' down."

He is on to Annie's bower,
   And tirled at the pin ;
And wha was sae ready as Annie hersel,
   To open and let him in.

" Ye are bidden come to Willie's weddin,
   The morn at twal at noon ;
Ye are bidden come to Willie's weddin',
   The heir of Duplin town.

" Ye manna put on the black, the black,
   Nor yet the dowie brown ;
But the scarlet sae red, and the kerches sae
      white,
   And your bonny locks hangin' down."

" Its I will come to Willie's weddin',
   The morn at twal at noon ;
Its I will come to Willie's weddin',
   But I rather the mass had been mine.

" Maidens, to my bower come,
   And lay gold on my hair ;

And whare ye laid ae plait before,
    Ye'll now lay ten times mair.

" Taylors, to my bower come,
    And mak to me a weed ;
And smiths unto my stable come,
    And shoe to me a steed."

At every tate o' Annie's horse' mane
    There hang a silver bell ;
And there came a wind out frae the south,
    Which made them a' to knell.

And whan she came to Mary-kirk,
    And sat down in the deas,
The light, that came frae fair Annie,
    Enlighten'd a' the place.

But up and stands the nut-brown bride,
    Just at her father's knee ;
" O wha is this, my father dear,
    That blinks in Willie's e'e ?"
" O this is Willie's first true love,
    Before he loved thee."

" If that be Willie's first true love,
    He might ha'e latten me be ;
She has as much gold on ae finger,
    As I'll wear till I die.

" O whare got ye that water, Annie,
　　That washes you sae white?"
" I got it in my mither's wambe,
　　Whare ye'll ne'er get the like.

" For ye've been wash'd in Dunny's well,
　　And dried on Dunny's dyke;
And a' the water in the sea
　　Will never wash ye white."

Willie's ta'en a rose out o' his hat,
　　Laid it in Annie's lap;
" [The bonniest to the bonniest fa's,]
　　Hae, wear it for my sake."

" Tak up and wear your rose, Willie,
　　And wear't wi' mickle care,
For the woman sall never bear a son,
　　That will mak my heart sae sair."

Whan night was come, and day was gane,
　　And a' man boun to bed,
Sweet Willie and the nut-brown bride
　　In their chamber were laid.

They werena weel lyen down,
　　And scarcely fa'n asleep,
Whan up and stands she, fair Annie,
　　Just up at Willie's feet.

" Weel brook ye o' your brown brown **bride,**
   Between ye and the wa';
And sae will I o' my winding sheet,
   That suits me best ava.

" Weel brook ye o' your brown brown bride,
   Between ye and the stock ;
And sae will I o' my black black kist,
   That has neither key nor lock."

Sad Willie raise, put on his claise,
   Drew till him his hose and **shoon,**
And he is on to Annie's bower,
   By the lei light o' the moon.

The firsten bower that he came till,
   There was right dowie wark ;
Her mither and her three sisters
   Were makin' to Annie a sark.

The nexten bower that he came till,
   There was right dowie cheir ;
Her father and her seven brethren
   Were makin' to Annie a bier.

The lasten bower, that he came till,
   [O heavy was his care !
The waxen lights were burning bright,]
   And fair Annie streekit there.

He's lifted up the coverlet,
  [Where she, fair Annie, lay ;
Sweet was her smile, but wan her cheek ;
  O wan, and cald as clay !]

" It's I will kiss your bonny cheek,
  And I will kiss your chin ;
And I will kiss your clay-cald lip ;
  But I'll never kiss woman again.

" The day ye deal at Annie's burial
  The bread but and the wine ;
Before the morn at twall o'clock,
  They'll deal the same at nine."

The tane was buried in Mary's kirk,
  The tither in Mary's quire ;
And out o' the tane there grew a birk,
  And out o' the tither a brier.

And ay they grew, and ay they drew,
  Untill they twa did meet ;
And every ane that past them by,
  Said, " Thae's been lovers sweet ! "

FAIR MARGARET AND SWEET WILLIAM.

From Percy's *Reliques*, iii. 164.

"This seems to be the old song quoted in Fletcher's *Knight of the Burning Pestle*, acts ii. and iii.; although the six lines there preserved are somewhat different from those in the ballad, as it stands at present. The reader will not wonder at this, when he is informed that this is only given from a modern printed copy picked up on a stall. Its full title is *Fair Margaret's misfortunes; or Sweet William's frightful dreams on his wedding night, with the sudden death and burial of those noble lovers.*

"The lines preserved in the play are this distich:

> " You are no love for me, Margaret,
>   I am no love for you."   Act iii. 5.

And the following stanza:

> " When it was grown to dark midnight,
>   And all were fast asleep,
> In came Margarets grimly ghost,
>   And stood at Williams feet.   Act ii. 8.

"These lines have acquired an importance by giving birth to one of the most beautiful ballads in our own or any other language: [Mallet's *Margaret's Ghost.*]

"Since the first edition, some improvements have been inserted, which were communicated by a lady of the first distinction, as she had heard this song repeated in her infancy."

The variations in Herd's copy, (i. 145,) and in Ritson's (*Ancient Songs*, ii. 92,) are unimportant.

In the main the same is the widely known ballad, *Der Ritter und das Mägdlein*, Erk, p. 81, Hoffmann's *Schlesische Volkslieder*, p. 9; *Herr Malmstens Drön*, *Svenska Folkvisor*, iii. 104, Arwidsson, ii. 21; *Volkslieder der Wenden*, by Haupt and Schmaler, i. 159–162 (Hoffmann); in Dutch, with a different close, Hoffmann's *Niederländische Volkslieder*, p. 61: also *Lord Lovel, post,* p. 162.

As it fell out on a long summer's day,
    Two lovers they sat on a hill;
They sat together that long summer's day,
    And could not talk their fill.

"I see no harm by you, Margaret,
    And you see none by mee;
Before to-morrow at eight o' the clock
    A rich wedding you shall see."

Fair Margaret sat in her bower-window,
    Combing her yellow hair;
There she spyed sweet William and his bride,
    As they were a riding near.

Then down she layd her ivory combe,
    And braided her hair in twain:
She went alive out of her bower,
    But ne'er came alive in't again.

When day was gone, and night was come,
    And all men fast asleep,
Then came the spirit of fair Marg'ret,
    And stood at Williams feet.

" Are you awake, sweet William ? " shee said,
    " Or, sweet William, are you asleep?
God give you joy of your gay bride-bed,
    And me of my winding-sheet." [1]

When day was come, and night 'twas gone,
    And all men wak'd from sleep,
Sweet William to his lady sayd,
    " My dear, I have cause to weep.

" I dreamt a dream, my dear ladye,
    Such dreames are never good:
I dreamt my bower was full of red swine,
    And my bride-bed full of blood."

" Such dreams, such dreams, my honoured sir,
    They never do prove good ;
To dream thy bower was full of red swine,
    And thy bride-bed full of blood."

[1] God give you joy, you lovers true,
    In bride-bed fast asleep;
Lo! I am going to my green-grass grave,
    And I'm in my winding sheet.   HERD's copy.

He called up his merry men all,
　By one, by two, and by three;
Saying, " I'll away to fair Marg'ret's bower,
　By the leave of my ladie."

And when he came to fair Marg'ret's bower,
　He knocked at the ring;
And who so ready as her seven brethren,
　To let sweet William in.

Then he turned up the covering-sheet;
　" Pray let me see the dead;
Methinks she looks all pale and wan,
　She hath lost her cherry red.

" I'll do more for thee, Margaret,
　Than any of thy kin:
For I will kiss thy pale wan lips,
　Though a smile I cannot win."

With that bespake the seven brethren,
　Making most piteous mone,
" You may go kiss your jolly brown bride,
　And let our sister alone."

"If I do kiss my jolly brown bride,
　I do but what is right;
I neer made a vow to yonder poor corpse,
　By day, nor yet by night.

" Deal on, deal on, my merry men all,
    Deal on your cake and your wine[1]:
For whatever is dealt at her funeral to-day,
    Shall be dealt to-morrow at mine."

Fair Margaret dyed to-day, to-day,
    Sweet William dyed the morrow :
Fair Margaret dyed for pure true love,
    Sweet William dyed for sorrow.

Margaret was buryed in the lower chancel,
    And William in the higher :
Out of her brest there sprang a rose,
    And out of his a briar.

They grew till they grew unto the church top,
    And then they could grow no higher ;
And there they tyed in a true lovers knot,
    Which made all the people admire.

Then came the clerk of the parish,
    As you the truth shall hear,
And by misfortune cut them down,
    Or they had now been there.

---

[1] Alluding to the dole anciently given at funerals. P.

As already remarked, is often made the sequel to other ballads. (See *Clerk Saunders*, p. 45.) It was first printed in the fourth volume of Ramsay's *Tea Table Miscellany*, with some imperfections, and with two spurious stanzas for a conclusion. We subjoin to Ramsay's copy the admirable version obtained by Motherwell from recitation, and still another variation furnished by Kinloch.

Closely similar in many respects are the Danish *Fæstemanden i Graven* (*Aage og Else*), Grundtvig, No. 90, and the Swedish *Sorgens Magt*, *Svenska F. V.*, i. 29, ii. 204, or Arwidsson, ii. 103. Also *Der Todte Freier*, Erk's *Liederhort*, 24, 24 a. In the Danish and Swedish ballads it is the uncontrolled grief of his mistress that calls the lover from his grave : in the English, the desire to be freed from his troth-plight. — See vol. i. p. 213, 217.

THERE came a ghost to Margaret's door,
  With many a grievous groan,
And ay he tirled at the pin,
  But answer made she none.

"Is that my father Philip,
  Or is't my brother John?
Or is't my true love Willy,
  From Scotland new come home? "

" Tis not thy father Philip,
 Nor yet thy brother John ;
But 'tis thy true love Willy,
 From Scotland new come home.

" O sweet Margaret ! O dear Margaret !
 I pray thee speak to mee :
Give me my faith and troth, Margaret,
 As I gave it to thee."

" Thy faith and troth thou's never get,
 Nor yet will I thee lend,
Till that thou come within my bower,
 And kiss my cheek and chin."

" If I should come within thy bower,
 I am no earthly man :
And should I kiss thy rosy lips,
 Thy days will not be lang.

" O sweet Margaret, O dear Margaret,
 I pray thee speak to mee :
Give me my faith and troth, Margaret,
 As I gave it to thee."

" Thy faith and troth thou's never get,
 Nor yet will I thee lend,
Till you take me to yon kirk-yard,
 And wed me with a ring."

" My bones are buried in yon kirk-yard,
   Afar beyond the sea,
And it is but my spirit, Margaret,
   That's now speaking to thee."

She stretched out her lily-white hand,
   And for to do her best ;
" Hae there[1] your faith and troth, Willy,
   God send your soul good rest."

Now she has kilted her robes of green
   A piece below her knee,
And a' the live-lang winter night
   The dead corps followed she.

" Is there any room at your head, Willy,
   Or any room at your feet ?
Or any room at your side, Willy,
   Wherein that I may creep ?"

" There's no room at my head, Margaret,
   There's no room at my feet ;
There's no room at my side, Margaret,
   My coffin's made so meet."

Then up and crew the red red cock,
   And up then crew the gray :
" Tis time, tis time, my dear Margaret,
   That you were going away."

<hr>

[1] ther's.

No more the ghost to Margaret said,
    But, with a grievous groan,
Evanish'd in a cloud of mist,
    And left her all alone.

" O stay, my only true love, stay,"
    The constant Margaret cried:
Wan grew her cheeks, she closed her een,
    Stretch'd her soft limbs, and died.

WILLIAM AND MARJORIE.

Motherwell's *Minstrelsy*, p. 186.

LADY MARJORIE, Lady Marjorie,
 Sat sewing her silken seam,
And by her came a pale, pale ghost,
 Wi' mony a sigh and mane.

" Are ye my father the king?" she says,
 " Or are ye my brither John?
Or are ye my true love, sweet William.
 From England newly come?"

"I'm not your father the king," he says,
 " No, no, nor your brither John ;
But I'm your true love, sweet William,
 From England that's newly come."

" Have ye brought me any scarlets sae red,
    Or any of the silks sae fine ;
Or have ye brought me any precious things,
    That merchants have for sale ? "

" I have not brought you any scarlets sae red,
    No, no, nor the silks sae fine ;
But I have brought you my winding-sheet
    Ower many a rock and hill.

" Lady Marjorie, Lady Marjorie,
    For faith and charitie,
Will ye gie to me my faith and troth,
    That I gave once to thee ? "

" O your faith and troth I'll not gie to thee,
    No, no, that will not I,
Until I get ae kiss of your ruby lips,
    And in my arms you lye."

" My lips they are sae bitter," he says,
    " My breath it is sae strang,
If you get ae kiss of my ruby lips,
    Your days will not be lang.

" The cocks are crawing, Marjorie," he says,—
    " The cocks are crawing again ;
It's time the dead should part the quick,—
    Marjorie, I must be gane."

She followed him high, she followed him low,
    Till she came to yon churchyard green;
And there the deep grave opened up,
    And young William he lay down.

" What three things are these, sweet William,"
      she says,
    " That stand here at your head ? "
" O it's three maidens, Marjorie," he says,
    "That I promised once to wed."

" What three things are these, sweet William,"
      she says,
    " That stand close at your side ? "
" O it's three babes, Marjorie," he says,
    " That these three maidens had."

" What three things are these, sweet William,"
      she says,
    " That lye close at your feet ? "
" O it's three hell-hounds, Marjorie," he says,
    " That's waiting my soul to keep."

O she took up her white, white hand,
    And she struck him on the breast,
Saying,—" Have there again your faith and
      troth,
    And I wish your saul gude rest."

SWEET WILLIAM AND MAY MARGARET.

Kinloch's *Ancient Scottish Ballads*, p. 241.

As May Marg'ret sat in her bouerie,
  In her bouer all alone,
At the very parting o' midnicht,
  She heard a mournfu' moan.

" O is it my father, O is it my mother,
  Or is it my brother John?
Or is it sweet William, my ain true love,
  To Scotland new come home ? "

" It is na your father, it is na your mother,
  It is na your brother John ;
But it is sweet William, your ain true love,
  To Scotland new come home."—

" Hae ye brought me onie fine things,
    Onie new thing for to wear?
Or hae ye brought me a braid o' lace,
    To snood up my gowden hair? "

" I've brought ye na fine things at all,
    Nor onie new thing to wear,
Nor hae I brought ye a braid of lace,
    To snood up your gowden hair.

" But Margaret, dear Margaret,
    I pray ye speak to me ;
O gie me back my faith and troth,
    As dear as I gied it thee ! "

" Your faith and troth ye sanna get,
    Nor will I wi' ye twin,
Till ye come within my bower,
    And kiss me, cheek and chin."

" O Margaret, dear Margaret,
    I pray ye speak to me ;
O gie me back my faith and troth,
    As dear as I gied it thee."

" Your faith and troth ye sanna get,
    Nor will I wi' ye twin,
Till ye tak me to yonder kirk,
    And wed me wi' a ring."

"O should I come within your bouer,
  I am na earthly man:
If I should kiss your red, red lips,
  Your days wad na be lang.

"My banes are buried in yon kirk-yard,
  It's far ayont the sea ;
And it is my spirit, Margaret,
  That's speaking unto thee."

"Your faith and troth ye sanna get,
  Nor will I twin wi' thee,
Tell ye tell me the pleasures o' Heaven,
  And pains of hell how they be."

"The pleasures of heaven I wat not of,
  But the pains of hell I dree ;
There some are lie hang'd for huring,
  And some for adulterie."

Then Marg'ret took her milk-white hand,
  And smooth'd it on his breast ;—
"Tak your faith and troth, William,
  God send your soul good rest !"

BONNY BARBARA ALLAN

WAS first published in Ramsay's *Tea-Table Miscellany*, (ii. 171,) from which it is transferred verbatim into Herd's *Scottish Songs*, Johnson's *Museum*, Ritson's *Scottish Songs*, &c. Percy printed it, " with a few conjectural emendations, from a written copy," *Reliques*, iii. 175, together with another version, which follows the present. Mr. G. F. Graham, *Songs of Scotland*, ii. 157, has pointed out an allusion to the " little Scotch Song of *Barbary Allen*," in Pepys's *Diary*, 2 Jan. 1665-6.

IT was in and about the Martinmas time,
   When the green leaves were a falling,
That Sir John Graeme in the west country
   Fell in love with Barbara Allan.

He sent his man down through the town,
   To the place where she was dwelling;
" O haste and come to my master dear,
   Gin ye be Barbara Allan."

O hooly, hooly rose she up,
　　To the place where he was lying,
And when she drew the curtain by,
　　" Young man, I think you're dying."

"O it's I'm sick, and very, very sick,
　　And 'tis a' for Barbara Allan : "
" O the better for me ye's never be,
　　Tho' your heart's blood were a spilling.

" O dinna ye mind, young man," said she,
　　" When ye was in the tavern a drinking,
That ye made the healths gae round and round,
　　And slighted Barbara Allan."

He turn'd his face unto the wall,
　　And death was with him dealing ;
" Adieu, adieu, my dear friends all,
　　And be kind to Barbara Allan."

And slowly, slowly raise she up,
　　And slowly, slowly left him ;
And sighing said, she cou'd not stay,
　　Since death of life had reft him.

She had not gane a mile but twa,
　　When she heard the dead-bell ringing,
And every jow that the dead-bell geid,
　　It cry'd " Woe to Barbara Allan ! "

" O mother, mother, make my bed,
   O make it saft and narrow ;
Since my love died for me today,
   I'll die for him tomorrow."

BARBARA ALLEN'S CRUELTY.

From Percy's *Reliques*, iii. 169.

"GIVEN, with some corrections, from an old black-letter copy, entitled, *Barbara Allen's Cruelty, or the Young Man's Tragedy.*"

In Scarlet towne, where I was borne,
    There was a faire maid dwellin,
Made every youth crye, Wel-awaye!
    Her name was Barbara Allen.

All in the merrye month of May,
    When greene buds they were swellin,
Yong Jemmye Grove on his death-bed lay,
    For love of Barbara Allen.

He sent his man unto her then,
    To the towne where shee was dwellin;
"You must come to my master deare,
    Giff your name be Barbara Allen.

" For death is printed on his face,
    And ore his hart is stealin :
Then haste away to comfort him,
    O lovelye Barbara Allen."

" Though death be printed on his face,
    And ore his harte is stealin,
Yet little better shall he bee
    For bonny Barbara Allen."

So slowly, slowly, she came up,
    And slowly she came nye him ;
And all she sayd, when there she came,
    " Yong man, I think y'are dying."

He turned his face unto her strait,
    With deadlye sorrow sighing ;
" O lovely maid, come pity mee,
    I'me on my death-bed lying."

" If on your death-bed you doe lye,
    What needs the tale you are tellin ?
I cannot keep you from your death ;
    Farewell," sayd Barbara Allen.

He turnd his face unto the wall,
    As deadlye pangs he fell in :
" Adieu ! adieu ! adieu to you all,
    Adieu to Barbara Allen !"

As she was walking ore the fields,
   She heard the bell a knellin ;
And every stroke did seem to saye,
   " Unworthy Barbara Allen ! "

She turnd her bodye round about,
   And spied the corps a coming :
" Laye down, laye down the corps," she sayd,
   " That I may look upon him."

With scornful eye she looked downe,
   Her cheeke with laughter swellin,
Whilst all her friends cryd out amaine,
   " Unworthye Barbara Allen ! "

When he was dead, and laid in grave,
   Her harte was struck with sorrowe ;
" O mother, mother, make my bed,
   For I shall dye to-morrowe.

" Hard-harted creature him to slight,
   Who loved me so dearlye :
O that I had beene more kind to him,
   When he was alive and neare me ! "

She, on her death-bed as she laye,
   Beg'd to be buried by him,
And sore repented of the daye,
   That she did ere denye him.

"Farewell," she sayd, "ye virgins all,
   And shun the fault I fell in:
Henceforth take warning by the fall
   Of cruel Barbara Allen."

LORD LOVEL.

" This ballad, taken down from the recitation of a
lady in Roxburghshire, appears to claim affinity to
Border Song ; and the title of the ' discourteous squire,'
would incline one to suppose that it has derived its origin from some circumstance connected with the county
of Northumberland, where Lovel was anciently a well-
known name." Kinloch's *Ancient Scottish Ballads*,
p. 31.

A version from a recent broadside is printed in
*Ancient Poems, Ballads, and Songs of the Peasantry
of England*, Percy Society, vol. xvii. p. 78.

A fragment of a similar story, the relations of the
parties being reversed, is *Lady Alice*, given in Bell's
Ballads of the Peasantry, p. 127, and *Notes and Queries*, 2d S, i. 418. —Compare also *Fair Margaret*, &c. p.
140.

Lord Lovel stands at his stable door,
    Mounted upon a grey steed ;
And bye came Ladie Nanciebel,
    And wish'd Lord Lovel much speed.

" O whare are ye going, Lord Lovel,
    My dearest tell to me ? "
" O I am going a far journey,
    Some strange countrie to see ;

" But I'll return in seven long years,
   Lady Nanciebel to see."
" O seven, seven, seven long years,
   They are much too long for me."

*   *   *   *   *   *   *

He was gane a year away,
   A year but barely ane,
When a strange fancy cam into his head,
   That fair Nanciebel was gane.

It's then he rade, and better rade,
   Until he cam to the toun,
And then he heard a dismal noise,
    ˙ For the church bells a' did soun'.

He asked what the bells rang for :
   They said, " It's for Nanciebel ;
She died for a discourteous squire,
   And his name is Lord Lovel."

The lid o' the coffin he opened up,
   The linens he faulded doun ;
And ae he kiss'd her pale, pale lips,
   And the tears cam trinkling doun.

" Weill may I kiss those pale, pale lips,
   For they will never kiss me ;—

I'll mak a vow, and keep it true,
   That they'll ne'er kiss ane but thee."

Lady Nancie died on Tuesday's nicht,
   Lord Lovel upon the niest day;
Lady Nancie died for pure, pure love,
   Lord Lovel, for deep sorray.

LORD SALTON AND AUCHANACHIE.

THE following fragment was first published in Maidment's *North Countrie Garland*, p. 10 ; shortly after, in Buchan's *Gleanings*, p. 161. A more complete copy, from Buchan's larger collection, is annexed.

*   *   *   *   *   *

BEN came her father,
　Skipping on the floor,
Said, " Jeanie, you're trying
　The tricks of a whore.

" You're caring for him
　That cares not for thee,
And I pray you take Salton,
　Let Auchanachie be."

" I will not have Salton,
　It lies low by the sea ;

He is bowed in the back,
    He's thrawen in the knee;
And I'll die if I get not
    My brave Auchanachie."

" I am bowed in the back,
    Lassie as ye see,
But the bonny lands of Salton
    Are no crooked tee."

And when she was married
    She would not lie down,
But they took out a knife,
    And cuttit her gown;

Likewise of her stays
    The lacing in three,
And now she lies dead
    For her Auchanachie.

Out comes her bower-woman,
    Wringing her hands,
Says, " Alas for the staying
    So long on the sands!

" Alas for the staying
    So long on the flood!
For Jeanie was married,
    And now she is dead."

LORD SALTON AND AUCHANACHIE.

From Buchan's *Ballads of the North of Scotland*, ii. 133.

"AUCHANACHIE Gordon is bonny and braw,
He would tempt any woman that ever he saw ;
He would tempt any woman, so has he tempted me,
And I'll die if I getna my love Auchanachie."

In came her father, tripping on the floor,
Says, "Jeanie, ye're trying the tricks o' a whore;
Ye're caring for them that cares little for thee,
Ye must marry Salton, leave Auchanachie.

"Auchanachie Gordon, he is but a man,
Altho' he be pretty, where lies his free land?
Salton's lands they lie broad, his towers they stand
    hie,
Ye must marry Salton, leave Auchanachie.

" Salton will gar you wear silk gowns fring'd to
    thy knee,
But ye'll never wear that wi' your love Auchana-
    chie."
" Wi' Auchanachie Gordon I would beg my bread,
Before that wi' Salton I'd wear gowd on my head;

" Wear gowd on my head, or gowns fring'd to the
    knee,
And I'll die if I getna my love Auchanachie;
O Salton's valley lies low by the sea,
He's bowed on the back, and thrawin on the knee."

" O Salton's a valley lies low by the sea;
Though he's bowed on the back, and thrawin on
    the knee,
Though he's bowed on the back, and thrawin on
    the knee,
The bonny rigs of Salton they're nae thrawin tee."

" O you that are my parents to church may me
    bring,
But unto young Salton I'll never bear a son;
For son, or for daughter, I'll ne'er bow my knee,
And I'll die if I getna my love Auchanachie."

When Jeanie was married, from church was
    brought hame,
When she wi' her maidens sae merry shou'd hae
    been,

When she wi' her maidens sae merry shou'd hae
    been,
She's called for a chamber to weep there her lane.

" Come to your bed, Jeanie, my honey and my
    sweet,
For to stile you mistress I do not think it meet."
" Mistress, or Jeanie, it is a' ane to me,
It's in your bed, Salton, I never will be."

Then out spake her father, he spake wi' renown,
" Some of you that are maidens, ye'll loose aff her
    gown ;
Some of you that are maidens, ye'll loose aff her
    gown,
And I'll mend the marriage wi' ten thousand
    crowns."

Then ane of her maidens they loosed aff her gown,
But bonny Jeanie Gordon, she fell in a swoon ;
She fell in a swoon low down by their knee ;
Says, " Look on, I die for my love Auchanachie !"

That very same day Miss Jeanie did die,
And hame came Auchanachie, hame frae the sea ;
Her father and mither welcom'd him at the gate ;
He said, " Where's Miss Jeanie, that she's nae
    here yet ?"

Then forth came her maidens, all wringing their
    hands,

Saying, "Alas! for your staying sae lang **frae**
    the land:
Sae lang frae the land, and sae lang fra the fleed,
They've wedded your Jeanie, and now she is
    dead!"

"Some of you, her maidens, take me by the hand,
And show me the chamber Miss Jeanie died in;"
He kiss'd her cold lips, which were colder than
    stane,
And he died in the chamber that Jeanie died in.

WILLIE AND MAY MARGARET.

A FRAGMENT obtained by Jamieson from the recitation of Mrs. Brown, of Falkland. *Popular Ballads,* i. 135. In connection with this we give the complete story from Buchan. Aytoun has changed the title to *The Mother's Malison.* An Italian ballad, containing a story similar to that of this ballad and the two following (but of independent origin), is *La Maledizione Materna,* in Marcoaldi's *Canti Popolari,* p. 170

" GIE corn to my horse, mither ;
   Gie meat unto my man ;
For I maun gang to Margaret's bower
   Before the nicht comes on."

" O stay at hame now, my son Willie !
   The wind blaws cald and sour ;
The nicht will be baith mirk and late,
   Before ye reach her bower."

" O tho' the nicht were ever sae dark,
   Or the wind blew never sae cald,
I will be in my Margaret's bower
   Before twa hours be tald."

"O gin ye gang to May Margaret,
   Without the leave of me,
Clyde's water's wide and deep enough ;—
   My malison drown thee!"

He mounted on his coal-black steed,
   And fast he rade awa' ;
But, ere he came to Clyde's water,
   Fu' loud the wind did blaw.

As he rode o'er yon hich, hich hill,
   And down yon dowie den,
There was a roar in Clyde's water
   Wad fear'd a hunder men.

His heart was warm, his pride was up ;
   Sweet Willie kentna fear ;
But yet his mither's malison
   Ay sounded in his ear.

O he has swam through Clyde's water,
   Tho' it was wide and deep ;
And he came to May Margaret's door,
   When a' were fast asleep.

O he's gane round and round about,
   And tirled at the pin ;
But doors were steek'd, and window's bar'd,
   And nane wad let him in.

" O open the door to me, Margaret,—
   O open and lat me in !
For my boots are full o' Clyde's water,
   And frozen to the brim."

" I darena open the door to you,
   Nor darena lat you in ;
For my mither she is fast asleep,
   And I darena mak nae din."

" O gin ye winna open the door,
   Nor yet be kind to me,
Now tell me o' some out-chamber,
   Where I this nicht may be."

" Ye canna win in this nicht, Willie,
   Nor here ye canna be ;
For I've nae chambers out nor in,
   Nae ane but barely three :

" The tane o' them is fu' o' corn,
   The tither is fu' o' hay ;
The tither is fu' o' merry young men ;—
   They winna remove till day."

' O fare ye weel, then, May Margaret,
   Sin better manna be ;
I've win my mither's malison,
   Coming this nicht to thee."

He's mounted on his coal-black steed,—
O but his heart was wae!
But, ere he came to Clyde's water,
'Twas half up o'er the brae.

*   *   *   *   *   *   *

———————— he plunged in,
But never raise again.

THE DROWNED LOVERS.

FROM Buchan's *Ballads of the North of Scotland,*
i. 140. The copy in the Appendix to Motherwell's
Minstrelsy, p. iii., is nearly the same.

WILLIE stands in his stable door,
  And clapping at his steed ;
And looking o'er his white fingers,
  His nose began to bleed.

" Gie corn to my horse, mother;
  And meat to my young man ;
And I'll awa' to Meggie's bower,
  I'll win ere she lie down."

" O bide this night wi' me, Willie
  O bide this night wi' me ;
The best an' cock o' a' the reest,
  At your supper shall be.

" A' your cocks, and a' your reests,
      I value not a prin ;
For I'll awa' to Meggie's bower,
      I'll win ere she lie down."

" Stay this night wi' me, Willie,
      O stay this night wi' me ;
The best an' sheep in a' the flock
      At your supper shall be."

" A' your sheep, and a' your flocks,
      I value not a prin ;
For I'll awa' to Meggie's bower,
      I'll win ere she lie down."

" O an' ye gang to Meggie's bower,
      Sae sair against my will,
The deepest pot in Clyde's water,
      My malison ye's feel."

" The guid steed that I ride upon
      Cost me thrice thretty pound ;
And I'll put trust in his swift feet,
      To hae me safe to land."

As he rade ower yon high, high hill,
      And down yon dowie den,
The noise that was in Clyde's water
      Wou'd fear'd five huner men.

" O roaring Clyde, ye roar ower loud,
   Your streams seem wond'rous strang;
Make me your wreck as I come back,
   But spare me as I gang."[1]

Then he is on to Meggie's bower,
   And tirled at the pin ;
" O sleep ye, wake ye, Meggie," he said,
" Ye'll open, lat me come in."

" O wha is this at my bower door,
   That calls me by my name ? "
" It is your first love, sweet Willie,
   This night newly come hame."

" I hae few lovers thereout, thereout,
   As few hae I therein;
The best an' love that ever I had,
   Was here just late yestreen."

" The warstan stable in a' your stables,
   For my puir steed to stand ;
The warstan bower in a' your bowers,
   For me to lie therein :
My boots are fu' o' Clyde's water,
   I'm shivering at the chin."

[1] Found also in *Leander on the bays*, and taken from
the epigram of Martial:

   " Clamabat tumidis audax Leander in undis,
      Mergite me fluctus, cum rediturus ero."

" My barns are fu' o' corn, Willie,
  My stables are fu' o' hay ;
My bowers are fu' o' gentlemen ;—
  They'll nae remove till day."

" O fare-ye-well, my fause Meggie,
  O farewell, and adieu ;
I've gotten my mither's malison,
  This night coming to you."

As he rode ower yon high, high hill,
  And down yon dowie den ;
The rushing that was in Clyde's water
  Took Willie's cane frae him.

He lean'd him ower his saddle bow,
  To catch his cane again ;
The rushing that was in Clyde's water
  Took Willie's hat frae him.

He lean'd him ower his saddle bow,
  To catch his hat thro' force ;
The rushing that was in Clyde's water
  Took Willie frae his horse.

His brither stood upo' the bank,
  Says, " Fye, man, will ye drown?
Ye'll turn ye to your high horse head,
  And learn how to sowm."

" How can I turn to my horse head,
  And learn how to sowm ?
I've gotten my mither's malison,
  Its here that I maun drown !"

The very hour this young man sank
  Into the pot sae deep,
Up it waken'd his love, Meggie,
  Out o' her drowsy sleep.

" Come here, come here, my mither **dear,**
  And read this dreary dream ;
I dream'd my love was at our gates,
  And nane wad let him in."

" Lye still, lye still now, my Meggie.
  Lye still and tak your rest ;
Sin' your true love was at your yates,
  It's but twa quarters past."

Nimbly, nimbly raise she up,
  And nimbly pat she on ;
And the higher that the lady cried,
  The louder blew the win.'

The first an' step that she stepp'd in,
  She stepped to the queet ;
" Ohon, alas !" said that lady,
  " This water's wond'rous deep."

The next an' step that she wade in,
  She wadit to the knee ;
Says she, " I cou'd wide farther in,
  If I my love cou'd see."

The next an' step that she wade in,
  She wadit to the chin ;
The deepest pot in Clyde's water
  She got sweet Willie in.

" You've had a cruel mither, Willie,
  And I have had anither ;
But we shall sleep in Clyde's water,
  Like sister an' like brither."

WILLIE'S DROWNED IN GAMERY.

From Buchan's *Ballads of the North of Scotland,*
i. 245. A fragment, exhibiting some differences, is
among those ballads of Buchan which are published in
the Percy Society's volumes, xvii. 66. Four stanzas,
of a superior cast, upon the same story, are printed in
the *Tea-Table Miscellany,* (ii. 141.)

Rare Willy drown'd in Yarrow.

" Willy's rare, and Willy's fair,
    And Willy's wond'rous bonny;
And Willy heght to marry me,
    Gin e'er he married ony.

" Yestreen I made my bed fu' braid,
    This night I'll make it narrow;
For a' the livelang winter night
    I ly twin'd of my marrow.

" O came you by yon water-side?
    Pou'd you the rose or lilly?
Or came you by yon meadow green?
    Or saw you my sweet Willy? "

She sought him east, she sought him west,
    She sought him braid and narrow;
Syne in the cleaving of a craig,
    She found him drown'd in Yarrow.

These stanzas furnished the theme to Logan's *Braes
of Yarrow.*

"O WILLIE is fair, and Willie is rare,
    And Willie is wond'rous bonny;
And Willie says he'll marry me,
    Gin ever he marry ony."

"O ye'se get James, or ye'se get George,
    Or ye's get bonny Johnnie;
Ye'se get the flower o' a' my sons,
    Gin ye'll forsake my Willie."

"O what care I for James or George,
    Or yet for bonny Peter?
I dinna value their love a leek,
    An' I getna Willie the writer."

"O Willie has a bonny hand,
    And dear but it is bonny;"
"He has nae mair for a' his land;
    What wou'd ye do wi' Willie?"

" O Willie has a bonny face,
   And dear but it is bonny ; "
" But Willie has nae other grace ;
   What wou'd ye do wi' Willie ? "

" Willie's fair, and Willie's rare,
   And Willie's wond'rous bonny ;
There's nane wi' him that can compare,
   I love him best of ony."

On Wednesday, that fatal day,
   The people were convening ;
Besides all this, threescore and ten,
   To gang to the bridesteel wi' him.

" Ride on, ride on, my merry men a',
   I've forgot something behind me ;
I've forgot to get my mother's blessing,
   To gae to the bridesteel wi' me."

" Your Peggy she's but bare fifteen,
   And ye are scarcely twenty ;
The water o' Gamery is wide and braid,
   My heavy curse gang wi' thee ! "

Then they rode on, and further on,
   Till they came on to Gamery ;
The wind was loud, the stream was proud,
   And wi' the stream gaed Willie.

Then they rode on, and further on,
    Till they came to the kirk o' Gamery;
And every one on high horse sat,
    But Willie's horse rade toomly.

When they were settled at that place,
    The people fell a mourning;
And a council held amo' them a',
    But sair, sair wept Kinmundy.

Then out it speaks the bride hersell,
    Says, "What means a' this mourning?"
Where is the man amo' them a',
    That shou'd gie me fair wedding?"

Then out it speaks his brother John,
    Says, "Meg, I'll tell you plainly;
The stream was strong, the clerk rade wrong,
    And Willie's drown'd in Gamery."

She put her hand up to her head,
    Where were the ribbons many;
She rave them a', let them down fa,'
    And straightway ran to Gamery.

She sought it up, she sought it down,
    Till she was wet and weary;
And in the middle part o' it,
    There she got her deary.

Then she stroak'd back his yellow hair,
  And kiss'd his mou' sae comely ;
"My mother's heart's be as wae as thine ;
  We'se baith asleep in the water o' Gam-
    ery."

ANNAN WATER.

Minstrelsy of the Scottish Border, iii. 282.

" The following verses are the original words of the
tune of *Allan Water*, by which name the song is
mentioned in Ramsay's *Tea-Table Miscellany*. The
ballad is given from tradition; and it is said that a
bridge over the Annan, was built in consequence of
the melancholy catastrophe which it narrates. Two
verses are added in this edition, from another copy of
the ballad, in which the conclusion proves fortunate.
By the *Gatehope-Slack*, is perhaps meant the *Gate-
Slack*, a pass in Annandale. The Annan, and the
Frith of Solway, into which it falls, are the frequent
scenes of tragical accidents. The Editor trusts he will
be pardoned for inserting the following awfully impres-
sive account of such an event, contained in a letter
from Dr. Currie, of Liverpool, by whose correspond-
ence, while in the course of preparing these volumes
for the press, he has been alike honoured and instruct-

ed. After stating that he had some recollection of the
ballad which follows, the biographer of Burns proceeds
thus :—" I once in my early days heard (for it was
night, and I could not see) a traveller drowning; not
in the Annan itself, but in the Frith of Solway, close
by the mouth of that river. The influx of the tide had
unhorsed him, in the night, as he was passing the sands
from Cumberland. The west wind blew a tempest,
and, according to the common expression, brought in
the water *three foot a-breast*. The traveller got upon
a standing net, a little way from the shore. There he
lashed himself to the post, shouting for half an hour
for assistance—till the tide rose over his head ! In the
darkness of the night, and amid the pauses of the hur-
ricane, his voice, heard at intervals, was exquisitely
mournful. No one could go to his assistance—no one
knew where he was—the sound seemed to proceed from
the spirit of the waters. But morning rose—the tide
had ebbed—and the poor traveller was found lashed to
the pole of the net, and bleaching in the wind.' "

SCOTT.

" ANNAN water's wading deep,
 And my love Annie's wondrous bonny ;
And I am laith she suld weet her feet,
 Because I love her best of ony.

" Gar saddle me the bonny black,
 Gar saddle sune, and make him ready :
For I will down the Gatehope-Slack,
 And all to see my bonny ladye." —

He has loupen on the bonny black,
   He stirr'd him wi' the spur right sairly ;
But, or he wan the Gatehope-Slack,
   I think the steed was wae and weary.

He has loupen on the bonny grey,
   He rade the right gate and the ready ;
I trow he would neither stint nor stay,
   For he was seeking his bonny ladye.

O he has ridden o'er field and fell,
   Through muir and moss, and mony a mire:
His spurs o' steel were sair to bide,
   And fra her fore-feet flew the fire.

" Now, bonny grey, now play your part!
   Gin ye be the steed that wins my deary,
Wi' corn and hay ye'se be fed for aye,
   And never spur sall make you wearie."—

The grey was a mare, and a right good mare ;
   But when she wan the Annan water,
She couldna hae ridden a furlong mair,
   Had a thousand merks been wadded at her.

" O boatman, boatman, put off your boat!
   Put off your boat for gowden money !
I cross the drumly stream the night,
   Or never mair I see my honey."—

"O I was sworn sae late yestreen,
  And not by ae aith, but by many ;
And for a' the gowd in fair Scotland,
  I dare na take ye through to Annie."

The side was stey, and the bottom deep,
  Frae bank to brae the water pouring ;
And the bonny grey mare did sweat for fear,
  For she heard the water-kelpy roaring.

O he has pou'd aff his dapperpy coat,
  The silver buttons glanced bonny ;
The waistcoat bursted aff his breast,
  He was sae full of melancholy.

He has ta'en the ford at that stream tail ;
  I wot he swam both strong and steady ;
But the stream was broad, and his strength did
      fail,
  And he never saw his bonny ladye !

"O wae betide the frush saugh wand !
  And wae betide the bush of brier !
It brake into my true love's hand,
  When his strength did fail, and his limbs did
      tire.

"And wae betide ye, Annan Water,
  This night that ye are a drumlie river !
For over thee I'll build a bridge,
  That ye never more true love may sever."—

"FROM a stall copy published at Glasgow several
years ago, collated with a recited copy, which has furnished one or two verbal improvements." Motherwell's *Minstrelsy*, p. 239.

Mr. Jamieson has published two other sets of this
simple, but touching ditty, (i. 126, ii. 382,) one of
which is placed after the present. Motherwell's text
is almost verbatim that of Buchan's *Gleanings*, p. 98.
The *Thistle of Scotland* copies Buchan and Jamieson
without acknowledgment.

The story has been made the foundation of a rude
drama in the North of Scotland. For a description of
similar entertainments, see Cunningham's Introduction
to his *Songs of Scotland*, i. 148.

The unfortunate maiden's name, according to Buchan, (*Gleanings*, p. 197,) "was Annie, or Agnes,
(which are synonymous in some parts of Scotland,)
Smith, who died of a broken heart on the 9th of Janu-
ary, 1631, as is to be found on a roughly cut stone,
broken in many pieces, in the green churchyard of

Fyvie." " What afterwards became of Bonny Andrew
Lammie," says Jamieson, " we have not been able to
learn ; but the current tradition of the ' Lawland leas
of Fyvie,' says, that some years subsequent to the melancholy fate of poor Tifty's Nanny, her sad story being
mentioned, and the ballad sung in a company in Edinburgh when he was present, he remained silent and
motionless, till he was discovered by a groan suddenly
bursting from him, and *several of the buttons flying
from his waistcoat.*"

At Mill o' Tifty liv'd a man,
   In the neighbourhood of Fyvie ·
He had a lovely daughter fair,
   Was called bonny Annie.

Her bloom was like the springing flower
   That salutes the rosy morning ;
With innocence and graceful mien
   Her beauteous form adorning.

Lord Fyvie had a trumpeter
   Whose name was Andrew Lammie ;
He had the art to gain the heart
   Of Mill o' Tiftie's Annie.

Proper he was, both young and gay,
   His like was not in Fyvie ;
No one was there that could compare
   With this same Andrew Lammie.

Lord Fyvie he rode by the door,
　　Where lived Tiftie's Annie;
His trumpeter rode him before,
　　Even this same Andrew Lammie.

Her mother call'd her to the door:
　　" Come here to me, my Annie;
Did you ever see a prettier man
　　Than this Trumpeter of Fyvie ? "

She sighed sore, but said no more,
　　Alas, for bonny Annie!
She durst not own her heart was won
　　By the Trumpeter of Fyvie.

At night when they went to their beds,
　　All slept full sound but Annie;
Love so opprest her tender breast,
　　Thinking on Andrew Lammie.

" Love comes in at my bed side,
　　And love lies down beyond me;
Love has possess'd my tender breast,
　　And love will waste my body.

" The first time I and my love met
　　Was in the woods of Fyvie;
His lovely form and speech so sweet
　　Soon gain'd the heart of Annie.

" He called me mistress; I said, No,
    I'm Tiftie's bonny Annie;
With apples sweet he did me treat,
    And kisses soft and many.

" It's up and down in Tiftie's den,
    Where the burn runs clear and bonny,
I've often gone to meet my love,
    My bonny Andrew Lammie."

But now, alas! her father heard
    That the Trumpeter of Fyvie
Had had the art to gain the heart
    Of Tiftie's bonny Annie.

Her father soon a letter wrote,
    And sent it on to Fyvie,
To tell his daughter was bewitch'd
    By his servant Andrew Lammie.

When Lord Fyvie had this letter read,
    O dear! but he was sorry;
The bonniest lass in Fyvie's land
    Is bewitched by Andrew Lammie.

Then up the stair his trumpeter
    He called soon and shortly:
" Pray tell me soon, what's this you've done
    To Tiftie's bonny Annie?"

" In wicked art I had no part,
  Nor therein am I canny;
True love alone the heart has won
  Of Tiftie's bonny Annie.

" Woe betide Mill o' Tiftie's pride,
  For it has ruin'd many;
He'll no ha'e 't said that she should wed
  The Trumpeter of Fyvie.

" Where will I find a boy so kind,
  That 'll carry a letter canny,
Who will run on to Tiftie's town,
  Give it to my love Annie?"

" Here you shall find a boy so kind,
  Who'll carry a letter canny,
Who will run on to Tiftie's town,
  And gi'e 't to thy love Annie."

" It's Tiftie he has daughters three,
  Who all are wondrous bonny;
But ye'll ken her o'er a' the lave,
  Gi'e that to bonny Annie."

" It's up and down in Tiftie's den,
  Where the burn runs clear and bonny,
There wilt thou come and meet thy love,
  Thy bonny Andrew Lammie.

" When wilt thou come, and I'll attend?
  My love, I long to see thee."
" Thou may'st come to the bridge of Sleugh,
  And there I'll come and meet thee."

" My love, I go to Edinbro',
  And for a while must leave thee;"
She sighed sore, and said no more
  But "I wish that I were wi' thee."

" I'll buy to thee a bridal gown,
  My love, I'll buy it bonny;"
" But I'll be dead, ere ye come back
  To see your bonnie Annie."

" If you'll be true and constant too,
  As my name's Andrew Lammie,
I shall thee wed, when I come back
  To see the lands of Fyvie."

" I will be true, and constant too,
  To thee, my Andrew Lammie;
But my bridal bed will ere then be made,
  In the green churchyard of Fyvie."

" Our time is gone, and now comes on,
  My dear, that I must leave thee;
If longer here I should appear,
  Mill o' Tiftie he would see me."

" I now for ever bid adieu
    To thee, my Andrew Lammie ;
Ere ye come back, I will be laid
    In the green churchyard of Fyvie."

He hied him to the head of the house,
    To the house top of Fyvie ;
He blew his trumpet loud and schill ;
    'Twas heard at Mill o' Tiftie.

Her father lock'd the door at night,
    Laid by the keys fu' canny ;
And when he heard the trumpet sound,
    Said, " Your cow is lowing, Annie."

" My father dear, I pray forbear,
    And reproach no more your Annie ;
For I'd rather hear that cow to low,
    Than ha'e a' the kine in Fyvie.

" I would not, for my braw new gown,
    And a' your gifts sae many,
That it were told in Fyvie's land
    How cruel you are to Annie.

" But if ye strike me, I will cry,
    And gentlemen will hear me ;
Lord Fyvie will be riding by,
    And he'll come in and see me."

At the same time, the Lord came in;
   He said, " What ails thee, Annie ? "
" 'Tis all for love now I must die,
   For bonny Andrew Lammie."

" Pray, Mill o' Tifty, gi'e consent,
   And let your daughter marry."
" It will be with some higher match
   Than the Trumpeter of Fyvie."

" If she were come of as high a kind
   As she's adorned with beauty,
I would take her unto myself,
   And make her mine own lady."

" It's Fyvie's lands are fair and wide,
   And they are rich and bonny;
I would not leave my own true love,
   For all the lands of Fyvie."

Her father struck her wondrous sore,
   And also did her mother;
Her sisters always did her scorn ;
   But woe be to her brother !

Her brother struck her wondrous sore,
   With cruel strokes and many;
He brake her back in the hall door,
   For liking Andrew Lammie.

" Alas ! my father and mother dear,
    Why so cruel to your Annie ?
My heart was broken first by love,
    My brother has broken my body.

"O mother dear, make ye my bed,
    And lay my face to Fyvie ;
Thus will I ly, and thus will die,
    For my love, Andrew Lammie !

" Ye neighbours, hear, both far and near;
    Ye pity Tiftie's Annie,
Who dies for love of one poor lad,
    For bonny Andrew Lammie.

" No kind of vice e'er stain'd my life,
    Nor hurt my virgin honour ;
My youthful heart was won by love,
    But death will me exoner."

Her mother then she made her bed,
    And laid her face to Fyvie ;
Her tender heart it soon did break,
    And ne'er saw Andrew Lammie.

But the word soon went up and down,
    Through all the lands of Fyvie,
That she was dead and buried,
    Even Tiftie's bonny Annie.

Lord Fyvie he did wring his hands,
 Said, " Alas, for Tiftie's Annie!
The fairest flower's cut down by love,
 That e'er sprung up in Fyvie.

" O woe betide Mill o' Tiftie's pride!
 He might have let them marry;
I should have giv'n them both to live
 Into the lands of Fyvie."

Her father sorely now laments
 The loss of his dear Annie,
And wishes he had gi'en consent
 To wed with Andrew Lammie.

Her mother grieves both air and late:
 Her sisters, 'cause they scorn'd her;
Surely her brother doth mourn and grieve,
 For the cruel usage he'd giv'n her.

But now, alas! it was too late,
 For they could not recal her;
Through life, unhappy is their fate,
 Because they did controul her.

When Andrew hame from Edinburgh came,
 With meikle grief and sorrow,
" My love has died for me to-day,
 I'll die for her to-morrow.

" Now I will on to Tiftie's den,
    Where the burn·runs clear and bonny ;
With tears I'll view the bridge of Sleugh,[1]
    Where I parted last with Annie.

* Then will I speed to the churchyard,
    To the green churchyard of Fyvie ;
With tears I'll water my love's grave,
    Till I follow Tiftie's Annie."

Ye parents grave, who children have,
    In crushing them be canny,
Lest when too late you do repent ;
    Remember Tiftie's Annie.

[1] " In one printed copy this is ' Sheugh,' and in a recited copy it was called ' Skew'; which is the right reading, the editor, from his ignorance of the topography of the
lands of Fyvie, is unable to say. It is a received superstition in Scotland, that, when friends or lovers part at a bridge,
they shall never again meet." MOTHERWELL.

THE TRUMPETER OF FYVIE.

" THE ballad was taken down by Dr. Leyden from
the recitation of a young lady (Miss Robson) of Edinburgh, who learned it in Teviotdale. It was current
in the Border counties within these few years, as it
still is in the northeast of Scotland, where the scene is
laid." Jamieson's *Popular Ballads*, i. 129.

AT Fyvie's yetts there grows a flower,
    It grows baith braid and bonny;
There's a daisie in the midst o' it,
    And it's ca'd by Andrew Lammie.

" O gin that flower war in my breast,
    For the love I bear the laddie ;
I wad kiss it, and I wad clap it,
    And daut it for Andrew Lammie.

" The first time me and my love met,
    Was in the woods of Fyvie ;

He kissed my lips five thousand times,
 And ay he ca'd me bonny ;
And a' the answer he gat frae me,
 Was, My bonny Andrew Lammie ! "

" ' Love, I maun gang to Edinburgh ;
 Love, I maun gang and leave thee ; '
I sighed right sair, and said nae mair,
 But, O gin I were wi' ye ! "

" But true and trusty will I be,
 As I am Andrew Lammie ;
I'll never kiss a woman's mouth,
 Till I come back and see thee."

" And true and trusty will I be,
 As I am Tiftie's Annie ;
I'll never kiss a man again,
 Till ye come back and see me."

Syne he's come back frae Edinburgh,
 To the bonny hows o' Fyvie ;
And ay his face to the nor-east,
 To look for Tiftie's Annie.

" I ha'e a love in Edinburgh,
 Sae ha'e I intill Leith, man ;
I hae a love intill Montrose,
 Sae ha'e I in Dalkeith, man.

" And east and west, where'er I go,
   My love she's always wi' me ;
For east and west, where'er I go,
   My love she dwells in Fyvie.

" My love possesses a' my heart,
   Nae pen can e'er indite her ;
She's ay sae stately as she goes,
   That I see nae mae like her.

" But Tiftie winna gi'e consent
   His dochter me to marry,
Because she has five thousand marks,
   And I have not a penny.

" Love pines away, love dwines away,
   Love, love, decays the body ;
For love o' thee, oh I must die ;
   Adieu, my bonny Annie ! "

Her mither raise out o' her bed,
   And ca'd on baith her women :
" What ails ye, Annie, my dochter dear ?
   O Annie, was ye dreamin' ?

" What dule disturb'd my dochter's sleep ?
   O tell to me, my Annie ! "
She sighed right sair, and said nae mair,
   But, " O for Andrew Lammie ! "

Her father beat her cruellie,
  Sae also did her mother;
Her sisters sair did scoff at her;
  But wae betide her brother!

Her brother beat her cruellie,
  Till his straiks they werena canny;
He brak her back, and he beat her sides,
  For the sake o' Andrew Lammie.

" O fie, O fie, my brother dear,
  The gentlemen 'll shame ye;
The laird o' Fyvie he's gaun by,
  And he'll come in and see me.

And he'll kiss me, and he'll clap me,
  And he will speer what ails me;
And I will answer him again,
  It's a' for Andrew Lammie."

Her sisters they stood in the door,
  Sair griev'd her wi' their folly;
" O sister dear, come to the door,
  Your cow is lowin on you."

" O fie, O fie, my sister dear,
  Grieve me not wi' your folly;
I'd rather hear the trumpet sound,
  Than a' the kye o' Fyvie.

" Love pines away, love dwines away,
    Love, love decays the body ;
For love o' thee now I maun die—
    Adieu to Andrew Lammie ! "

But Tiftie's wrote a braid letter,
    And sent it into Fyvie,
Saying, his daughter was bewitch'd
    By bonny Andrew Lammie.

" Now, Tiftie, ye maun gi'e consent,
    And lat the lassie marry."
" I'll never, never gi'e consent
    To the Trumpeter of Fyvie."

When Fyvie looked the letter on,
    He was baith sad and sorry :
Says—" The bonniest lass o' the country-side
    Has died for Andrew Lammie."

O Andrew's gane to the house-top
    O' the bonny house o' Fyvie ;
He's blawn his horn baith loud and shill
    O'er the lawland leas o' Fyvie.

" Mony a time ha'e I walk'd a' night,
    And never yet was weary ;
But now I may walk wae my lane,
    For I'll never see my deary.

" Love pines away, love dwines away,
  Love, love, decays the body :
For the love o' thee, now I maun die—
  I come, my bonny Annie ! "

FAIR HELEN OF KIRCONNELL.

" THE following very popular ballad has been hand-
ed down by tradition in its present imperfect state.
The affecting incident on which it is founded is well
known.   A lady, of the name of Helen Irving, or Bell,
(for this is disputed by the two clans,) daughter of the
Laird of Kirconnell, in Dumfries-shire, and celebrated
for her beauty, was beloved by two gentlemen in the
neighbourhood.   The name of the favoured suitor was
Adam Fleming of Kirkpatrick ; that of the other has
escaped tradition : though it has been alleged that he
was a Bell, of Blacket House.   The addresses of the
latter were, however, favoured by the friends of the
lady, and the lovers were therefore obliged to meet in
secret, and by night, in the churchyard of Kirconnell,
a romantic spot, almost surrounded by the river Kirtle.
During one of these private interviews, the jealous and
despised lover suddenly appeared on the opposite bank
of the stream, and levelled his carabine at the breast of
his rival.   Helen threw herself before her lover, received in her bosom the bullet, and died in his arms.

A desperate and mortal combat ensued between Fleming and the murderer, in which the latter was cut to pieces. Other accounts say, that Fleming pursued his enemy to Spain, and slew him in the streets of Madrid.

" The ballad, as now published, consists of two parts. The first seems to be an address, either by Fleming or his rival, to the lady; if, indeed, it constituted any portion of the original poem. For the Editor cannot help suspecting, that these verses have been the production of a different and inferior bard, and only adapted to the original measure and tune. But this suspicion being unwarranted by any copy he has been able to procure, he does not venture to do more than intimate his own opinion. The second part, by far the most beautiful, and which is unquestionably original, forms the lament of Fleming over the grave of fair Helen.

" The ballad is here given, without alteration or improvement, from the most accurate copy which could be recovered. The fate of Helen has not, however, remained unsung by modern bards. A lament, of great poetical merit, by the learned historian, Mr. Pinkerton, with several other poems on this subject, have been printed in various forms.[1]

" The grave of the lovers is yet shown in the churchyard of Kirconnell, near Springkell. Upon the tombstone can still be read—*Hic jacet Adamus Fleming ;*

---

[1] For Pinkerton's elegy, see his *Select Scottish Ballads,* I. 109; for Mayne's, the *Gentleman's Magazine,* vol. 86, Part ii. 64. Jamieson has enfeebled the story in *Popular Ballads,* i. 205, and Wordsworth's *Ellen Irwin* hardly deserves more praise. ED.

a cross and sword are sculptured on the stone. The
former is called by the country people, the gun with
which Helen was murdered; and the latter the aveng-
ing sword of her lover. *Sit illis terra levis !* A heap
of stones is raised on the spot where the murder was
committed; a token of abhorrence common to most
nations." *Minstrelsy of the Scottish Border*, iii. 98.

Versions of the Second Part, (which alone deserves
notice,) nearly agreeing with Scott's, are given in the
Illustrations to the new edition of Johnson's *Museum*,
p. 143, by Mr. Stenhouse, p. 210, by Mr. Sharpe. Inferior and fragmentary ones in Herd's *Scottish Songs*,
i. 257; Johnson's *Museum*, 163; Ritson's *Scottish Song*,
i. 145; Jamieson's *Popular Ballads*, i. 203.

FAIR HELEN.

PART FIRST.

O! SWEETEST sweet, and fairest fair,
Of birth and worth beyond compare,
Thou art the causer of my care,
    Since first I loved thee.

Yet God hath given to me a mind,
The which to thee shall prove as kind
As any one that thou shalt find,
    Of high or low degree.

The shallowest water makes maist din,
The deadest pool the deepest linn;
The richest man least truth within,
    Though he preferred be.

Yet, nevertheless, I am content,
And never a whit my love repent,
But think the time was a' weel spent,
  Though I disdained be.

O ! Helen sweet, and maist complete,
My captive spirit's at thy feet !
Thinks thou still fit thus for to treat
  Thy captive cruelly ?

O ! Helen brave ! but this I crave,
Of thy poor slave some pity have,
And do him save that's near his grave,
  And dies for love of thee.

FAIR HELEN.

PART SECOND.

I wish I were where Helen lies,
Night and day on me she cries;
O that I were where Helen lies,
   On fair Kirconnell Lee!

Curst be the heart that thought the thought,
And curst the hand that fired the shot,
When in my arms burd Helen dropt,
   And died to succour me!

O think na ye my heart was sair,
When my love dropt down and spak nae mair!
There did she swoon wi' meikle care,
   On fair Kirconnell Lee.

As I went down the water side,
None but my foe to be my guide,
None but my foe to be my guide,
   On fair Kirconnell Lee;

I lighted down my sword to draw,
I hacked him in pieces sma',
I hacked him in pieces sma',
    For her sake that died for me.

O Helen fair, beyond compare !
I'll make a garland of thy hair,
Shall bind my heart for evermair,
    Until the day I die.

O that I were where Helen lies !
Night and day on me she cries ;
Out of my bed she bids me rise,
    Says, " Haste and come to me ! " —

O Helen fair ! O Helen chaste !
If I were with thee, I were blest,
Where thou lies low, and takes thy rest,
    On fair Kirconnell Lee.

I wish my grave were growing green,
A winding-sheet drawn ower my een,
And I in Helen's arms lying,
    On fair Kirconnell Lee.

I wish I were where Helen lies !
Night and day on me she cries ;
And I am weary of the skies,
    For her sake that died for me.

THE LOWLANDS OF HOLLAND.

Mr. STENHOUSE was informed that this ballad was composed, about the beginning of the last century, by a young widow in Galloway, whose husband was drowned on a voyage to Holland. (*Musical Museum,* ed. 1853, iv. 115.) But some of the verses appear to be old, and one stanza will be remarked to be of common occurrence in ballad poetry.

A fragment of this piece was published in Herd's collection, (ii. 49.) Our copy is from Johnson's *Museum,* p. 118, with the omission, however, of one spurious and absurd stanza, while another, not printed by Johnson, is supplied from the note above cited to the new edition. Cunningham makes sense of the interpolated verses and retains them; otherwise his version is nearly the same as the present. (*Songs of Scotland,* ii. 181.)

" THE love that I have chosen,
    I'll therewith be content,
The saut sea shall be frozen
    Before that I repent;

Repent it shall I never,
    Until the day I die,
But the lowlands of Holland
    Hae twinn'd my love and me.

" My love lies in the saut sea,
    And I am on the side,
Enough to break a young thing's heart,
    Wha lately was a bride ;
Wha lately was a bonnie bride,
    And pleasure in her e'e,
But the lowlands of Holland
    Hae twinn'd my love and me.

" My love he built a bonnie ship,
    And set her to the sea,
Wi' seven score brave mariners
    To bear her companie ;
Threescore gaed to the bottom,
    And threescore died at sea,
And the lowlands of Holland
    Hae twinn'd my love and me.

" My love has built another ship
    And set her to the main ;
He had but twenty mariners,
    And all to bring her hame ;
The stormy winds did roar again,
    The raging waves did rout,

And my love and his bonnie ship
    Turn'd widdershins about.

" There shall nae mantle cross my back,
    Nor kame gae in my hair,
Neither shall coal nor candle light
    Shine in my bower mair ;
Nor shall I chuse anither love,
    Until the day I die,
Since the lowlands of Holland
    Hae twinn'd my love and me."

" O haud your tongue, my daughter dear,
    Be still, and be content ;
There are mair lads in Galloway,
    Ye need nae sair lament."
" O there is nane in Galloway,
    There's nane at a' for me ;
For I never loved a lad but ane,
    And he's drowned in the sea." [1]

---

[1] With the conclusion of this piece may be compared a passage from *Bonny Bee-Ho'm*, vol. iii. p. 57.

    " Ohon, alas ! what shall I do,
        Tormented night and day !
    I never loved a love but ane,
        And now he's gone away.

    " But I will do for my true love
        What ladies would think sair ;

For seven years shall come and gae,
   Ere a kaime gae in my hair.

" There shall neither a shoe gae on my foot,
   Nor a kaime gae in my hair,
Nor ever a coal or candle light
   Shine in my bower nae mair."

See also *The Weary Coble o' Cargill.*

BOOK III.

THE TWA BROTHERS.

From Jamieson's *Popular Ballads*, i. 59.

The ballad of the *Twa Brothers*, like many of the domestic tragedies with which it is grouped in this volume, is by no means the peculiar property of the island of Great Britain. It finds an exact counterpart in the Swedish ballad *Sven i Rosengård, Svenska F. V.*, No. 67, Arwidsson, No. 87, A, B, which, together with a Finnish version of the same story, thought to be derived from the Swedish, will be found translated in our Appendix. *Edward*, in Percy's *Reliques*, has the same general theme, with the difference that a father is murdered instead of a brother. Motherwell [1] has printed a ballad (*Son Davie*) closely agreeing with *Edward*, except

---

[1] The stanza mentioned by Motherwell, as occurring in Werner's *Twenty Fourth of February*, (Scene i.) is apparently only a quotation from memory of Herder's translation of *Edward*. When Motherwell became aware that a similar tradition was common to the Northern nations of Europe, he could no longer have thought it possible that an occurrence in the family history of the Somervilles gave rise to *The Twa Brothers*.

that the crime is again fratricide. He has also furnished another version of *The Twa Brothers*, in which
the catastrophe is the consequence of an accident, and
this circumstance has led the excellent editor to tax
Jamieson with altering one of the most essential
features of the ballad, by filling out a defective
stanza with four lines that make one brother to
have slain the other in a quarrel. Jamieson is, however, justified in giving this more melancholy character
to the story, by the tenor of all the kindred pieces,
and by the language of his own. It will be observed
that both in *Edward* and *Son Davie*, the wicked act
was not only deliberate, but was even instigated
by the mother. The departure from the original is
undoubtedly on the part of Motherwell's copy, which
has softened down a shocking incident to accommodate
a modern and refined sentiment. But Jamieson is ar-
tistically, as well as critically right, since the effect of
the contrast of the remorse of one party and the gener-
osity of the other is heightened by representing the
terrible event as the result of ungoverned passion.

The three Scottish ballads mentioned above, here
follow, and Motherwell's *Twa Brothers* will be found
in the Appendix. Mr. Sharpe has inserted a third
copy of this in his *Ballad Book*, p. 56. Another is said to
be in *The Scot's Magazine*, for June, 1822. Placing no
confidence in any of Allan Cunningham's *souvenirs* of
Scottish Song, we simply state that one of them, composed upon the theme of the *Twa Brothers*, is included
in the *Songs of Scotland*, ii. 16.

" The common title of this ballad is, *The Twa Brothers*, or, *The Wood o' Warslin*, but the words o' *Wars-*

lin appearing to the editor, as will be seen in the text,
to be a mistake for *a-wrestling*, he took the liberty of
altering it accordingly. After all, perhaps, the title
may be right; and the wood may afterwards have obtained its denomination from the tragical event here
celebrated. A very few lines inserted by the editor
to fill up chasms, [some of which have been omitted,]
are inclosed in brackets; the text, in other respects, is
given genuine, as it was taken down from the recitation of Mrs. Arrott." JAMIESON.

"O WILL ye gae to the school, brother?
　　Or will ye gae to the ba'?
Or will ye gae to the wood a-warslin.
　　To see whilk o's maun fa'?"

" It's I winna gae to the school, brother;
　　Nor will I gae to the ba'?
But I will gae to the wood a-warslin:
　　And it is you maun fa'."

They warstled up, they warstled down,
　　The lee-lang simmer's day;
[And nane was near to part the strife,
　　That raise atween them tway,
Till out and Willie's drawn his sword.
　　And did his brother slay.]

" O lift me up upon your back;
　　Tak me to yon wall fair;

You'll wash my bluidy wounds o'er and o'er,
    And syne they'll bleed nae mair.

"And ye'll tak aff my Hollin sark,
    And riv't frae gair to gair ;
Ye'll stap it in my bluidy wounds,
    And syne they'll bleed nae mair."

He's liftit his brother upon his back ;
    Ta'en him to yon wall fair ;
He's washed his bluidy wounds o'er and o'er,
    But ay they bled mair and mair.

And he's ta'en aff his Hollin sark,
    And riven't frae gair to gair ;
He's stappit it in his bluidy wounds ;
    But ay they bled mair and mair.

" Ye'll lift me up upon your back,
    Tak me to Kirkland fair ;[1]
Ye'll mak my greaf baith braid and lang,
    And lay my body there.

" Ye'll lay my arrows at my head,
    My bent bow at my feet ;

---

[1] " The house of Inchmurry, formerly called Kirkland, was built of old by the abbot of Holyrood-house, for his accommodation when he came to that country, and was formerly the minister's manse." *Stat. Ac. of Scotland*, vol. xiii. p. 506. J.

My sword and buckler at my side,
    As I was wont to sleep.

" Whan ye gae hame to your father,
    He'll speer for his son John :—
Say, ye left him into Kirkland fair,
    Learning the school alone.

" When ye gae hame to my sister,
    She'll speer for her brother John :—
Ye'll say, ye left him in Kirkland fair,
    The green grass growin aboon.

" Whan ye gae hame to my true love,
    She'll speer for her lord John :—
Ye'll say, ye left him in Kirkland fair,
    But hame ye fear he'll never come."—

He's gane hame to his father ;
    He speered for his son John :
" It's I left him into Kirkland fair,
    Learning the school alone."

And whan he gaed hame to his sister,
    She speered for her brother John :—
" It's I left him into Kirkland fair,
    The green grass growin aboon."

And whan he gaed hame to his true love,
    She speer'd for her lord John :

" It's I left him into Kirkland fair,
    And hame I fear he'll never come."

" But whaten bluid's that on your sword, Wil-
      lie?
    Sweet Willie, tell to me."
" O it is the bluid o' my grey hounds;
    They wadna rin for me."

" It's nae the bluid o' your hounds, Willie;
    Their bluid was never so red;
But it is the bluid o' my true love,
    That ye hae slain indeed."

That fair may wept, that fair may mourn'd,
    That fair may mourn'd and pin'd;
" When every lady looks for her love,
    I ne'er need look for mine."

" O whaten a death will ye die, Willie?
    Now, Willie, tell to me."
" Ye'll put me in a bottomless boat,
    And I'll gae sail the sea."

" Whan will ye come hame again, Willie?
    Now, Willie, tell to me."
" Whan the sun and moon dances on the
      green,
    And that will never be."

EDWARD, EDWARD.

" This curious Song was transmitted to the Editor
by Sir David Dalrymple, Bart., late Lord Hailes."

PERCY, *Reliques*, i. 61.

" Quhy dois zour brand sae drop w' bluid,
          Edward, Edward ?
Quhy dois zour brand sae drop wi' bluid,
          And quhy sae sad gang zee O ? "
" O I hae killed my hauke sae guid,
          Mither, mither :
O I hae killed my hauke sae guid,
          And I had nae mair bot hee O."

" Zour haukis bluid was nevir sae reid,
          Edward, Edward :
Zour haukis bluid was nevir sae reid,
          My deir son I tell thee O."

" O I hae killed my reid-roan steid,
           Mither, mither :
O I hae killed my reid-roan steid,
           That erst was sae fair and free O."

" Zour steid was auld, and ze hae gat mair,
           Edward, Edward :
Zour steid was auld, and ze hae gat mair,
           Sum other dule ze drie O."
" O I hae killed my fadir deir,
           Mither, mither :
O I hae killed my fadir deir,
           Alas ! and wae is mee O !"

" And quhatten penance wul ze drie, for that,
           Edward, Edward ?
And quhatten penance will ze drie for that ?
           My deir son, now tell me O."
" Ile set my feit in zonder boat,
           Mither, mither :
Ile set my feit in zonder boat,
           And Ile fare ovir the sea O."

" And quhat wul ze doe wi' zour towirs and zour
     ha',
           Edward, Edward ?
And quhat wul ze doe wi' zour towirs and zour ha',
           That were sae fair to see O ? "
" Ile let thame stand til they doun fa',
           Mither, mither :

Ile let thame stand til they doun fa',
   For here nevir mair maun I bee O."

And quhat wul ze leive to zour bairns and
  zour wife,
     Edward, Edward?
And quhat wul ze leive to zour bairns and zour
  wife,
   Quhan ze gang ovir the sea O?"
" The warldis room, late them beg throw life,
    Mither, mither:
The warldis room, late them beg throw life,
   For thame nevir mair wul I see O."

" And quhat wul ze leive to zour ain mither deir,
    Edward, Edward?
And quhat wul ze leive to zour ain mither deir?
   My deir son, now tell me O."
" The curse of hell frae me sall ze beir,
    Mither, mither:
The curse of hell frae me sall ze beir,
   Sic counseils ze gave to me O."

SON DAVIE, SON DAVIE.

From the recitation of an old woman. Motherwell's *Minstrelsy*, 339.

" WHAT bluid's that on thy coat lap?
    Son Davie! son Davie!
What bluid's that on thy coat lap?
    And the truth come tell to me O."

" It is the bluid of my great hawk,
    Mother lady! mother lady!
It is the bluid of my great hawk,
    And the truth I hae tald to thee O."

" Hawk's bluid was ne'er sae red,
    Son Davie! son Davie!
Hawk's bluid was ne'er sae red,
    And the truth come tell to me O."

" It is the bluid o' my grey hound,
    Mother lady ! mother lady !
It is the bluid of my grey hound,
    And it wudna rin for me O."

" Hound's bluid was ne'er sae red,
    Son Davie ! son Davie !
Hound's bluid was ne'er sae red,
    And the truth come tell to me O."

" It is the bluid o' my brother John,
    Mother lady ! mother lady !
It is the bluid o' my brother John,
    And the truth I hae tald to thee O."

" What about did the plea begin ?
    Son Davie ! son Davie ! "
" It began about the cutting o' a willow wand,
    That would never hae been a tree O."

" What death dost thou desire to die ?
    Son Davie ! son Davie !
What death dost thou desire to die ?
    And the truth come tell to me O."

" I'll set my foot in a bottomless ship,
    Mother lady ! mother lady !
I'll set my foot in a bottomless ship,
    And ye'll never see mair o' me O."

" What wilt thou leave to thy poor wife?
   Son Davie ! son Davie ! "
" Grief and sorrow all her life,
   And she'll never get mair frae me O."

" What wilt thou leave to thy auld son?
   Son Davie ! son Davie ! "
" The weary warld to wander up and down,
   And he'll never get mair o' me O."

" What wilt thou leave to thy mother dear?
   Son Davie ! son Davie ! "
" A fire o' coals to burn her wi' hearty cheer,
   And she'll never get mair o' me O."

THE CRUEL SISTER.

THE earliest printed copy of this ballad is the curious piece in *Wit Restor'd*, (1658,) called *The Miller
and the King's Daughter*, improperly said to be a parody, by Jamieson and others. (See Appendix.) Pinkerton inserted in his *Tragic Ballads*, (p. 72,) a ballad
on the subject, which preserves many genuine lines,
but is half his own composition. Complete versions
were published by Scott and Jamieson, and more recently a third has been furnished in Sharpe's *Ballad
Book*, p. 30, and a fourth in Buchan's *Ballads of the
North of Scotland* (given at the end of this volume).
The burden of Mr. Sharpe's copy is nearly the same
as that of the *Cruel Mother*, *post*, p. 372. Jamieson's
copy had also this burden, but he exchanged it for the
more popular, and certainly more tasteful, *Binnorie*.
No ballad furnishes a closer link than this between the
popular poetry of England and that of the other
nations of Northern Europe. The same story is found
in Icelandic, Norse, Faroish, and Estnish ballads, as
well as in the Swedish and Danish, and a nearly related one in many other ballads or tales, German, Pol-
ish, Lithuanian, etc., etc. — See *Svenska Folk-Visor*, iii.
16, i. 81, 86, Arwidsson, ii. 139, and especially *Den
Talende Strengeleg*, Grundtvig, No. 95, and the notes
to *Der Singende Knochen*, *K. u. H. Märchen*, iii. 55,
ed. 1856.

Of the edition in the *Border Minstrelsy*, Scott gives the following account, (iii. 287.)

" It is compiled from a copy in Mrs. Brown's MSS., intermixed with a beautiful fragment, of fourteen verses, transmitted to the Editor by J. C. Walker, Esq. the ingenious historian of the Irish bards. Mr. Walker, at the same time, favored the Editor with the following note : ' I am indebted to my departed friend, Miss Brook, for the foregoing pathetic fragment. Her account of it was as follows : This song was transscribed, several years ago, from the memory of an old woman, who had no recollection of the concluding verses ; probably the beginning may also be lost, as it seems to commence abruptly.' The first verse and burden of the fragment ran thus :—

' O sister, sister, reach thy hand!
Hey ho, my Nanny, O ;
And you shall be heir of all my land,
While the swan swims bonney, O.' "

THERE were two sisters sat in a bour ;
                Binnorie, O Binnorie ;
There came a knight to be their wooer ;
        By the bonny milldams of Binnorie.

He courted the eldest with glove and ring,
                Binnorie, O Binnorie ;
But he lo'ed the youngest abune a' thing ;
        By the bonny milldams of Binnorie.

He courted the eldest with broach and knife,
       Binnorie, O Binnorie ;
But he lo'ed the youngest abune his life ;
       By the bonny milldams of Binnorie.

The eldest she was vexed sair,
       Binnorie, O Binnorie ;
And sore envied her sister fair ;
       By the bonny milldams of Binnorie.

The eldest said to the youngest ane,
       Binnorie, O Binnorie ;
" Will ye go and see our father's ships come in ? "
       By the bonny milldams of Binnorie.

She's ta'en her by the lily hand,
       Binnorie, O Binnorie ;
And led her down to the river strand ;
       By the bonny milldams of Binnorie.

The youngest stude upon a stane,
       Binnorie, O Binnorie ;
The eldest came and pushed her in ;
       By the bonny milldams of Binnorie

She took her by the middle sma',
       Binnorie, O Binnorie ;
And dash'd her bonny back to the jaw ;
       By the bonny milldams of Binnorie.

" O sister, sister, reach your hand,
          Binnorie, O Binnorie ;
And ye shall be heir of half my land."—
       By the bonny milldams of Binnorie.

" O sister, I'll not reach my hand,
          Binnorie, O Binnorie ;
And I'll be heir of all your land ;
       By the bonny milldams of Binnorie.

" Shame fa' the hand that I should take,
          Binnorie, O Binnorie ;
It's twin'd me and my world's make."—
       By the bonny milldams of Binnorie.

" O sister, reach me but your glove,
          Binnorie, O Binnorie ;
And sweet William shall be your love."—
       By the bonny milldams of Binnorie.

" Sink on, nor hope for hand or glove !
          Binnorie, O Binnorie ;
And sweet William shall better be my love,
       By the bonny milldams of Binnorie.

" Your cherry cheeks and your yellow hair,
          Binnorie, O Binnorie,
Garr'd me gang maiden evermair."—
       By the bonny milldams of Binnorie.

Sometimes she sunk, and sometimes she swam,
      Binnorie, O Binnorie ;
Until she cam to the miller's dam ;
      By the bonny milldams of Binnorie.

" O father, father, draw your dam !
      Binnorie, O Binnorie ;
There's either a mermaid, or a milk-white swan."
      By the bonny milldams of Binnorie.

The miller hasted and drew his dam,
      Binnorie, O Binnorie ;
And there he found a drown'd woman ;
      By the bonny milldams of Binnorie.

You could not see her yellow hair,
      Binnorie, O Binnorie ;
For gowd and pearls that were so rare ;
      By the bonny milldams of Binnorie.

You could not see her middle sma',
      Binnorie, O Binnorie ;
Her gowden girdle was sae bra' ;
      By the bonny milldams of Binnorie.

A famous harper passing by,
      Binnorie, O Binnorie ;
The sweet pale face he chanced to spy ;
      By the bonny milldams of Binnorie.

And when he looked that lady on,
   Binnorie, O Binnorie ;
He sigh'd and made a heavy moan ;
   By the bonny milldams of Binnorie.

He made a harp of her breast-bone,
   Binnorie, O Binnorie ;
Whose sounds would melt a heart of stone ;
   By the bonny milldams of Binnorie.

The strings he framed of her yellow hair,
   Binnorie, O Binnorie ;
Whose notes made sad the listening ear ;
   By the bonny milldams of Binnorie.

He brought it to her father's hall,
   Binnorie, O Binnorie ;
And there was the court assembled all ;
   By the bonny milldams of Binnorie.

He laid his harp upon a stone,
   Binnorie, O Binnorie ;
And straight it began to play alone ;
   By the bonny milldams of Binnorie.

" O yonder sits my father, the king,
   Binnorie, O Binnorie ;
And yonder sits my mother, the queen ;"
   By the bonny milldams of Binnorie

" And yonder stands my brother Hugh,
         Binnorie, O Binnorie ;
And by him my William, sweet and true."
      By the bonny milldams of Binnorie.

But the last tune that the harp play'd then,
         Binnorie, O Binnorie ;
Was—" Woe to my sister, false Helen ! "
      By the bonny milldams of Binnorie.

THE TWA SISTERS.

Verbatim (with one interpolated stanza) from the recitation of Mrs. Brown. Jamieson's *Popular Ballads*, i. 50.

THERE was twa sisters liv'd in a bower,
   Binnorie, O Binnorie!
There came a knight to be their wooer,
   By the bonny mill-dams o' Binnorie.

He courted the eldest wi' glove and ring,
   Binnorie, O Binnorie!
But he loved the youngest aboon a' thing,
   By the bonny mill-dams o' Binnorie.

He courted the eldest wi' broach and knife,
   Binnorie, O Binnorie!
But he loved the youngest as his life,
   By the bonny mill-dams o' Binnorie.

The eldest she was vexed sair,
  Binnorie, O Binnorie!
And sair envied her sister fair,
  By the bonny mill-dams o' Binnorie.

Intill her bower she coudna rest,
  Binnorie, O Binnorie!
Wi' grief and spite she maistly brast,
  By the bonny mill-dams o' Binnorie.

Upon a morning fair and clear,
  Binnorie, O Binnorie!
She cried upon her sister dear,
  By the bonny mill-dams o' Binnorie.

"O sister, come to yon sea strand,
  Binnorie, O Binnorie!
And see our father's ships come to land,"
  By the bonny mill-dams o' Binnorie.

She's ta'en her by the milk-white hand,
  Binnorie, O Binnorie!
And led her down to yon sea strand,
  By the bonny mill-dams o' Binnorie.

The youngest stood upon a stane,
  Binnorie, O Binnorie!
The eldest came and threw her in,
  By the bonny mill-dams o' Binnorie.

She took her by the middle sma'
  Binnorie, O Binnorie !
And dashed her bonny back to the jaw,
  By the bonny mill-dams o' Binnorie.

" O sister, sister, tak my hand,
  Binnorie, O Binnorie !
And I'se mak ye heir to a' my land,
  By the bonny mill-dams o' Binnorie.

" O sister, sister, tak my middle,
  Binnorie, O Binnorie !
And ye's get my goud and my gouden girdle,
  By the bonny mill-dams o' Binnorie.

" O sister, sister, save my life,
  Binnorie, O Binnorie !
And I swear I'se never be nae man's wife,"
  By the bonny mill-dams o' Binnorie.

" Foul fa' the hand that I should tak,
  Binnorie, O Binnorie !
It twin'd me o' my warldes mak,
  By the bonny mill-dams o' Binnorie.

" Your cherry cheeks and yellow hair
  Binnorie, O Binnorie !
Gars me gang maiden for evermair,"
  By the bonny mill-dams o' Binnorie.

Sometimes she sank, sometimes she swam,
Binnorie, O Binnorie!
Till she came to the mouth o' yon mill-dam,
By the bonny mill-dams o' Binnorie.

O out it came the miller's son,
Binnorie, O Binnorie!
And saw the fair maid soummin in,
By the bonny mill-dams o' Binnorie.

"O father, father, draw your dam,
Binnorie, O Binnorie!
There's either a mermaid or a swan,"
By the bonny mill-dams o' Binnorie.

[The miller quickly drew the dam,
Binnorie, O Binnorie!
And there he found a drown'd woman,
By the bonny mill-dams o' Binnorie.]

"And sair and lang mat their teen last,
Binnorie, O Binnorie!
That wrought thee sic a dowie cast,"
By the bonny mill-dams o' Binnorie!

You coudna see her yellow hair
Binnorie, O Binnorie!
For goud and pearl that was sae rare,
By the bonny mill-dams o' Binnorie.

You coudna see her middle sma
  Binnorie, O Binnorie!
For gouden girdle that was sae braw,
  By the bonny mill-dams o' Binnorie.

You coudna see her fingers white,
  Binnorie, O Binnorie!
For gouden rings that were sae gryte,
  By the bonny mill-dams o' Binnorie.

And by there came a harper fine,
  Binnorie, O Binnorie!
That harped to the king at dine,
  By the bonny mill-dams o' Binnorie.

Whan he did look that lady upon,
  Binnorie, O Binnorie!
He sigh'd and made a heavy moan,
  By the bonny mill-dams o' Binnorie.

He's ta'en three locks o' her yellow hair,
  Binnorie, O Binnorie!
And wi' them strung his harp sae fair,
  By the bonny mill-dams o' Binnorie.

The first tune it did play and sing,
  Binnorie, O Binnorie!
Was, " Fareweel to my father the king,"
  By the bonny mill-dams o' Binnorie.

The nexten tune that it play'd seen,
  Binnorie, O Binnorie!
Was, " Fareweel to my mither the queen,"
  By the bonny mill-dams o' Binnorie.

The thirden tune that it play'd then,
  Binnorie, O Binnorie!
Was, " Wae to my sister, fair Ellen,"
  By the bonny mill-dams o' Binnorie!

LORD DONALD.

Kinloch's *Ancient Scottish Ballads*, p. 110.

LIKE the two which preceded it, this ballad is common to the Gothic nations. It exists in a great variety of forms. Two stanzas, recovered by Burns, were printed in Johnson's *Museum*, i. 337 ; two others were inserted by Jamieson, in his *Illustrations*, p. 319. The *Border Minstrelsy* furnished five stanzas, giving the *story*, without the bequests. Allan Cunningham's alteration of Scott's version, (*Scottish Songs*, i. 285,) has one stanza more. Kinloch procured from the North of Scotland the following complete copy.

In the Appendix, we have placed a nursery song on the same subject, still familiar in Scotland, and translations of the corresponding German and Swedish ballads—both most remarkable cases of parallelism in popular romance.

Lord Donald, as Kinloch remarks, would seem to have been poisoned by eating toads prepared as fishes. Scott, in his introduction to *Lord Randal*, has quoted from an old chronicle, a fabulous account of the poisoning of King John by means of a cup of ale, in which the venom of this reptile had been infused.

"O WHARE hae ye been a' day, Lord Donald, my
    son?
O whare hae ye been a' day, my jollie young
    man?"
" I've been awa courtin :—mither, mak my bed
    sune,
For I'm sick at the heart, and I fain wad lie
    doun."

" What wad ye hae for your supper, Lord Don-
    ald, my son?
What wad ye hae for your supper, my jollie young
    man?"
" I've gotten my supper :—mither, mak my bed
    sune,
For I'm sick at the heart, and I fain wad lie
    doun."

" What did ye get for your supper, Lord Donald,
    my son?
What did ye get for your supper, my jollie young
    man?"
" A dish of sma' fishes:—mither mak my bed
    sune,
For I'm sick at the heart, and I fain wad lie
    doun."

" Whare gat ye the fishes, Lord Donald, my son?
Whare gat ye the fishes, my jollie young man?"

" In my father's black ditches :—mither, mak my
  bed sune,
For I'm sick at the heart, and I fain wad lie
  doun."

" What like were your fishes, Lord Donald, my
  son ?
What like were your fishes, my jollie young
  man ? "
" Black backs and spreckl'd bellies :—mither, mak
  my bed sune,
For I'm sick at the heart, and I fain wad lie
  doun."

" O I fear ye are poison'd, Lord Donald, my son !
O I fear ye are poison'd, my jollie young man !"
" O yes ! I am poison'd :—mither mak my bed
  sune,
For I'm sick at the heart, and I fain wad lie
  doun."

" What will ye leave to your father, Lord Donald my son?
What will ye leave to your father, my jollie young
  man ? "
" Baith my houses and land :—mither, mak my
  bed sune,
For I'm sick at the heart, and I fain wad lie
  doun."

"What will ye leave to your brither, Lord Donald,
  my son?
What will ye leave to your brither, my jollie
  young man?"
" My horse and the saddle :—mither, mak my bed
  sune,
For I'm sick at the heart, and I fain wad lie
  doun."

" What will ye leave to your sister, Lord Donald,
  my son?
What will ye leave to your sister, my jollie young
  man?"
" Baith my gold box and rings :—mither, mak my
  bed sune,
For I'm sick at the heart, and I fain wad lie
  doun."

" What will ye leave to your true-love, Lord
  Donald, my son?
What will ye leave to your true-love, my jollie
  young man?"
" The tow and the halter, for to hang on yon tree,
And lat her hang there for the poysoning o'
  me."

LORD RANDAL (B).

From *Minstrelsy of the Scottish Border*, (iii. 49.)

Scott changed the name of the hero of this piece from *Lord Ronald* to *Lord Randal*, on the authority of a single copy. The change is unimportant, but the reason will appear curious, if we remember that the Swedes and Germans have the ballad as well as the Scotch;—" because, though the circumstances are so very different, I think it not impossible, that the ballad may have originally regarded the death of Thomas Randolph, or Randal, Earl of Murray, nephew to Robert Bruce, and governor of Scotland."

" O where hae ye been Lord Randal, my son?
O where hae ye been, my handsome young
    man?"—
" I hae been to the wild wood; mother make my
    bed soon,
For I'm weary wi' hunting, and fain wald lie
    down."—

" Where gat ye your dinner, Lord Randal, my
    son ?

Where gat ye your dinner, my handsome young
    man ? "

" I dined wi' my true-love ; mother, make my bed
    soon,

For I'm weary wi' hunting, and fain wald lie
    down."—

" What gat ye to your dinner, Lord Randal, my
    son ?

What gat ye to your dinner, my handsome young
    man ? "—

" I gat eels bóil'd in broo ; mother, make my bed
    soon,

For I'm weary wi' hunting, and fain wald lie
    down."—

" What became of your bloodhounds, Lord Ran-
    dal, my son?

What became of your bloodhounds, my handsome
    young man ? "—

" O they swell'd and they died ; mother, make my
    bed soon,

For I'm weary wi' hunting, and fain wald lie
    down."—

" O I fear ye are poison'd, Lord Randal, my
    son !

O I fear ye are poisoned, my handsome young
    man ! "—
" O yes! I am poison'd ; mother, make my bed
    soon,
For I'm sick at the heart, and I fain wad lie
    down."

THE CRUEL BROTHER:

OR,

THE BRIDE'S TESTAMENT.

Of this ballad, which is still commonly recited and sung in Scotland, four copies have been published. The following is from Jamieson's collection, i. 66, where it was printed *verbatim* after the recitation of Mrs. Arrott. A copy from Aytoun's collection is subjoined, which is nearly the same as a less perfect one in Herd, i. 149, and the fourth, from Gilbert's *Ancient Christmas Carols*, &c., is in the Appendix to this volume.

The conclusion, or testamentary part, occurs very frequently in ballads, e. g. *Den lillas Testamente*, *Svenska Folk-Visor*, No. 68, translated in the Appendix to this volume, the end of *Den onde Svigermoder*, *Danske Viser*, i. 261, translated in *Illustrations of Northern Antiquities*, p. 344, *Möen paa Baalet*, Grundtvig, No. 109, A, st. 18–21, and *Kong Valdemar og hans Söster*, Grundtvig, No. 126, A, st. 101–105. See also *Edward*, and *Lord Donald*, p. 225, p. 244.

THERE was three ladies play'd at the ba',
With a heigh-ho! and a lily gay;
There came a knight, and play'd o'er them a',
As the primrose spreads so sweetly.

The eldest was baith tall and fair,
  With a heigh-ho ! and a lily gay ;
But the youngest was beyond compare,
  As the primrose spreads so sweetly.

The midmost had a gracefu' mien,
  With a heigh-ho ! and a lily gay ;
But the youngest look'd like beauty's queen,
  As the primrose spreads so sweetly.

The knight bow'd low to a' the three,
  With a heigh-ho ! and a lily gay ;
But to the youngest he bent his knee,
  As the primrose spreads so sweetly.

The lady turned her head aside,
  With a heigh-ho ! and a lily gay ;
The knight he woo'd her to be his bride,
  As the primrose spreads so sweetly.

The lady blush'd a rosy red,
  With a heiyh-ho ! and a lily gay ;
And said, " Sir knight, I'm o'er young to wed,"
  As the primrose spreads so sweetly.

" O lady fair, give me your hand,
  With a heigh-ho ! and a lily gay ;
And I'll mak you ladie of a' my land,"
  As the primrose spreads so sweetly.

" Sir knight, ere you my favor win,
  With a heigh-ho ! and a lily gay ;
Ye maun get consent frae a' my kin,"
  As the primrose spreads so sweetly.

He has got consent fra her parents dear,
  With a heigh-ho ! and a lily gay ;
And likewise frae her sisters fair,
  As the primrose spreads so sweetly.

He has got consent frae her kin each one,
  With a heigh-ho ! and a lily gay ;
But forgot to speer at her brother John,
  As the primrose spreads so sweetly.

Now, when the wedding day was come,
  With a heigh-ho ! and a lily gay ;
The knight would take his bonny bride home.
  As the primrose spreads so sweetly.

And many a lord and many a knight,
  With a heigh-ho ! and a lily gay ;
Came to behold that lady bright,
  As the primrose spreads so sweetly.

And there was nae man that did her see,
  With a heigh-ho ! and a lily gay,
But wished himself bridegroom to be,
  As the primrose spreads so sweetly.

Her father dear led her down the stair,
  With a heigh-ho ! and a lily gay ;
And her sisters twain they kiss'd her there,
  As the primrose spreads so sweetly.

Her mother dear led her through the close,
  With a heigh-ho ! and a lily gay ;
And her brother John set her on her horse,
  As the primrose spreads so sweetly.

She lean'd her o'er the saddle-bow,
  With a heigh-ho ! and a lily gay,
To give him a kiss ere she did go,
  As the primrose spreads so sweetly.

He has ta'en a knife, baith lang and sharp,
  With a heigh-ho ! and a lily gay,
And stabb'd the bonny bride to the heart,
  As the primrose spreads so sweetly.

She hadna ridden half thro' the town,
  With a heigh-ho ! and a lily gay,
Until her heart's blood stained her gown,
  As the primrose spreads so sweetly.

" Ride saftly on," said the best young man,
  With a heigh-ho ! and a lily gay ;
" For I think our bonny bride looks pale and
    wan,"
  As the primrose spreads so sweetly.

"O lead me gently up yon hill,
With a heigh-ho ! and a lily gay,
And I'll there sit down, and make my will,"
As the primrose spreads so sweetly.

"O what will you leave to your father dear?"
With a heigh-ho ! and a lily gay ;
"The silver-shod steed that brought me here,"
As the primrose spreads so sweetly.

"What will you leave to your mother dear?"
With a heigh-ho ! and a lily gay ;
"My velvet pall and silken gear,"
As the primrose spreads so sweetly.

"And what will ye leave to your sister Ann?"
With a heigh-ho ! and a lily gay ;
"My silken scarf, and my golden fan,"
As the primrose spreads so sweetly.

"What will ye leave to your sister Grace?"
With a heigh-ho ! and a lily gay ;
"My bloody cloaths to wash and dress,"
As the primrose spreads so sweetly.

"What will ye leave to your brother John?"
With a heigh-ho ! and a lily gay ;
"The gallows-tree to hang him on,"
As the primrose spreads so sweetly.

" What will ye leave to your brother John's wife ? '
With a heigh-ho! and a lily gay ;
" The wilderness to end her life,"
As the primrose spreads so sweetly.

This fair lady in her grave was laid,
With a heigh-ho! and a lily gay ;
And a mass was o'er her said,
As the primrose spreads so sweetly.

But it would have made your heart right sair,
With a heigh-ho! and a lily gay ;
To see the bridegroom rive his hair,
As the primrose spreads so sweetly.

THE CRUEL BROTHER.

From Aytoun's *Ballads of Scotland* (2d ed.), i. 232, "taken down from recitation." Found also, but with several stanzas wanting, in Herd's *Scottish Songs*, i. 149. The title in both collections is *Fine Flowers i' the Valley*. This part of the refrain is found in one of the versions of the *Cruel Mother*, p. 269. To Herd's copy are annexed two fragmentary stanzas with nearly the same burden as that of the foregoing ballad.

She louted down to gie a kiss,
  With a hey and a lily gay;
He stuck his penknife in her hass,
  And the rose it smells so sweetly.

" Ride up, ride up," cry'd the foremost man,
  With a hey and a lily gay;
I think our bride looks pale and wan,"
  And the rose it smells so sweetly.

THERE were three sisters in a ha',
  Fine flowers i' the valley,
There came three lords amang them a',
  The red, green, and the yellow.

The first o' them was clad in red,
Fine flowers i' the valley ;
" O lady, will ye be my bride ? "
Wi' the red, green, and the yellow.

The second o' them was clad in green,
Fine flowers i' the valley ;
" O lady, will ye be my queen ? "
Wi' the red, green, and the yellow.

The third o' them was clad in yellow,
Fine flowers i' the valley ;
" O lady, will ye be my marrow ? "
Wi' the red, green, and the yellow.

" O ye maun ask my father dear,'
Fine flowers i' the valley,
" Likewise the mother that did me bear,"
Wi' the red, green, and the yellow.

" And ye maun ask my sister Ann,"
Fine flowers i' the valley ;
" And not forget my brother John,"
Wi' the red, green, and the yellow.

" O I have asked thy father dear,"
Fine flowers i' the valley,
" Likewise the mother that did thee bear,"
Wi' the red, green, and the yellow.

" And I have asked your sister Ann,"
Fine flowers i' the valley;
" But I forgot your brother John ; "
Wi' the red, green, and the yellow.

Now when the wedding-day was come,
Fine flowers i' the valley,
The knight would take his bonny bride home,
Wi' the red, green, and the yellow.

And mony a lord, and mony a knight,
Fine flowers i' the valley,
Cam to behold that lady bright,
Wi' the red, green, and the yellow.

There was nae man that did her see,
Fine flowers i' the valley,
But wished himsell bridegroom to be,
Wi' the red, green, and the yellow.

Her father led her down the stair,
Fine flowers i' the valley,
And her sisters twain they kissed her there,
Wi' the red, green, and the yellow.

Her mother led her through the close,
Fine flowers i' the valley;
Her brother John set her on her horse,
Wi' the red, green, and the yellow.

" You are high and I am low,"
  Fine flowers i' the valley ;
" Give me a kiss before you go,"
  Wi' the red, green, and the yellow.

She was louting down to kiss him sweet,
  Fine flowers i' the valley ;
When wi' his knife he wounded her deep,
  Wi' the red, green, and the yellow.

She hadna ridden through half the town,
  Fine flowers i' the valley,
Until her heart's blood stained her gown,
  Wi' the red, green, and the yellow.

" Ride saftly on," said the best young man,
  Fine flowers i' the valley ;
" I think our bride looks pale and wan ! "
  Wi' the red, green, and the yellow.

" O lead me over into yon stile,"
  Fine flowers i' the valley,
" That I may stop and breathe awhile,"
  Wi' the red, green, and the yellow.

" O lead me over into yon stair,"
  Fine flowers i' the valley,
" For there I'll lie and bleed nae mair,"
  Wi' the red, green, and the yellow.

"O what will you leave to your father dear?"
  Fine flowers i' the valley :
"The siller-shod steed that brought me here,"
  Wi' the red, green, and the yellow.

"What will you leave to your mother dear?"
  Fine flowers i' the valley ;
"My velvet pall, and my pearlin' gear,"
  Wi' the red, green, and the yellow.

"What will you leave to your sister Ann?"
  Fine flowers i' the valley ;
"My silken gown that stands its lane,"
  Wi' the red, green, and the yellow.

"What will you leave to your sister Grace?"
  Fine flowers i' the valley ;
"My bluidy shirt to wash and dress,"
  Wi' the red, green, and the yellow.

"What will you leave to your brother John?"
  Fine flowers i' the valley ;
"The gates o' hell to let him in,"
  Wi' the red, green, and the yellow.

LADY ANNE.

From *Minstrelsy of the Scottish Border*, iii. 18.

" This ballad was communicated to me by Mr. Kirkpatrick Sharpe of Hoddom, who mentions having copied it from an old magazine. Although it has probably
received some modern corrections, the general turn
seems to be ancient, and corresponds with that of a
fragment which I have often heard sung in my child-
hood."

The version to which Sir Walter Scott refers, and
part of which he proceeds to quote, had been printed
in Johnson's *Museum*. It is placed immediately after
the present, with other copies of the ballad from Motherwell and Kinloch.

In Buchan's *Ballads of the North of Scotland* there
are two more, which are repeated with slight variations in the XVII. Vol. of the Percy Society, p. 46,
p. 50. Both will be found in the Appendix. The
copy in Buchan's *Gleanings*, p. 90, seems to be taken
from Scott. Smith's *Scottish Minstrel*, iv. 33, affords
still another variety.

In German, *Die Kindesmörderin*, Erk's *Liederhort*,
No. 41, five copies; Erlach, iv. 148; Hoffmann, *Schlesische V. L.*, No. 31, 32; *Wunderhorn*, ii. 202; Zuccalmaglio, No. 97; Meinert, No. 81; Simrock, p. 87.
(But some of these are repetitions.) Wendish, Haupt
and Schmaler, I. No. 292, and with considerable differences, I. No. 290, II. 197. This last reference is
taken from Grundtvig, ii. 531.

FAIR Lady Anne sate in her bower,
   Down by the greenwood side,
And the flowers did spring, and the birds did
     sing,
   'Twas the pleasant May-day tide.

But fair Lady Anne on Sir William call'd,
   With the tear grit in her ee,
"O though thou be fause, may Heaven thee
     guard,
   In the wars ayont the sea!"—

Out of the wood came three bonnie boys,
   Upon the simmer's morn,
And they did sing and play at the ba',
   As naked as they were born.

"O seven lang years wad I sit here,
   Amang the frost and snaw,
A' to hae but ane o' these bonnie boys,
   A playing at the ba' "—

Then up and spake the eldest boy,
   " Now listen, thou fair ladie,
And ponder well the rede that I tell,
   Then make ye a choice of the three.

" 'Tis I am Peter, and this is Paul,
   And that ane, sae fair to see,

But a twelve-month sinsyne to paradise came,
    To join with our companie."—

" O I will hae the snaw-white boy,
    The bonniest of the three."—
" And if I were thine, and in thy propine,
    O what wad ye do to me ? "—

" 'Tis I wad clead thee in silk and gowd,
    And nourice thee on my knee."—
" O mither ! mither ! when I was thine,
    Sic kindness I couldna see.

" Beneath the turf, where now I stand,
    The fause nurse buried me ;
The cruel penknife sticks still in my heart,
    And I come not back to thee."—

        *   *   *   *   *   *   *

FINE FLOWERS IN THE VALLEY.

From Johnson's *Musical Museum*, p. 331.

THE first line of the burden is found also in *The Cruel Brother*, p. 258.

SHE sat down below a thorn,
 Fine flowers in the valley ;
And there she has her sweet babe born,
 And the green leaves they grow rarely.

" Smile na sae sweet, my bonnie babe,
 Fine flowers in the valley,
And ye smile sae sweet, ye'll smile me dead,"
 And the green leaves they grow rarely.

She's taen out her little penknife,
 Fine flowers in the valley,
And twinn'd the sweet babe o' its life,
 And the green leaves they grow rarely.

She's howket a grave by the light o' the moon,
  Fine flowers in the valley,
And there she's buried her sweet babe in,
  And the green leaves they grow rarely.

As she was going to the church,
  Fine flowers in the valley,
She saw a sweet babe in the porch,
  And the green leaves they grow rarely.

" O sweet babe, and thou were mine,
  Fine flowers in the valley,
I wad cleed thee in the silk so fine,"
  And the green leaves they grow rarely.

" O mother dear, when I was thine,
  Fine flowers in the valley,
Ye did na prove to me sae kind,"
  And the green leaves they grow rarely.

THE CRUEL MOTHER.

From Motherwell's *Minstrelsy*, p. 161.

SHE leaned her back unto a thorn,
 Three, three, and three by three ;
And there she has her two babes born,
 Three, three, and thirty-three.

She took frae 'bout her ribbon-belt,
And there she bound them hand and foot.

She has ta'en out her wee penknife,
And there she ended baith their life.

She has howked a hole baith deep and wide,
She has put them in baith side by side.

She has covered them o'er wi' a marble stane,
Thinking she would gang maiden hame.

As she was walking by her father's castle wa',
She saw twa pretty babes playing at the ba'.

"O bonnie babes ! gin ye were mine,
I would dress you up in satin fine !

" O I would dress you in the silk,
And wash you ay in morning milk ! "

" O cruel mother ! we were thine,
And thou made us to wear the twine.

" O cursed mother ! heaven 's high,
And that's where thou will ne'er win nigh.

"O cursed mother ! hell is deep,
And there thou'll enter step by step. "

THE CRUEL MOTHER.

From Kinloch's *Ancient Scottish Ballads*, p. 46.

THREE stanzas of a Warwickshire version closely resembling Kinloch's are given in *Notes and Queries*, vol. viii. p. 358.

THERE lives a lady in London—
All alone, and alonie ;
She's gane wi' bairn to the clerk's son—
Doun by the greenwud sae bonnie.

She has tane her mantel her about—
All alone, and alonie ;
She's gane aff to the gude greenwud—
Doun by the greenwud sae bonnie.

She has set her back until an aik—
All alone, and alonie ;
First it bowed, and syne it brake—
Doun by the greenwud sae bonnie.

She has set her back until a brier—
All alone, and alonie ;

Bonnie were the twa boys she did bear—
Doun by the greenwud sae bonnie.

But out she's tane a little penknife—
All alone, and alonie;
And she's parted them and their sweet life—
Doun by the greenwud sae bonnie.

She's aff unto her father's ha'—
All alone, and alonie;
She seem'd the lealest maiden amang them a'—
Doan by the greenwud sae bonnie.

As she lookit our the castle wa'—
All alone, and alonie;
She spied twa bonnie boys playing at the ba'—
Doun by the greenwud sae bonnie.

"O an thae twa babes were mine"—
All alone, and alonie;
"They should wear the silk and the sabelline"—
Doun by the greenwud sae bonnie.

"O mother dear, when we were thine,"
All alone, and alonie;
"We neither wore the silks nor the sabelline"—
Doun by the greenwud sae bonnie.

"But out ye took a little penknife"—
All alone, and alonie;

" An ye parted us and our sweet life "—
Doun by the greenwud sae bonnie.

" But now we're in the heavens hie " —
All alone, and alonie ;
"And ye have the pains o' hell to dree "—
Doun by the greenwud sae bonnie.

MAY COLVIN, OR FALSE SIR JOHN.

In the very ancient though corrupted ballads of
Lady Isabel and the Elf-Knight, and *The Water o
Wearie's Well* (vol. i. p. 195, 198), an Elf or a Mer-
man occupies the place here assigned to False Sir
John. Perhaps *May Colvin* is the result of the same
modernizing process by which *Hynde Etin* has been
converted into *Young Hastings the Groom* (vol. i. p.
294, 189). The coincidence of the name with *Clerk
Colvill,* in vol. i. p. 192, may have some significance.
This, however, would not be the opinion of Grundtvig,
who regards the Norse and German ballads resembling
Lady Isabel, &c., as compounded of two independent
stories. If this be so, then we should rather say that
a ballad similar to *May Colvin* has been made to furnish the conclusion to the pieces referred to.

The story of this ballad has apparently some connection with *Bluebeard*, but it is hard to say what the connection is. (See *Fitchers Vogel* in the Grimms' *K. u. H.-Märchen*, No. 46, and notes.) The versions of the ballad in other languages are all but innumerable: e. g. *Röfvaren Rymer*, *Röfvaren Brun*, *Svenska F.-V.*, No. 82, 83 ; *Den Falske Riddaren*, Arwidsson, No. 44 ; *Ulrich und Aennchen*, *Schön Ulrich u. Roth-Aennchen*, *Schön Ulrich und Rautendelein*, *Ulinger*, *Herr Halewyn*, etc., in *Wunderhorn*, i. 274 ; Uhland, 141– 157 (four copies) ; Erk, *Liederhort*, 91, 93 ; Erlach, iii. 450 ; Zuccalmaglio, *Deutsche Volkslieder*, No. 15 ; Hoffmann, *Schlesische Volkslieder*, No. 12, 13, and *Niederländische Volkslieder*, No. 9, 10 ; etc. etc. A very brief Italian ballad will be found in the Appendix, p. 391, which seems to have the same theme. In some of the ballads the treacherous seducer is an enchanter, who prevails upon the maid to go with him by the power of a spell.

May Colvin was first published in Herd's Collection, vol. i. 153. The copy here given is one obtained from recitation by Motherwell, (*Minstrelsy*, p. 67,) collated by him with that of Herd. It is defective at the end. The other versions in Sharpe's *Ballad Book*, p. 45, and Buchan's *Ballads of the North of Scotland*, ii. 45, though they are provided with some sort of conclusion, are not worth reprinting. A modernized version, styled *The Outlandish Knight*, is inserted in the Notes to *Scottish Traditional Versions of Ancient Ballads*, Percy Society, vol. xvii. 101.

Carlton Castle, on the coast of Carrick, is affirmed by the country people, according to Mr. Chambers, to have been the residence of the perfidious knight, and

a precipice overhanging the sea, called " Fause Sir
John's Loup," is pointed out as the place where he was
wont to drown his wives. May Colvin is equally well
ascertained to have been " a daughter of the family of
Kennedy of Colzean, now represented by the Earl of
Cassilis." Buchan's version assigns a different locality
to the transaction — that of " Binyan's Bay," which,
says the editor, is the old name of the mouth of the
river Ugie.

FALSE Sir John a wooing came
　　To a maid of beauty fair ;
May Colvin was the lady's name,
　　Her father's only heir.

He's courted her butt, and he's courted her ben,
　　And he's courted her into the ha',
Till once he got this lady's consent
　　To mount and ride awa'.

She's gane to her father's coffers,
　　Where all his money lay ;
And she's taken the red, and she's left the white,
　　And so lightly as she tripped away.

She's gane down to her father's stable,
　　Where all his steeds did stand ;
And she's taken the best, and she's left tle
　　warst,
　　That was in her father's land.

He rode on, and she rode on,
  They rode a lang simmer's day,
Until they came to a broad river,
  An arm of a lonesome sea.

" Loup off the steed," says false Sir John ;
  " Your bridal bed you see ;
For it's seven king's daughters I have drowned
      here,
  And the eighth I'll out make with thee.

" Cast off, cast off your silks so fine,
  And lay them on a stone,
For they are o'er good and o'er costly
  To rot in the salt sea foam.

" Cast off, cast off your Holland smock,
  And lay it on this stone,
. For it is too fine and o'er costly
  To rot in the salt sea foam."

" O turn you about, thou false Sir John,
  And look to the leaf o' the tree ;
For it never became a gentleman
  A naked woman to see."

He's turn'd himself straight round about,
  To look to the leaf o' the tree ;
She's twined her arms about his waist,
  And thrown him into the sea.

"O hold a grip of me, May Colvin,
　For fear that I should drown ;
I'll take you hame to your father's gates,
　And safely I'll set you down."

"O lie you there, thou false Sir John,
　O lie you there," said she ;
" For you lie not in a caulder bed
　Than the ane you intended for me."

So she went on her father's steed,
　As swift as she could flee,
And she came hame to her father's gates
　At the breaking of the day.

Up then spake the pretty parrot :
　"May Colvin, where have you been ?
What has become of false Sir John,
　That wooed you so late yestreen ? "

Up then spake the pretty parrot,
　In the bonnie cage where it lay :
" O what hae ye done with the false Sir John,
　That he behind you does stay ?

" He wooed you butt, he wooed you ben,
　He wooed you into the ha',
Until he got your own consent
　For to mount and gang awa'."

"O hold your tongue, my pretty parrot,
    Lay not the blame upon me ;
Your cage will be made of the beaten gold,
    And the spakes of ivorie."

Up then spake the king himself,
    In the chamber where he lay :
"O what ails the pretty parrot,
    That prattles so long ere day ?"

"It was a cat cam to my cage door ;
    I thought 't would have worried me ;
And I was calling on fair May Colvin
    To take the cat from me."

BABYLON,

OR,

THE BONNIE BANKS O' FORDIE.

" This ballad is given from two copies obtained from recitation, which differ but little from each other. Indeed, the only variation is in the verse where the outlawed brother unweetingly slays his sister. One reading is, —

> ' He's taken out his wee penknife,
>   *Hey how bonnie ;*
> And he's twined her o' her ain sweet life,
>   *On the bonnie banks o' Fordie.*'

The other reading is that adopted in the text. This ballad is popular in the southern parishes of Perthshire : but where the scene is laid the editor has been unable to ascertain. Nor has any research of his enabled him to throw farther light on the history of its hero with the fantastic name, than what the ballad itself supplies." Motherwell's *Minstrelsy*, p. 88.

Another version is subjoined, from Kinloch's collection.

This ballad is found in Danish ; *Herr Truels's Doetre, Danske Viser*, No. 164. In a note the editor endeavors to show that the story is based on fact !

THERE were three ladies lived in a bower,
Eh vow bonnie,
And they went out to pull a flower,
On the bonnie banks o' Fordie.

They hadna pu'ed a flower but ane,
Eh vow bonnie,
When up started to them a banisht man,
On the bonnie banks o' Fordie.

He's ta'en the first sister by her hand,
Eh vow bonnie,
And he's turned her round and made her stand,
On the bonnie banks o' Fordie.

" It's whether will ye be a rank robber's wife,
Eh vow bonnie,
Or will ye die by my wee penknife,"
On the bonnie banks o' Fordie?

" It's I'll not be a rank robber's wife,
Eh vow bonnie,
But I'll rather die by your wee penknife,"
On the bonnie banks o' Fordie.

He's killed this may and he's laid her by,
Eh vow bonnie,
For to bear the red rose company,
On the bonnie banks o' Fordie.

He's taken the second ane by the hand,
　Eh vow bonnie,
And he's turned her round and made her stand,
　On the bonnie banks o' Fordie.

" It's whether will ye be a rank robber's wife,
　Eh vow bonnie,
Or will ye die by my wee penknife,"
　On the bonnie banks o' Fordie?

" I'll not be a rank robber's wife,
　Eh vow bonnie,
But I'll rather die by your wee penknife,"
　On the bonnie banks o' Fordie.

He's killed this may and he's laid her by,
　Eh vow bonnie,
For to bear the red rose company,
　On the bonnie banks o' Fordie.

He's taken the youngest ane by the hand,
　Eh vow bonnie,
And he's turned her round and made her stand,
　On the bonnie banks o' Fordie.

Says, " Will ye be a rank robber's wife,
　Eh vow bonnie,
Or will ye die by my wee penknife,"
　On the bonnie banks o' Fordie?

"I'll not be a rank robber's wife,
  Eh vow bonnie,
Nor will I die by your wee penknife,
  On the bonnie banks o' Fordie.

" For I hae a brother in this wood,
  Eh vow bonnie,
And gin ye kill me, it's he'll kill thee,"
  On the bonnie banks o' Fordie.

" What's thy brother's name? come tell to me,"
  Eh vow bonnie;
" My brother's name is Babylon,"
  On the bonnie banks o' Fordie.

"O sister, sister, what have I done,
  Eh vow bonnie?
O have I done this ill to thee,
  On the bonnie banks o' Fordie?

" O since I've done this evil deed,
  Eh vow bonnie,
Good sall never be seen o' me,"
  On the bonnie banks o' Fordie.

He's taken out his wee penknife,
  Eh vow bonnie,
And he's twyned himsel o' his ain sweet life,
  On the bonnie banks o' Fordie.

DUKE OF PERTH'S THREE DAUGHTERS

From Kinloch's *Ancient Scottish Ballads*, p. 212.

THE Duke o' Perth had three daughters,
  Elizabeth, Margaret, and fair Marie ;
And Elizabeth's to the greenwud gane,
  To pu' the rose and the fair lilie.

But she hadna pu'd a rose, a rose,
  A double rose, but barely three,
Whan up and started a Loudon lord,
  Wi' Loudon hose, and Loudon sheen.

" Will ye be called a robber's wife ?
Or will ye be stickit wi' my bloody knife ?
For pu'in the rose and the fair lilie,
For pu'in them sae fair and free."

" Before I'll be called a robber's wife,
I'll rather be stickit wi' your bloody knife,
For pu'in the rose and the fair lilie,
For pu'in them sae fair and free."

The out he's tane his little penknife,
And he's parted her and her sweet life,
And thrown her o'er a bank o' brume,
There never more for to be found.

The Duke o' Perth had three daughters,
   Elizabeth, Margaret, and fair Marie;
And Margaret's to the greenwud gane,
   To pu' the rose and the fair lilie.

She hadna pu'd a rose, a rose,
   A double rose, but barely three,
When up and started a Loudon lord,
   Wi' Loudon hose, and Loudon sheen.

" Will ye be called a robber's wife?
Or will ye be stickit wi' my bloody knife?
For pu'in the rose and the fair lilie,
For pu'in them sae fair and free."

" Before I'll be called a robber's wife,
I'll rather be sticket wi' your bloody knife,
For pu'in the rose and the fair lilie,
For pu'in them sae fair and free."

Then out he's tane his little penknife,
And he's parted her and her sweet life,
For pu'in the rose and the fair lilie,
For pu'in them sae fair and free.

The Duke o' Perth had three daughters,
   Elizabeth, Margaret, and fair Marie ;
And Mary's to the greenwud gane,
   To pu' the rose and the fair lilie.

She hadna pu'd a rose, a rose,
   A double rose, but barely three,
When up and started a Loudon lord,
   Wi' Loudon hose, and Loudon sheen.

"O will ye be called a robber's wife ?
Or will ye be stickit wi' my bloody knife ?
For pu'in the rose and the fair lilie,
For pu'in them sae fair and free."

" Before I'll be called a robber's wife,
I'll rather be stickit wi' your bloody knife,
For pu'in the rose and the fair lilie,
For pu'in them sae fair and free."

But just as he took out his knife,
To tak frae her her ain sweet life,
Her brother John cam ryding bye,
And this bloody robber he did espy.

But when he saw his sister fair,
He kenn'd her by her yellow hair ;
He call'd upon his pages three,
To find this robber speedilie.

" My sisters twa that are dead and gane,
For whom we made a heavy maene,
It's you that's twinn'd them o' their life,
And wi' your cruel bloody knife.

Then for their life ye sair shall dree :
Ye sall be hangit on a tree,
Or thrown into the poison'd lake,
To feed the toads and rattle-snake."

JELLON GRAME.

From *Minstrelsy of the Scottish Border*, iii. 162.

" This ballad is published from tradition, with some conjectural emendations. It is corrected by a copy in Mrs. Brown's MS., from which it differs in the concluding stanzas. Some verses are apparently modernized.

" *Jellon* seems to be the same name with *Jyllian*, or *Julian*. 'Jyl of Brentford's Testament' is mentioned in Warton's *History of Poetry*, vol. ii. p. 40. The name repeatedly occurs in old ballads, sometimes as that of a man, at other times as that of a woman. Of the former is an instance in the ballad of *The Knight and the Shepherd's Daughter*. [See this collection, vol. iii. p. 253.]

> ' Some do call me Jack, sweetheart,
> And some do call me *Jille*.'

" Witton Gilbert, a village four miles west of Durham, is, throughout the bishopric, pronounced Witton Jilbert. We have also the common name of Giles, always in Scotland pronounced Jill. For Gille or

Juliana, as a female name, we have *Fair Gillian* of Croyden, and a thousand authorities. Such being the case, the Editor must enter his protest against the conversion of *Gil* Morrice into *Child* Maurice, an epithet of chivalry. All the circumstances in that ballad argue, that the unfortunate hero was an obscure and very young man, who had never received the honour of knighthood. At any rate there can be no reason, even were internal evidence totally wanting, for altering a well-known proper name, which, till of late years, has been the uniform title of the ballad." SCOTT.

May-a-Row, in Buchan's larger collection, ii. **231,** is another, but an inferior, version of this ballad.

O JELLON GRAME sat in Silverwood, [1]
　　He sharp'd his broadsword lang ;
And he has call'd his little foot-page
　　An errand for to gang.

" Win up, my bonny boy," he says,
　　" As quickly as ye may ;
For ye maun gang for Lillie Flower
　　Before the break of day."—

1. Silverwood, mentioned in this ballad, occurs in a medey MS. song, which seems to have been copied from the first edition of the Aberdeen Cantus, *penes* John G. Dalyell, Esq. advocate. One line only is cited, apparently the beginning of some song:—

　　" Silverwood, gin ye were mine." SCOTT.

The boy has buckled his belt about,
   And through the green-wood ran ;
And he came to the ladye's bower
   Before the day did dawn.

" O sleep ye, wake ye, Lillie Flower ?
   The red sun's on the rain :
Ye're bidden come to Silverwood,
   But I doubt ye'll never win hame."—

She hadna ridden a mile, a mile,
   A mile but barely three,
Ere she came to a new-made grave,
   Beneath a green aik tree.

O then up started Jellon Grame,
   Out of a bush thereby ;
" Light down, light down, now, Lillie Flower,
   For it's here that ye maun lye."—

She lighted aff her milk-white steed,
   And kneel'd upon her knee ;
" O mercy, mercy, Jellon Grame,
   For I'm no prepared to die !

" Your bairn, that stirs between my sides,
   Maun shortly see the light :
But to see it weltering in my blood,
   Would be a piteous sight."—

" O should I spare your life," he says,
  " Until that bairn were born,
Full weel I ken your auld father
  Would hang me on the morn."—

" O spare my life, now, Jellon Grame!
  My father ye needna dread:
I'll keep my babe in gude green-wood,
  Or wi' it I'll beg my bread."—

He took no pity on Lillie Flower,
  Though she for life did pray;
But pierced her through the fair body
  As at his feet she lay.

He felt nae pity for Lillie Flower,
  Where she was lying dead;
But he felt some for the bonny bairn,
  That lay weltering in her bluid.

Up has he ta'en that bonny boy,
  Given him to nurses nine;
Three to sleep, and three to wake,
  And three to go between.

And he bred up that bonny boy,
  Call'd him his sister's son;
And he thought no eye could ever see
  The deed that he had done.

O so it fell upon a day,
　　When hunting they might be,
They rested them in Silverwood,
　　Beneath that green aik tree.

And many were the green-wood flowers
　　Upon the grave that grew,
And marvell'd much that bonny boy
　　To see their lovely hue.

" What's paler than the prymrose wan ?
　　What's redder than the rose ?
What's fairer than the lilye flower
　　On this wee know that grows ? "—

O out and answer'd Jellon Grame,
　　And he spak hastilie—
" Your mother was a fairer flower,
　　And lies beneath this tree.

" More pale she was, when she sought my grace,
　　Than prymrose pale and wan ;
And redder than rose her ruddy heart's blood,
　　That down my broadsword ran."—

Wi' that the boy has bent his bow,
　　It was baith stout and lang ;
An thro' and thro' him, Jellon Grame,
　　He gar'd an arrow gang.

Says,—" Lie ye there, now, Jellon Grame !
  My malisoun gang you wi' !
The place that my mother lies buried in
  Is far too good for thee."

YOUNG JOHNSTONE.

A FRAGMENT of this fine ballad (which is commonly called *The Cruel Knight*) was published by Herd,
(i. 222,) and also by Pinkerton, (*Select Scottish Ballads*, i. 69,) with variations. Finlay constructed a
nearly complete edition from two recited copies, but
suppressed some lines. (*Scottish Ballads*, ii. 72.) The
present copy is one which Motherwell obtained from
recitation, with a few verbal emendations by that
editor from Finlay's.

With respect to the sudden and strange catastrophe,
Motherwell remarks :—

" The reciters of old ballads frequently supply the
best commentaries upon them, when any obscurity or
want of connection appears in the poetical narrative.
This ballad, as it stands, throws no light on young
Johnstone's motive for stabbing his lady ; but the person from whose lips it was taken down alleged that the
barbarous act was committed unwittingly, through
young Johnstone's suddenly waking from sleep, and, in
that moment of confusion and alarm, unhappily mis-
taking his mistress for one of his pursuers. It is not
improbable but the ballad may have had, at one time,

a stanza to the above effect, the substance of which is
still remembered, though the words in which it was
couched have been forgotten." *Minstrelsy*, p. 193.

Buchan's version, (*Lord John's Murder*, ii. 20,) it
will be seen, supplies this deficiency.

Young Johnstone and the young Col'nel
    Sat drinking at the wine :
"O gin ye wad marry my sister,
    It's I wad marry thine."

"I wadna marry your sister,
    For a' your houses and land ;
But I'll keep her for my leman,
    When I come o'er the strand.

"I wadna marry your sister,
    For a' your gowd so gay ;
But I'll keep her for my leman,
    When I come by the way."

Young Johnstone had a nut-brown sword,
    Hung low down by his gair,
And he ritted [1] it through the young Col'nel,
    That word he ne'er spak mair.

---

[1] In the copy obtained by the Editor, the word "ritted"
did not occur, instead of which the word "stabbed" was
used. The "nut-brown sword" was also changed into "a
little small sword." MOTHERWELL.

But he's awa' to his sister's bower,
    He's tirled at the pin :
" Whare hae ye been, my dear brither,
    Sae late a coming in ? "
" I hae been at the school, sister,
    Learning young clerks to sing."

" I've dreamed a dreary dream this night,
    I wish it may be for good ;
They were seeking you with hawks and hounds,
    And the young Col'nel was dead."

" Hawks and hounds they may seek me,
    As I trow well they be ;
For I have killed the young Col'nel,
    And thy own true love was he."

" If ye hae killed the young Col'nel,
    O dule and wae is me ;
But I wish ye may be hanged on a hie gallows,
    And hae nae power to flee."

And he's awa' to his true love's bower,
    He's tirled at the pin :
" Whar hae ye been, my dear Johnstone,
    Sae late a coming in ? "
" It's I hae been at the school," he says,
    " Learning young clerks to sing."

" I have dreamed a dreary dream," she says,
    " I wish it may be for good ;
They were seeking you with hawks and hounds,
    And the young Col'nel was dead."

" Hawks and hounds they may seek me,
    As I trow well they be ;
For I hae killed the young Col'nel,
    And thy ae brother was he."

" If ye hae killed the young Col'nel,
    O dule and wae is me ;
But I care the less for the young Col'nel,
    If thy ain body be free.

" Come in, come in, my dear Johnstone,
    Come in and take a sleep ;
And I will go to my casement,
    And carefully I will thee keep."

He had not weel been in her bower door,
    No not for half an hour,
When four-and-twenty belted knights
    Came riding to the bower.

" Well may you sit and see, Lady,
    Well may you sit and say ;
Did you not see a bloody squire
    Come riding by this way ? "

" What colour were his hawks?" she says,
    " What colour were his hounds?
What colour was the gallant steed
    That bore him from the bounds?"

" Bloody, bloody were his hawks,
    And bloody were his hounds;
But milk-white was the gallant steed
    That bore him from the bounds."

" Yes, bloody, bloody were his hawks,
    And bloody were his hounds;
And milk-white was the gallant steed
    That bore him from the bounds.

" Light down, light down now, gentlemen,
    And take some bread and wine;
And the steed be swift that he rides on,
    He's past the brig o' Lyne."

" We thank you for your bread, fair Lady,
    We thank you for your wine;
But I wad gie thrice three thousand pound,
    That bloody knight was ta'en."

" Lie still, lie still, my dear Johnstone,
    Lie still and take a sleep;
For thy enemies are past and gone,
    And carefully I will thee keep."

But young Johnstone had a little wee sword,
   Hung low down by his gair,
And he stabbed it in fair Annet's breast,
   A deep wound and a sair. [1]

" What aileth thee now, dear Johnstone ?
   What aileth thee at me ?
Hast thou not got my father's gold,
   Bot and my mither's fee ? "

" Now live, now live, my dear Ladye,
   Now live but half an hour,
And there's no a leech in a' Scotland
   But shall be in thy bower."

" How can I live, how shall I live ?
   Young Johnstone, do not you see
The red, red drops o' my bonny heart's blood
   Rin trinkling down my knee ?

" But take thy harp into thy hand,
   And harp out owre yon plain,

[1] Buchan's version furnishes the necessary explanation of
Young Johnstone's apparent cruelty :—

        " Ohon, alas, my lady gay,
          To come sae hastilié !
        I thought it was my deadly foe,
          Ye had trysted in to me."

And ne'er think mair on thy true love
　Than if she had never been."

He hadna weel been out o' the stable,
　And on his saddle set,
Till four-and-twenty broad arrows
　Were thrilling in his heart.

YOUNG BENJIE.

From the *Minstrelsy of the Scottish Border*, iii. 10. *Bondsey and Maisry*, another version of the same story, from Buchan's collection, is given in the Appendix.

" In this ballad the reader will find traces of a singular superstition, not yet altogether discredited in the wilder parts of Scotland. The lykewake, or watching a dead body, in itself a melancholy office, is rendered, in the idea of the assistants, more dismally awful, by the mysterious horrors of superstition. In the interval betwixt death and interment, the disembodied spirit is supposed to hover round its mortal habitation, and, if invoked by certain rites, retains the power of communicating, through its organs, the cause of its dissolution. Such inquiries, however, are always dangerous, and never to be resorted to, unless the deceased is suspected to have suffered *foul play*, as it is called. It is the more unsafe to tamper with this charm in an unauthorized manner, because the inhabitants of the infernal regions are, at such periods, peculiarly active. One of the most potent ceremonies in the charm, for causing the dead body to speak, is, setting the door ajar, or half open. On this account, the peasants of Scotland sedulously avoid leaving the door ajar, while a corpse lies in the house. The door must either be left wide open, or quite shut; but the first is always preferred, on account of the exercise of hospitality usual on such occasions. The attendants must be likewise careful never to leave the corpse for a moment alone, or, if it is left alone, to avoid, with a degree of superstitious horror, the first sight of it.

" The following story, which is frequently related by the peasants of Scotland, will illustrate the imaginary danger of leaving the door ajar. In former times, a man and his wife lived in a solitary cottage, on one of the extensive Border fells. One day the husband died suddenly; and his wife, who was equally afraid of staying alone by the corpse, or leaving the dead body by itself, repeatedly went to the door, and looked anxiously over the lonely moor for the sight of some person approaching. In her confusion and alarm she accidentally left the door ajar, when the corpse suddenly started up, and sat in the bed, frowning and grinning at her frightfully. She sat alone, crying bitterly, unable to avoid the fascination of the dead man's eye, and too much terrified to break the sullen silence, till a Catholic priest, passing over the wild, entered the cottage. He first set the door quite open, then put his little finger in his mouth, and said the paternoster backwards; when the horrid look of the corpse relaxed, it fell back on the bed, and behaved itself as a dead man ought to do.

" The ballad is given from tradition. I have been informed by a lady, [Miss Joanna Baillie,] of the highest literary eminence, that she has heard a ballad on

the same subject, in which the scene was laid upon the
banks of the Clyde. The chorus was,

> " O Bothwell banks bloom bonny,"

and the watching of the dead corpse was said to have
taken place in Bothwell church. SCOTT.

OF a' the maids o' fair Scotland,
    The fairest was Marjorie ;
And young Benjie was her ae true love,
    And a dear true love was he.

And wow but they were lovers dear,
    And loved fu' constantlie ;
But aye the mair when they fell out,
    The sairer was their plea.

And they hae quarrell'd on a day,
    Till Marjorie's heart grew wae ;
And she said she'd chuse another luve,
    And let young Benjie gae.

And he was stout, and proud-hearted,
    And thought o't bitterlie ;
And he's gane by the wan moonlight,
    To meet his Marjorie.

" O open, open, my true love,
    O open, and let me in ! "—

" I darena open, young Benjie,
    My three brothers are within."—

" Ye lied, ye lied, ye bonny burd,
    Sae loud's I hear ye lie ;
As I came by the Lowden banks,
    They bade gude e'en to me.

" But fare ye weel, my ae fause love,
    That I have loved sae lang !
It sets ye chuse another love,
    And let young Benjie gang."—

Then Marjorie turn'd her round about,
    The tear blinding her ee,—
" I darena, darena let thee in,
    But I'll come down to thee."—

Then saft she smiled, and said to him,
    " O what ill hae I done ? "—
He took her in his armis twa,
    And threw her o'er the linn.

The stream was strang, the maid was stout,
    And laith, laith to be dang,
But, ere she wan the Lowden banks,
    Her fair colour was wan.

Then up bespak her eldest brother,
    " O see na ye what I see ? "—

And out then spak her second brother,
  " It's our sister Marjorie ! " —

Out then spak her eldest brother,
  " O how shall we her ken ? "—
And out then spak her youngest brother,
  " There's a honey mark on her chin."—

Then they've ta'en up the comely corpse,
  And laid it on the ground :
" O wha has killed our ae sister,
  And how can he be found ?

" The night it is her low lykewake,
  The morn her burial day,
And we maun watch at mirk midnight,
  And hear what she will say."—

Wi' doors ajar, and candle light,
  And torches burning clear,
The streikit corpse, till still midnight,
  They waked, but naething hear.

About the middle o' the night,
  The cocks began to craw ;
And at the dead hour o' the night,
  The corpse began to thraw.

" O whae has done the wrang, sister,
  Or dared the deadly sin ?

Whae was sae stout, and fear'd nae dout,
   As thraw ye o'er the linn?"

" Young Benjie was the first ae man
   I laid my love upon ;
He was sae stout and proud-hearted,
   He threw me o'er the linn."—

" Sall we young Benjie head, sister,
   Sall we young Benjie hang,
Or sall we pike out his twa gray een,
   And punish him ere he gang?"

" Ye maunna Benjie head, brothers,
   Ye maunna Benjie hang,
But ye maun pike out his twa gray een,
   And punish him ere he gang.

" Tie a green gravat round his neck,
   And lead him out and in,
And the best ae servant about your house
   To wait young Benjie on.

" And aye, at every seven years' end,
   Ye'l tak him to the linn ;
For that's the penance he maun dree,
   To scug his deadly sin."

APPENDIX.

LORD BARNABY.

Scottish version of *Little Musgrave and Lady Barnard.* See p. 15.

From Jamieson's *Popular Ballads and Songs*, i. 170.

" I HAVE a tower in Dalisberry,
    Which now is dearly dight,
And I will gie it to young Musgrave
    To lodge wi' me 'i' night."

" To lodge wi' thee a' night, fair lady,
    Wad breed baith sorrow and strife ;
For I see by the rings on your fingers,
    You're good lord Barnaby's wife."

" Lord Barnaby's wife although I be,
    Yet what is that to thee ?
For we'll beguile him for this ae night—
    He's on to fair Dundee.

" Come here, come here, my little foot-page,
    This gold I will give thee,
If ye will keep thir secrets close
    'Tween young Musgrave and me.

" But here I hae a little pen-knife,
    Hings low down by my gare ;
Gin ye winna keep thir secrets close
    Ye'll find it wonder sair."

Then she's ta'en him to her chamber,
    And down in her arms lay he :
The boy coost aff his hose and shoon,
    And ran to fair Dundee.

When he cam to the wan water,
    He slack'd[1] his bow and swam ;
And when he cam to growin grass,
    Set down his feet and ran.

And when he cam to fair Dundee,
    Wad neither chap nor ca' ;
But set his brent bow to his breast,
    And merrily jump'd the wa'.

" O waken ye, waken ye, my good lord,
    Waken, and come away ! "—
" What ails, what ails my wee foot page,
    He cries sae lang ere day.

" O is my bowers brent, my boy ?
    Or is my castle won ?

---

1 For *slack'd* read *bent.*   J.

Or has the lady that I lo'e best
    Brought me a daughter or son ? "

" Your ha's are safe, your bowers are safe,
    And free frae all alarms ;
But, oh ! the lady that ye lo'e best
    Lies sound in Musgrave's arms."

" Gae saddle to me the black," he cried,
    " Gae saddle to me the gray ;
Gae saddle to me the swiftest steed,
    To hie me on my way."

" O lady, I heard a wee horn toot,
    And it blew wonder clear ;
And ay the turning o' the note,
    Was, ' Barnaby will be here ! '

" I thought I heard a wee horn blaw,
    And it blew loud and high ;
And ay at ilka turn it said,
    ' Away, Musgrave, away ! ' "

" Lie still, my dear ; lie still, my dear ;
    Ye keep me frae the cold ;
For it is but my father's shepherds
    Driving their flocks to the fold."

Up they lookit, and down they lay,
    And they're fa'en sound asleep ;
Till up stood good lord Barnaby,
    Just close at their bed feet.

" How do you like my bed, Musgrave ?
    And how like ye my sheets ?

And how like ye my fair lady,
    Lies in your arms and sleeps?"

"Weel like I your bed, my lord,
    And weel like I your sheets;
But ill like I your fair lady,
    Lies in my arms and sleeps.

"You got your wale o' se'en sisters,
    And I got mine o' five;
Sae tak ye mine, and I's tak thine,
    And we nae mair sall strive."

"O my woman's the best woman
    That ever brak world's bread;
And your woman's the worst woman
    That ever drew coat o'er head.

"I hae twa swords in ae scabbert,
    They are baith sharp and clear;
Take ye the best, and I the warst,
    And we'll end the matter here.

"But up, and arm thee, young Musgrave,
    We'll try it han' to han';
It's ne'er be said o' lord Barnaby,
    He strack at a naked man."

The first straik that young Musgrave got,
    It was baith deep and sair;
And down he fell at Barnaby's feet,
    And word spak never mair.

    *   *   *   *   *   *

" A grave, a grave !" lord Barnaby cried,
   " A grave to lay them in ;
My lady shall lie on the sunny side,
   Because of her noble kin."

But oh, how sorry was that good lord,
   For a' his angry mood,
Whan he beheld his ain young son
   All welt'ring in his blood !

NOTE. [In v. 31] the term " *braid* bow " has been altered
by the editor into " *brent* bow," i. e. *straight*, or *unbent* bow.
In most of the old ballads, where a page is employed as the
bearer of a message, we are told, that,

   " When he came to wan water,
     He *bent* his bow and swam;"

And

   " He set his *bent* bow to his breast,
     And lightly lap the wa'," &c.

The application of the term *bent*, in the latter instance, does
not seem correct, and is probably substituted for *brent*.

In the establishment of a feudal baron, every thing wore a
military aspect; he was a warrior by profession; every man
attached to him, particularly those employed about his person, was a soldier; and his little foot-page was very appropri-
ately equipped in the light accoutrements of an archer. His
bow, in the old ballad, seems as inseparable from his character as the bow of Cupid or of Apollo, or the caduceus of his ce-
lestial prototype Mercury. This bow, which he carried unbent,
he seems to have *bent* when he had occasion to swim, in order
that he might the more easily carry it in his teeth, to prevent
the string from being injured by getting wet. At other times
he availed himself of its length and elasticity in the *brent*, or
straight state, and used it (as hunters do a leaping pole) in

vaulting over the wall of the outer court of a castle, when his business would not admit of the tedious formality of blowing a horn, or ringing a bell, and holding a long parley with the porter at the gate, before he could gain admission. This, at least, appears to the editor to be the meaning of these passages in the old ballads. JAMIESON.

CHILDE MAURICE. See p. 30.

From Jamieson's *Popular Ballads and Songs*, i. 8.

CHILDE MAURICE hunted i' the silver wood,
  He hunted it round about,
And noebody yt he found theren,
  Nor noebody without.

* * * * * * *
* * * * * * *

And tooke his silver combe in his hand
  To kembe his yellow lockes.

He sayes, " come hither, thou litle footpage,
  That runneth lowly by my knee ;
Ffor thou shalt goe to John Steward's wiffe,
  And pray her speake with mee.

1. MS. silven.

" And as it ffalls out,[1] many times
    As knotts been knitt on a kell,
Or merchant men gone to leeve London,
    Either to buy ware or sell,

*   *   *   *   *   *   *
*   *   *   *   *   *   *

And grete thou doe that ladye well,
    Ever soe well ffroe mee.

" And as it ffalls out, many times
    As any harte can thinke,
As schoole masters are in any schoole house,
    Writting with pen and inke,

*   *   *   *   *   *   *
*   *   *   *   *   *   *

Ffor if I might as well as shee may,
    This night I wold with her speake.

" And heere I send a mantle of greene,
    As greene as any grasse,
And bid her come to the silver wood,
    To hunt with Child Maurice.

" And there I send her a ring of gold,
    A ring of precyous stone ;
And bid her come to the silver wood,
    Let for no kind of man."

One while this litle boy he yode,
    Another while he ran ;

---

[1] out out.

Until he came to John Steward's hall,
   Iwis he never blan.

And of nurture the child had good ;
   He ran up hall and bower ffree,
And when he came to this lady ffaire,
   Sayes, " God you save and see.

" I am come ffrom Childe Maurice,
   A message unto thee,
And Childe Maurice he greetes you well,
   And ever soe well ffrom me.

" And as it ffalls out, oftentimes
   As knotts been knitt on a kell,
Or merchant men gone to leeve London
   Either to buy or sell ;

" And as oftentimes he greetes you well,
   As any hart can thinke,
Or schoolemaster in any schoole,
   Wryting with pen and inke.

" And heere he sends a mantle of greene,
   As greene as any grasse,
And he bidds you come to the silver wood,
   To hunt with child Maurice.

" And heere he sends you a ring of gold,
   A ring of precyous stone ;
He prayes you to come to the silver wood,
   Let for no kind of man."

" Now peace, now peace, thou litle fotpage,
   Ffor Christes sake I pray thee ;

Ffor if my lord heare one of those words,
   Thou must be hanged hye."

John Steward stood under the castle wall,
   And he wrote the words every one;
*   *   *   *   *   *   *

*   *   *   *   *   *   *

And he called unto his horssekeeper,
   " Make ready you my steede ; "
And soe he did to his chamberlaine,
   " Make readye then my weed."

And he cast a lease upon his backe,
   And he rode to the silver wood,
And there he sought all about,
   About the silver wood.

And there he found him Childe Maurice,
   Sitting upon a blocke,
With a silver combe in his hand,
   Kembing his yellow locke.

He sayes, " how now, how now, Childe Maurice,
   Alacke how may this bee ? "
But then stood by him Childe Maurice,
   And sayd these words trulye :

" I do not know your ladye," he said,
   " If that I doe her see."
" Ffor thou hast sent her love tokens,
   More now than two or three.

" For thou hast sent her a mantle of greene,
   As greene as any grasse,

And bade her come to the silver wood,
   To hunt with Childe Maurice.

" And by my faith now, Childe Maurice,
   The tane of us shall dye ; "
" Now by my troth," sayd Childe Maurice,
   " And that shall not be I."

But he pulled out a bright browne sword,
   And dryed it on the grasse,
And soe fast he smote at John Steward,
   Iwis he never rest.

Then hee pulled forth his bright browne swoid,
   And dryed itt on his sleeve,
And the flirst good stroke John Steward stroke,
   Child Maurice head he did cleeve.

And he pricked it on his swords poynt,
   Went singing there beside,
And he rode till he came to the ladye ffaire,
   Whereas his ladye lyed.

And sayes, " dost thou know Child Maurice head,
   Iff that thou dost it see ?
And llap it soft, and kisse itt offt,
   Ffor thou lovedst him better than mee."

But when shee looked on Child Maurice head,
   Shee never spake words but three :
" I never beare noe child but one,
   And you have slain him trulye."

Sayes, " wicked be my merry men all,
   I gave meate, drinke, and clothe ;

But cold they not have holden me,
  When I was in all that wrath !

" Ffor I have slaine one of the courteousest
    knights
That ever bestrode a steede ;
Soe have I done one of the fairest ladyes
  That ever ware womans weede."

CLERK SAUNDERS.　See p. 45.

From Jamieson's *Popular Ballads and Songs*, i. 83.

" The following copy was transmitted by Mrs. Arrott of Aberbrothick. The stanzas, where the seven brothers are introduced, have been enlarged from two fragments, which, although very defective in themselves, furnished lines which, when incorporated with the text, seemed to improve it. Stanzas 21 and 22, were written by the editor ; the idea of the *rose* being suggested by the gentleman who recited, but who could not recollect the language in which it was expressed."

This copy of *Clerk Saunders* bears traces of having been made up from several sources. A portion of the concluding stanzas (v. 107–130) have a strong resemblance to the beginning and end of *Proud Lady Margaret* (vol. viii. 83, 278), which ballad is itself in a corrupt condition. It may also be doubted whether the fragments Jamieson speaks of did not belong to a ballad resembling *Lady Maisry*, p. 78 of this volume.

Accepting the ballad as it stands here, there is certainly likeness enough in the first part to suggest a community of origin with the Swedish ballad *Den Grymma Brodern, Svenska Folk-Visor*, No. 86 (translated in *Lit. and Rom. of Northern Europe*, p. 261). W. Grimm mentions (*Altdän. Heldenl.*, p. 519) a Spanish ballad, *De la Blanca Niña*, in the *Romancero de Amberes*, in which the similarity to *Den Grymma Brodern* is very striking. The series of questions (v. 30–62) sometimes appears apart from the story, and with a comic turn, as in *Det Hurtige Svar, Danske V.*, No. 204, or *Thore och hans Syster*, Arwidsson, i. 358. In this shape they closely resemble the familiar old song, *Our gudeman came hame at e'en*, Herd, *Scottish Songs*, ii. 74.

CLERK SAUNDERS was an earl's son,
   He liv'd upon sea-sand;
May Margaret was a king's daughter,
   She liv'd in upper land.

Clerk Saunders was an earl's son,
   Weel learned at the scheel;
May Margaret was a king's daughter;
   They baith lo'ed ither weel.

He's throw the dark, and throw the mark,
   And throw the leaves o' green ;
Till he came to May Margaret's door,
   And tirled at the pin.

" O sleep ye, wake ye, May Margaret,
   Or are ye the bower within ? "
" O wha is that at my bower door,
   Sae weel my name does ken ? "
" It's I, Clerk Saunders, your true love,
   You'll open and lat me in.

" O will ye to the cards, Margaret,
   Or to the table to dine ?
Or to the bed, that's weel down spread,
   And sleep when we get time."

" I'll no go to the cards," she says,
   " Nor to the table to dine ;
But I'll go to a bed, that's weel down spread,
   And sleep when we get time.'

They were not weel lyen down,
   And no weel fa'en asleep,
When up and stood May Margaret's brethren,
   Just up at their bed feet.

" O tell us, tell us, May Margaret,
   And dinna to us len,
O wha is aught yon noble steed,
   That stands your stable in ?

" The steed is mine, and it may be thine,
   To ride whan ye ride in hie——

*   *   *   *   *   *   *

" But awa', awa', my bald brethren,
 Awa', and mak nae din ;
For I am as sick a lady the nicht
 As e'er lay a bower within."

" O tell us, tell us, May Margaret,
 And dinna to us len,
O wha is aught yon noble hawk,
 That stands your kitchen in ? "

" The hawk is mine, and it may be thine,
 To hawk whan ye hawk in hie——

*   *   *   *   *   *   *

" But awa', awa', my bald brethren !
 Awa', and mak nae din ;
For I'm ane o' the sickest ladies this nicht
 That e'er lay a bower within."

" O tell us, tell us, May Margaret,
 And dinna to us len,
O wha is that, May Margaret,
 You and the wa' between ? "

" O it is my bower-maiden," she says,
 " As sick as sick can be ;
O it is my bower maiden," she says,
 And she's thrice as sick as me."

" We hae been east, and we've been west,
 And low beneath the moon ;

But a' the bower-women e'er we saw
 Hadna goud buckles in their shoon."

Then up and spak her eldest brither,
 Ay in ill time spak he:
" It is Clerk Saunders, your true love,
 And never mat I the,
But for this scorn that he has done,
 This moment he sall die."

But up and spak her youngest brother,
 Ay in good time spak he:
" O but they are a gudelie pair !—
 True lovers an ye be,
The sword that hangs at my sword belt
 Sall never sinder ye !"

Syne up and spak her nexten brother,
 And the tear stood in his ee:
" You've lo'ed her lang, and lo'ed her weel,
 And pity it wad be,
The sword that hangs at my sword-belt
 Shoud ever sinder ye !"

But up and spak her fifthen brother,
 " Sleep on your sleep for me ;
But we baith sall never sleep again,
 For the tane o' us sall die !"

[But up and spak her midmaist brother ;
 And an angry laugh leugh he :
" The thorn that dabs, I'll cut it down,
 Though fair the rose may be.

" The flower that smell'd sae sweet yestreen
  Has lost its bloom wi' thee ;
And though I'm wae it should be sae,
  Clerk Saunders, ye maun die."]

And up and spak her thirden brother,
  Ay in ill time spak he :
" Curse on his love and comeliness !—
  Dishonour'd as ye be,
The sword that hangs at my sword-belt
  Sall quickly sinder ye ! "

Her eldest brother has drawn his sword ;
  Her second has drawn anither ;
Between Clerk Saunders' hause and collar bane
  The cald iron met thegither.

" O wae be to you, my fause brethren,
  And an ill death mat ye die !
Ye mith slain Clerk Saunders in open field,
  And no in the bed wi' me."

When seven years were come and gane,
  Lady Margaret she thought lang ;
And she is up to the hichest tower,
  By the lee licht o' the moon.

She was lookin o'er her castle high,
  To see what she might fa' ;
And there she saw a grieved ghost
  Comin waukin o'er the wa.' [1]

---

[1] The *wa'* here is supposed to mean the wall, which, in
some old castles, surrounded the court.   J.

" O are ye a man of mean," she says,
  " Seekin ony o' my meat ?
Or are you a rank robber,
  Come in my bower to break ? "

" O I'm Clerk Saunders, your **true love** ;
  Behold, Margaret, and see,
And mind, for a' your meikle pride,
  Sae will become of thee."

" Gin ye be Clerk Saunders, my true love,
  This meikle marvels me :
O wherein is your bonny arms
  That wont to embrace me ? "

" By worms they're eaten, in mools they're **rotten,**
  Behold, Margaret, and see ;
And mind, for a' your mickle pride,
  Sae will become o' thee ! "

*　*　*　*　*　*　*

O, bonny, bonny sang the bird,
  Sat on the coil o' hay ;
But dowie, dowie was the maid,
  That follow'd the corpse o' clay.

" Is there ony room at your head, Saunders,
  Is there ony room at your feet ?
Is there ony room at your twa sides,
  For a lady to lie and sleep ? "

" There is nae room at my head, Margaret,
  As little at my feet ;

There is nae room at my twa sides,
  For a lady to lie and sleep.

" But gae hame, gae hame, now, May Margaret,
  Gae hame and sew your seam ;
For if ye were laid in your weel-made bed.
  Your days will nae be lang."

LORD WA'YATES AND AULD INGRAM.

A FRAGMENT. See p. 72.

Jamieson's *Popular Ballads*, ii. 265.

" From Mr. Herd's MS., transmitted by Mr. Scott."

LADY MAISERY was a lady fair,
  She made her mother's bed ;
Auld Ingram was an aged knight,
  And her he sought to wed.

" Its I forbid ye, auld Ingram,
  For to seek me to spouse ;
For Lord Wa'yates, your sister's son,
  Has been into my bowers.

" Its I forbid ye, auld Ingram,
  For to seek me to wed ;
For Lord Wa'yates, your sister's son,
  Has been into my bed."

He has brocht to this ladie
   The robis of the brown ;
And ever, " Alas ! " says this ladie,
   " Thae robes will put me down."

And he has brocht to that ladie
   The robis of the red ;
And ever, " Alas ! " says that ladie,
   " Thae robes will be my dead."

And he has brocht to that ladie
   The chrystal and the laumer ;
Sae has he brocht to her mither
   The curches o' the cannel.

Every ane o' her seven brethren
   They had a hawk in hand,
And every lady in the place
   They got a goud garland.

Every cuik in that kitchen
   They got a noble claith ;
A' was blyth at auld Ingram's coming,
   But Lady Maisery was wraith.

" Whare will I get a bonny boy,
   Wad fain win hose and shoon,
That wad rin on to my Wa'yates,
   And quickly come again ? "

" Here am I, a bonny boy,
   Wad fain win hose and shoon ;
Wha will rin on to your Wa'yates,
   And quickly come again."

" Ye'll bid him, and ye'll pray him baith,
 Gin ony prayer may dee,
To Marykirk to come the morn,
 My weary wadding to see."

Lord Wa'yates lay o'er his castle wa',
 Beheld baith dale and down ;
And he beheld a bonny boy
 Come running to the town.

" What news, what news, ye bonny boy ?
 What news hae ye to me ?
*   *   *   *   *   *   *
*   *   *   *   *   *   *

" O are my ladie's fauldis brunt,
 Or are her towers won ?
Or is my Maisery lichter yet
 O' a dear dochter or son ? "

" Your ladie's faulds are neither brunt,
 Nor are her towers won ;
Nor is your Maisery lichter yet
 O' a dear dochter or son :

" But she bids you, and she prays you baith,
 Gin ony prayer can dee,
To Mary Kirk to come the morn,
 Her weary wadding to see."

He dang the buird up wi' his fit,
 Sae did he wi' his knee ;
The silver cup, that was upon't,
 I' the fire he gar'd it flee :

" O whatten a lord in a' Scotland
   Dare marry my Maisery ?

" O it is but a feeble thocht,
   To tell the tane and nae the tither ;
O it is but a feeble thocht
   To tell it's your ain mither's brither."

" Its I will send to that wadding,
   And I will follow syne,
The fitches o' the fallow deer,
   And the gammons o' the swine ;
And the nine hides o' the noble cow—
   'Twas slain in season time.

" Its I will send to that wadding
   Ten tun o' the red wine ;
And mair I'll send to that waddin',
   And I will follow syne."

Whan he came in into the ha',
   Lady Maisery she did ween ;
And twenty times he kist her mou',
   Afore auld Ingram's een.

And till the kirk she wadna gae,
   Nor tillt she wadna ride,
Till four-and-twenty men she gat her before,
   And twenty on ilka side,
And four-and-twenty milk white dows,
   To flee aboon her head.

A loud lauchter gae Lord Wa'yates,
   'Mang the mids o' his men ;

" Marry that lady wha that will,
  A maiden she is nane."

" O leuch ye at my men, Wa'yates,
  Or did ye lauch at me ?
Or leuch ye at the bierdly bride,
  That's gaun to marry me ? "

" I leuchna at your men, uncle,
  Nor yet leuch I at thee ;
But I leuch at my lands so braid,
  Sae weel's I do them see."

When e'en was come, and e'en-bells rung,
  And a' man gane to bed,
The bride but and the silly bridegroom
  In ae chamber were laid.

Wasna't a fell thing for to see
  Twa heads upon a cod ;
Lady Maisery's like the mo'ten goud,
  Auld Ingram's like a toad.

He turn'd his face unto the stock,
  And sound he fell asleep ;
She turn'd her face unto the wa',
  And saut tears she did weep.

It fell about the mirk midnicht,
  Auld Ingram began to turn him ;
He put his hand on's ladie's side,
  And waly, sair was she mournin'.

" What aileth thee, my lady dear ?
  Ever alas, and wae is me !

There is a babe betwixt thy sides,—
  Oh ! sae sair's it grieves me ! "

" O didna I tell ye, auld Ingram,
  Ere ye socht me to wed,
That Lord Wa'yates, your sister's son,
  Had been into my bed ? "

" Then father that bairn on me, Maisery,
  O father that bairn on me ;
And ye sall hae a rigland shire
  Your mornin' gift to be."

" O sarbit!" says the Ladie Maisery,
  " That ever the like me befa',
To father my bairn on auld Ingram,
  Lord Wa'yates in my father's ha'.

" O sarbit!" says the Ladie Maisery,
  " That ever the like betide,
To father my bairn on auld Ingram,
  And Lord Wa'yates beside."

   *   *   *   *   *   *   *   *

From Buchan's *Ballads of the North of Scotland*, i. 97

" HEY love Willie, and how love Willie,
　And Willie my love shall be ;
They're thinking to sinder our lang love, Willie;
　It's mair than man can dee.

" Ye'll mount me quickly on a steed,
　A milk-white steed or gray ;
And carry me on to gude greenwood
　Before that it be day."

He mounted her upon a steed,
　He chose a steed o' gray ;
He had her on to gude greenwood
　Before that it was day.

" O will ye gang to the cards, Meggie
　Or will ye gang wi' me ?
Or will ye ha'e a bower woman,
　To stay ere it be day ? "

" I winna gang to the cards," she said,
  " Nor will I gae wi' thee,
Nor will I hae a bower woman,
  To spoil my modestie.

" Ye'll gie me a lady at my back,
  An' a lady me beforn ;
An' a midwife at my twa sides
  Till your young son be born.

" Ye'll do me up, and further up,
  To the top o' yon greenwood tree ;
For every pain myself shall ha'e,
  The same pain ye maun drie."

The first pain that did strike sweet Willie,
  It was into the side ;
Then sighing sair said sweet Willie,
  " These pains are ill to bide."

The nextan pain that strake sweet Willie,
  It was into the back ;
Then sighing sair said sweet Willie,
  " These pains are women's wreck."

The nextan pain that strake sweet Willie,
  It was into the head ;
Then sighing sair said sweet Willie,
  " I fear my lady's dead."

Then he's gane on, and further on,
  At the foot o' yon greenwood tree ;
There he got his lady lighter,
  Wi' his young son on her knee.

Then he's ta'en up his little young son,
　　And kiss'd him cheek and chin;
And he is on to his mother,
　　As fast as he could gang.

"Ye will take in my son, mother,
　　Gi'e him to nurses nine;
Three to wauk, and three to sleep,
　　And three to gang between."

Then he has left his mother's house,
　　And frae her he has gane;
And he is back to his lady,
　　And safely brought her hame.

Then in it came her father dear,
　　Was belted in a brand;
"It's nae time for brides to lye in bed,
　　When the bridegroom's send's in town.

"There are four-and-twenty noble lords
　　A' lighted on the green;
The fairest knight amang them a',
　　He must be your bridegroom."

"O wha will shoe my foot, my foot?
　　And wha will glove my hand?
And wha will prin my sma' middle,
　　Wi' the short prin and the lang?"

Now out it speaks him, sweet Willie,
　　Who knew her troubles best;
"It is my duty for to serve,
　　As I'm come here as guest.

" Now I will shoe your foot, Maisry,
  And I will glove your hand,
And I will prin your sma' middle,
  Wi' the sma' prin and the lang."

" Wha will saddle my steed," she says,
  " And gar my bridle ring ?
And wha will ha'e me to gude church-door,
  This day I'm ill abound ? "

" I will saddle your steed, Maisry,
  And gar your bridle ring ;
And I'll hae you to gude church-door,
  And safely set you down."

" O healy, healy take me up,
  And healy set me down ;
And set my back until a wa',
  My foot to yird-fast stane."

He healy took her frae her horse,
  And healy set her down ;
And set her back until a wa',
  Her foot to yird-fast stane.

When they had eaten and well drunken,
  And a' had thorn'd fine ;
The bride's father he took the cup,
  For to serve out the wine.

Out it speaks the bridegroom's brother
  An ill death mat he die !
" I fear our bride she's born a bairn,
  Or else has it a dee."

She's ta'en out a Bible braid,
   And deeply has she sworn ;
" If I ha'e born a bairn," she says,
   " Sin' yesterday at morn ;

" Or if I've born a bairn," she says,
   " Sin' yesterday at noon ;
There's nae a lady amang you a'
   That wou'd been here sae soon."

Then out it spake the bridegroom's man,
   Mischance come ower his heel !
" Win up, win up, now bride," he says,
   " And dance a shamefu' reel." [1]

Then out it speaks the bride hersell,
   And a sorry heart had she ;
" Is there nae ane amang you a'
   Will dance this dance for me ? "

Then out it speaks him, sweet Willie,
   And he spake aye thro' pride ;
" O draw my boots for me, bridegroom,
   Or I dance for your bride."

Then out it spake the bride hersell,
   " O na, this maunna be ;
For I will dance this dance mysell,
   Tho' my back shou'd gang in three."

[1] The first reel, danced with the bride, her maiden, and
two young men, and called the Shame Spring, or Reel, as
the bride chooses the tune that is to be played. B.

She hadna well gane thro' the reel,
  Nor yet well on the green,
Till she fell down at Willie's feet
  As cauld as ony stane.

He's ta'en her in his arms twa,
  And ha'ed her up the stair ;
Then up it came her jolly bridegroom,
  Says, " What's your business there ? "

Then Willie lifted up his foot,
  And dang him down the stair ;
And brake three ribs o' the bridegroom's side,
  And a word he spake nae mair.

Nae meen was made for that lady,
  When she was lying dead ;
But a' was for him, sweet Willie,
  On the fields for he ran mad.

LADY MARJORIE. See p. 92.

" GIVEN from the recitation of an old woman in Kilbarchan, Renfrewshire, from whom the Editor has obtained several valuable pieces of a like nature. In singing, O is added at the end of the second and fourth line of each stanza." Motherwell's *Minstrelsy*, **p. 234.**

LADY Marjorie was her mother's only daughter,
    Her father's only heir ;
And she is awa to Strawberry Castle,
    To get some unco lair.

She had na been in Strawberry Castle
    A twelvemonth and a day,
Till Lady Marjorie she gangs big wi' child,
    As big as she can gae.

Word is to her father gane,
    Before he got on his shoon,
That Lady Majorie she gaes wi' child,
    And it is to an Irish groom.

But word is to her mother gone,
  Before she got on her goun,
That Lady Marjorie she gaes wi' child
  To a lord of high renown.

" O wha will put on the pat," they said,
  " Or wha will put on the pan,
Or wha will put on a bauld, bauld fire,
  To burn Lady Marjorie in ? "

Her father he put on the pat,
  Her sister put on the pan,
And her brother he put on a bauld, bauld fire,
  To burn Lady Marjorie in ;
And her mother she sat in a golden chair,
  To see her daughter burn.

" But where will I get a pretty little boy,
  That will win hose and shoon ;
That will go quickly to Strawberry Castle,
  And bid my lord come doun ? "

" O here am I, a pretty little boy,
  That will win hose and shoon ;
That will rin quickly to Strawberry Castle,
  And bid thy lord come doun."

O when he cam to broken brigs,
  He bent his bow and swam ;
And when he cam to gude dry land,
  He set doun his foot and ran.

When he cam to Strawberry Castle,
  He tirled at the pin ;

Nane was sae ready as the gay lord himsell
　　To open and let him in.

“ O is there any of my towers burnt,
　　Or any of my castles won ?
Or is Lady Marjorie brought to bed,
　　Of a daughter or a son ? ”

“ O there is nane of thy towers burnt,
　　Nor nane of thy castles broken ;
But Lady Marjorie is condemned to die,
　　To be burnt in a fire of oaken.”

“ O gar saddle to me the black,” he says,
　　“ Gar saddle to me the broun ;
Gar saddle to me the swiftest steed
　　That e’er carried a man frae toun ! ”

He left the black into the slap,
　　The broun into the brae ;
But fair fa’ that bonnie apple-gray
　　That carried this gay lord away !

“ Beet on, beet on, my brother dear,
　　I value you not one straw ;
For yonder comes my ain true luve,
　　I hear his horn blaw.

“ Beet on, beet on, my father dear,
　　I value you not a pin ;
For yonder comes my ain true luve,
　　I hear his bridle ring.”

He took a little horn out of his pocket,
　　And he blew’t baith loud and schill ;

And wi' the little life that was in her,
   She hearken'd to it full weel.

But when he came into the place,
   He lap unto the wa' ;
He thought to get a kiss o' her bonnie lips,
   But her body fell in twa !

" O vow ! O vow ! O vow ! " he said,
   " O vow ! but ye've been cruel :
Ye've taken the timber out of my ain wood,
   And burnt my ain dear jewel !

" Now for thy sake, Lady Marjorie,
   I'll burn baith father and mother ;
And for thy sake, Lady Marjorie,
   I'll burn baith sister and brother.

" And for thy sake, Lady Marjorie,
   I'll burn baith kith and kin ;
But I'll aye remember the pretty little boy
   That did thy errand rin."

LEESOME BRAND.

Buchan's *Ballads of the North of Scotland*, i. 38
This is properly a tragic story, as may be perceived by
comparing the present corrupted version (evidently
made up from several different sources) with the Danish and Swedish ballads. See *Herr Medelvold, Danske
Viser*, iii. 361, *Die wahrsagenden Nachtigallen*, in
Grimm's *Altdänische Heldenlieder*, p. 88, *Fair Midel
and Kirsten Lyle*, translated by Jamieson, *Illustrations*,
p. 377; and *Herr Redevall, Svenska Folkvisor*, ii. 189,
Krist' Lilla och Herr Tideman, Arwidsson, i. 352, *Sir
Wal and Lisa Lyle*, translated by Jamieson, p. 373.

My boy was scarcely ten years auld,
 Whan he went to an unco land,
Where wind never blew, nor cocks ever crew,
 Ohon ! for my son, Leesome Brand.

Awa' to that king's court he went,
 It was to serve for meat an' fee ;
Gude red gowd it was his hire,
 And lang in that king's court stay'd he.

He hadna been in that unco land,
 But only twallmonths twa or three ;
Till by the glancing o' his ee,
 He gain'd the love o' a gay ladye.

This ladye was scarce eleven years auld,
    When on her love she was right bauld ;
She was scarce up to my right knee,
    When oft in bed wi' men I'm tauld.

But when nine months were come and gane,
This ladye's face turn'd pale and wane ;
To Leesome Brand she then did say,
" In this place I can nae mair stay.

" Ye do you to my father's stable,
Where steeds do stand baith wight and able ;
Strike ane o' them upo' the back,
The swiftest will gie his head a wap.

" Ye take him out upo' the green,
And get him saddled and bridled seen ;
Get ane for you, anither for me,
And lat us ride out ower the lee.

" Ye do you to my mother's coffer,
And out of it ye'll take my tocher ;
Therein are sixty thousand pounds,
Which all to me by right belongs."

He's done him to her father's stable,
Where steeds stood baith wicht and able ;
Then he strake ane upon the back,
The swiftest gae his head a wap.

He's ta'en him out upo' the green,
And got him saddled and bridled seen ;
Ane for him, and another for her,
To carry them baith wi' might and virr.

He's done him to her mother's coffer,
And there he's taen his lover's tocher;
Wherein were sixty thousand pounds,
Which all to her by right belong'd.

When they had ridden about six mile,
His true love then began to fail;
" O wae's me," said that gay ladye,
" I fear my back will gang in three !

" O gin I had but a gude midwife,
Here this day to save my life,
And ease me o' my misery,
O dear, how happy I wou'd be !"

" My love, we're far frae ony town;
There is nae midwife to be foun';
But if ye'll be content wi' me,
I'll do for you what man can dee."

" For no, for no, this maunna be,"
Wi' a sigh, replied this gay ladye;
" When I endure my grief and pain,
My companie ye maun refrain.

" Ye'll take your arrow and your bow,
And ye will hunt the deer and roe;
Be sure ye touch not the white hynde,
For she is o' the woman kind."

He took sic pleasure in deer and roe,
Till he forgot his gay ladye;
Till by it came that milk-white hynde,
And then he mind on his ladye syne.

He hasted him to yon greenwood tree,
For to relieve his gay ladye;
But found his ladye lying dead,
Likeways her young son at her head.

His mother lay ower her castle wa',
　　And she beheld baith dale and down;
And she beheld young Leesome Brand,
　　As he came riding to the town.

" Get minstrels for to play," she said,
　　" And dancers to dance in my room;
For here comes my son, Leesome Brand,
　　And he comes merrilie to the town."

" Seek nae minstrels to play, mother,
　　Nor dancers to dance in your room;
But tho' your son comes, Leesome Brand,
　　Yet he comes sorry to the town.

" O I hae lost my gowden knife,
I rather had lost my ain sweet life;
And I hae lost a better thing,
The gilded sheath that it was in."

" Are there nae gowdsmiths here in Fife,
Can make to you anither knife?
Are there nae sheath-makers in the land,
Can make a sheath to Leesome Brand?"

" There are nae gowdsmiths here in Fife,
　　Can make me sic a gowden knife;
Nor nae sheath-makers in the land,
　　Can make to me a sheath again.

" There ne'er was man in Scotland born,
Ordain'd to be so much forlorn ;
I've lost my ladye I lov'd sae dear,
Likeways the son she did me bear."

" Put in your hand at my bed head,
    There ye'll find a gude grey horn ;
In it three draps o' Saint Paul's ain blude,
    That hae been there sin' he was born.

" Drap twa o' them o' your ladye,
    And ane upo' your little young son ;
Then as lively they will be
    As the first night ye brought them hame."

He put his hand at her bed head,
    And there he found a gude grey horn ;
Wi' three draps o' Saint Paul's ain blude,
    That had been there sin' he was born.

Then he drapp'd twa on his ladye,
    And ane o' them on his young son ;
And now they do as lively be,
    As the first day he brought them hame.

NOTE to v. 49–72. — A similar passage is found at p. 94 of this volume, v. 33–36, also vol. v. p. 178, v. 97–108, and p. 402, v. 169–176, and in the Scandinavian ballads cited in the preface to this ballad. In these last the lady frees herself from the presence of the knight by sending him to get her some water, and she is found dead on his return. This incident, remarks Grimm, (*Altdänische Heldenlieder*, p. 508), is also found in *Wolfdietrich*, Str. 1680–96.

BOOK IV.

THE YOUTH OF ROSENGORD. See p. 219.

Sven i Rosengård, Svenska Folk-Visor, iii. 3, and
Arwidsson's *Fornsånger,* ii. 83 : translated in *Literature
and Romance of Northern Europe,* i. 263.

> " So long where hast thou tarried,
>   Young man of Rosengord ? "
> " I have been into my stable,
>   Our mother dear."
> Long may you look for me, or look for me never.

> " What hast thou done in the stable,
>   Young man of Rosengord ? "
> " I have watered the horses,
>   Our mother dear."
> Long may ye look for me, or look for me never.

> " Why is thy foot so bloody,
>   Young man of Rosengord ? "
> " The black horse has trampled me,
>   Our mother dear."
> Long may you look for me, or look for me never.

" Why is thy sword so bloody,
　　Young man of Rosengord ? "
" I have murdered my brother,
　　Our mother dear."
Long may you look for me, or look for me never.

" Whither wilt thou betake thee,
　　Young man of Rosengord ? "
" I shall flee my country,
　　Our mother dear."
Long may you look for me, or look for me never.

" What will become of thy wedded wife,
　　Young man of Rosengord ? "
" She must spin for her living,
　　Our mother dear."
Long may you look for me, or look for me never.

" What will become of thy children small,
　　Young man of Rosengord ? "
" They must beg from door to door,
　　Our mother dear."
Long may you look for me, or look for me never.

" When comest thou back again,
　　Young man of Rosengord ? "
" When the swan is black as night,
　　Our mother dear."
Long may you look for me, or look for me never.

" And when will the swan be black as night,
　　Young man of Rosengord ? "
" When the raven shall be white as snow,
　　Our mother dear."
Long may you look for me, or look for me never.

" And when will the raven be white as snow,
　　Young man of Rosengord ? "
" When the grey rocks take to flight,
　　Our mother dear."
Long may you look for me, or look for me never.

" And when will fly the grey rocks,
　　Young man of Rosengord ? "
" The rocks they will fly never,
　　Our mother dear."
Long may you look for me, or look for me never.

A translation, nearly word for word, of *Der Blutige Sohn*, printed from oral tradition in Schröter's *Finnische Runen*, (*Finnisch und Deutsch*,) ed. 1834, p. 151.

" SAY whence com'st thou, say whence com'st thou,
  Merry son of mine ? "
" From the lake-side, from the lake-side,
  O dear mother mine."

" What hast done there, what hast done there,
  Merry son of mine ? "
" Steeds I watered, steeds I watered,
  O dear mother mine."

" Why thus clay-bedaubed thy jacket,
  Merry son of mine ? "
" Steeds kept stamping, steeds kept stamping,
  O dear mother mine."

" But how came thy sword so bloody,
 Merry son of mine ? "
" I have stabbed my only brother,
 O dear mother mine."

" Whither wilt thou now betake thee,
 Merry son of mine ? "
" Far away to foreign countries,
 O dear mother mine."

" Where leav'st thou thy gray-haired father,
 Merry son of mine ? "
" Let him chop wood in the forest,
 Never wish to see me more,
  O dear mother mine."

" Where leav'st thou thy gray-haired mother,
 Merry son of mine ? "
" Let her sit, her flax a-picking,
Never wish to see me more,
  O dear mother mine."

" Where leav'st thou thy wife so youthful,
 Merry son of mine ? "
" Let her deck her, take another,
Never wish to see me more,
  O dear mother mine."

" Where leav'st thou thy son so youthful,
 Merry son of mine ? "
" He to school, and bear the rod there,
[Never wish to see me more,]
  O dear mother mine."

" Where leav'st thou thy youthful daughter,
   Merry son of mine ?
" She to the wood and eat wild berries,
Never wish to see me more,
   O dear mother mine."

" Home when com'st thou back from roaming,
   Merry son of mine ? "
" In the north when breaks the morning,
   O dear mother mine."

" In the north when breaks the morning,
   Merry son of mine ? "
" When stones dance upon the water,
   O dear mother mine."

" When shall stones dance on the water,
   Merry son of mine ? "
" When a feather sinks to the bottom,
   O dear mother mine."

" When shall feathers sink to the bottom,
   Merry son of mine ? "
" When we all shall come to judgment,
   O dear mother mine."

From Motherwell's *Minstrelsy*, p. 61.

THERE were twa brothers at the scule,
  And when they got awa,'—
" It's will ye play at the stane-chucking,
  Or will ye play at the ba',
Or will ye gae up to yon hill head,
  And there we'll warsel a fa' ? "

" I winna play at the stane-chucking,
  Nor will I play at the ba' ;
But I'll gae up to yon bonnie green hill,
  And there we'll warsel a fa'."

They warsled up, they warsled down,
  Till John fell to the ground ;
A dirk fell out of William's pouch,
  And gave John a deadly wound.

" O lift me upon your back,
  Take me to yon well fair,

And wash my bluidy wounds o'er and o'er,
And they'll ne'er bleed nae mair."

He's lifted his brother upon his back,
Ta'en him to yon well fair;
He's wash'd his bluidy wounds o'er and o'er,
But they bleed ay mair and mair.

" Tak ye aff my Holland sark,
And rive it gair by gair,
And row it in my bluidy wounds,
And they'll ne'er bleed nae mair."

He's taken aff his Holland sark,
And torn it gair by gair;
He's rowit it in his bluidy wounds,
But they bleed ay mair and mair.

" Tak now aff my green cleiding,
And row me saftly in;
And tak me up to yon kirk style,
Whare the grass grows fair and green."

He's taken aff the green cleiding,
And rowed him saftly in;
He's laid him down by yon kirk style,
Whare the grass grows fair and green.

" What will ye say to your father dear,
When ye gae hame at e'en ?"
" I'll say ye're lying at yon kirk style,
Whare the grass grows fair and green."

" O no, O no, my brother dear,
O you must not say so;

But say that I'm gane to a foreign land,
. Whare nae man does me know."

When he sat in his father's chair,
  He grew baith pale and wan :
" O what blude 's that upon your brow ?
  O dear son, tell to me."
" It is the blude o' my gude gray steed,
  He wadna ride wi' me."

" O thy steed's blude was ne'er sae red,
  Nor e'er sae dear to me :
O what blude 's this upon your cheek ?
  O dear son, tell to me."
" It is the blude of my greyhound,
  He wadna hunt for me."

" O thy hound's blude was ne'er sae red,
  Nor e'er sae dear to me :
O what blude 's this upon your hand ?
  O dear son, tell to me."
" It is the blude of my gay goss hawk,
  He wadna flee for me."

" O thy hawk's blude was ne'er sae red,
  Nor e'er sae dear to me :
O what blude 's this upon your dirk ?
  Dear Willie, tell to me."
" It is the blude of my ae brother,
  O dule and wae is me ! "

" O what will ye say to your father ?
  Dear Willie, tell to me."
" I'll saddle my steed, and awa I'll ride
  To dwell in some far countrie."

" O when will ye come hame again ?
  Dear Willie, tell to me."
" When sun and mune leap on yon hill,
  And that will never be."

She turn'd hersel' right round about,
  And her heart burst into three :
" My ae best son is deid and gane,
  And my tother ane I'll ne'er see."

THE MILLER AND THE KING'S DAUGH-
TER. See p. 231.

FROM *Wit Restor'd*, (1658,) reprinted, London,
1817, i. 153. It is there ascribed to " Mr. Smith," (Dr.
James Smith, the author of many of the pieces in that
collection,) who may have written it down from tradition, and perhaps added a verse or two. Mr. Rimbault
has printed the same piece from a broadside dated 1656,
in *Notes and Queries*, v. 59'. A fragment of it is given
from recitation at p. 316 of that volume, and a copy
quite different from any before published, at p. 102 of
vol. vi. Although two or three stanzas are ludicrous,
and were probably intended for burlesque, this ballad
is by no means to be regarded as a parody.

THERE were two sisters, they went a-playing,
 With a lie downe, downe, a downe a ;
To see their fathers ships sayling in.
 With a hy downe, downe, a downe o.

And when they came into the sea brym,
 With, &c.
The elder did push the younger in.
 With, &c.

" O sister, O sister, take me by the gowne,
 With, &c.
And drawe me up upon the dry ground."
 With, &c.

" O sister, O sister, that may not bee,
    With, &c.
Till salt and oatmeale grow both of a tree."
    With, &c.

Somtymes she sanke, somtymes she swam,
    With, &c.
Untill she came unto the mildam.
    With, &c.

The miller runne hastily downe the cliffe,
    With, &c.
And up he betook her withouten her life.
    With, &c.

What did he doe with her brest bone ?
    With, &c.
He made him a viall to play thereupon.
    With, &c.

What did he doe with her fingers so small ?
    With, &c.
He made him peggs to his violl withall.
    With, &c.

What did he doe with her nose-ridge ?
    With, &c.
Unto his violl he made him a bridge.
    With, &c.

What did he do with her veynes so blewe ?
    With, &c.
He made him strings to his viole thereto.
    With, &c.

What did he doe with her eyes so bright?
With, &c.
Upon his violl he played at first sight.
With, &c.

What did he doe with her tongue soe rough?
With, &c.
Unto the violl it spake enough.
With, &c.

What did he doe with her two shinnes?
With, &c.
Unto the violl they danct Moll Syms.
With, &c.

Then bespake the treble string,
With, &c.
" O yonder is my father the king."
With, &c.

Then bespake the second string,
With, &c.
" O yonder sitts my mother the queen."
With, &c.

And then bespake the stringes all three,
With, &c.
" O yonder is my sister that drowned mee."
With, &c.

Now pay the miller for his payne,
With, &c.
And let him bee gone in the divels name.
With, &c.

THE BONNY BOWS O' LONDON. See p. 231.

From Buchan's *Ballads of the North of Scotland*, ii. **128**

THERE were twa sisters in a bower,
Hey wi' the gay and the grinding;
And ae king's son hae courted them baith,
At the bonny, bonny bows o' London.

He courted the youngest wi' broach and ring,
Hey wi' the gay and the grinding;
He courted the eldest wi' some other thing,
At the bonny, bonny bows o' London.

It fell ance upon a day,
Hey wi' the gay and the grinding,
The eldest to the youngest did say,
At the bonny, bonny bows o' London:

" Wil ye gae to yon Tweed mill dam,"
Hey wi' the gay and the grinding,
" And see our father's ships come to land ?"
At the bonny, bonny bows o' London.

They baith stood up upon a stane,
   Hey wi' the gay and the grinding;
The eldest dang the youngest in,
   At the bonny, bonny bows o' London.

She swimmed up, sae did she down,
   Hey wi' the gay and the grinding;
Till she came to the Tweed mill-dam,
   At the bonny, bonny bows o' London.

The miller's servant he came out,
   Hey wi' the gay and the grinding;
And saw the lady floating about,
   At the bonny, bonny bows o' London.

" O master, master, set your mill,"
   Hey wi' the gay and the grinding;
" There is a fish, or a milk-white swan,"
   At the bonny, bonny bows o' London.

They could not ken her yellow hair,
   Hey wi' the gay and the grinding;
[For] the scales o' gowd that were laid there
   At the bonny, bonny bows o' London.

They could not ken her fingers sae white,
   Hey wi' the gay and the grinding;
The rings o' gowd they were sae bright,
   At the bonny, bonny bows o' London.

They could not ken her middle sae jimp,
   Hey wi' the gay and the grinding;
The stays o' gowd were so well laced,
   At the bonny, bonny bows o' London.

They could not ken her foot sae fair,
Hey wi' the gay and the grinding;
The shoes o' gowd they were so rare,
At the bonny, bonny bows o' London.

Her father's fiddler he came by,
Hey wi' the gay and the grinding;
Upstarted her ghaist before his eye,
At the bonny, bonny bows o' London.

" Ye'll take a lock o' my yellow hair,"
Hey wi' the gay and the grinding;
" Ye'll make a string to your fiddle there,"
At the bonny, bonny bows o' London.

" Ye'll take a lith o' my little finger bane,"
Hey wi' the gay and the grinding;
" And ye'll make a pin to your fiddle then,"
At the bonny, bonny bows o' London.

He's ta'en a lock o' her yellow hair,
Hey wi' the gay and the grinding;
And made a string to his fiddle there,
At the bonny, bonny bows o' London.

He's taen a lith o' her little finger bane,
Hey wi' the gay and the grinding;
And he's made a pin to his fiddle then,
At the bonny, bonny bows o' London.

The firstand spring the fiddle did play,
Hey wi' the gay and the grinding;
Said, " Ye'll drown my sister, as she's dune me,"
At the bonny, bonny bows o' London.

L.

THE CROODLIN DOO.   See *Lord Donald*, p. 244.

FROM Chambers's *Scottish Ballads*, p. 324.   Other copies in *The Scot's Musical Museum*, (1853,) vol. iv. 364*, and Buchan's *Ballads of the North of Scotland*, ii. 179.

" O WHAUR hae ye been a' the day,
  My little wee croodlin doo ? "
" O I've been at my grandmother's ;
  Mak my bed, mammie, noo."

" O what gat ye at your grandmother's,
  My little wee croodlin doo ? "
" I got a bonnie wee fishie ;
  Mak my bed, mammie, noo."

" O whaur did she catch the fishie,
  My bonnie wee croodlin doo ?"
" She catch'd it in the gutter-hole ;
  Mak my bed, mammie, noo."

" And what did she do wi' the fish,
  My little wee croodlin doo ? "

" She boiled it in a brass pan ;
   O mak my bed, mammie, noo."

" And what did ye do wi' the banes o't,
   My bonnie wee croodlin doo ? "
"I gied them to my little dog ;
   Mak my bed, mammie, noo."

" And what did your little doggie do,
   My bonnie wee croodlin doo ? "
" He stretch'd out his head, his feet, and dee'd,
   And so will I, mammie, noo ! "

II.
THE SNAKE-COOK.

FROM oral tradition, in Erk's *Deutscher Leiderhort*,
p. 6. Our homely translation is, as far as possible, word
for word. Other German versions are *The Stepmother*,
at p. 5 of the same collection, (or Uhland, i. 272.) and
Grandmother Adder-cook, at p. 7. The last is translated
by Jamieson, *Illustrations of Northern Antiquities*, p. 320.

" WHERE hast thou been away so long,
   Henry, my dearest son ? "
" O I have been at my true-love's,
   Lady mother, ah me !
My young life,
She has poisoned for me."

" What gave she thee to eat,
   Henry, my dearest son ? "

" She cooked me a speckled fish,
   Lady mother, ah me ! " &c.

" And how many pieces cut she thee,
   Henry my dearest son ? "
" She cut three little pieces from it,
   Lady mother, ah me ! " &c.

" Where left she then the third piece,
   Henry, my dearest son ? "
" She gave it to her dark-brown dog,
   Lady mother, ah me ! " &c.

" And what befell the dark-brown dog,
   Henry, my dearest son ? "
" His belly burst in the midst in two,
   Lady mother, ah me ! " &c.

" What wishest thou for thy father,
   Henry, my dearest son ? "
" I wish him a thousandfold boon and blessing,
   Lady mother, ah me ! " &c.

" What wishest thou for thy mother,
   Henry, my dearest son ? "
" I wish for her eternal bliss,
   Lady mother, ah me ! " &c.

" What wishest thou for thy true-love,
   Henry, my dearest son ? "
" I wish her eternal hell and torment,
   Lady mother, ah me ! " &c.

III.

THE CHILD'S LAST WILL.

Den lillas Testamente: Svenska Folk-Visor, iii. 13.
Translated in *Literature and Romance of Northern
Europe,* i. 265. See also Arwidsson's *Fornsånger,* ii. 90.

" So LONG where hast thou tarried,
  Little daughter dear ? "
" I have tarried with my old nurse,
  Sweet step-mother mine."
For ah, ah !—I am so ill—ah !

" What gave she thee for dinner,
  Little daughter dear ? "
" A few small speckled fishes,
  Sweet step-mother mine."
For ah, ah !—I am so ill—ah !

" What didst thou do with the fish-bones,
  Little daughter dear ? "
" Gave them to the beagle,
  Sweet step-mother mine."
For ah, ah !—I am so ill—ah !

" What wish leav'st thou thy father,
  Little daughter dear ? "
" The blessedness of heaven,
  Sweet step-mother mine."
For ah, ah !—I am so ill—ah !

" What wish leav'st thou thy mother,
  Little daughter dear ? "
" All the joys of heaven,
  Sweet step-mother mine."
For ah, ah !—I am so ill—ah !

" What wish leav'st thou thy brother,
  Little daughter dear ? "
" A fleet ship on the waters,
  Sweet step-mother mine."
For ah, ah !—I am so ill—ah !

" What wish leav'st thou thy sister,
  Little daughter dear ? "
" Golden chests and caskets,
  Sweet step-mother mine."
For ah, ah !—I am so ill—ah !

" What wish leav'st thou thy step-mother,
  Little daughter dear ? "
" Of hell the bitter sorrow
  Sweet step-mother mine."
For ah, ah !—I am so ill—ah !

" What wish leav'st thou thy old nurse,
  Little daughter dear ? "
" For her I wish the same pangs,
  Sweet step-mother mine.
For ah, ah !—I am so ill—ah !

" But now the time is over
  When I with you can stay ;
The little bells of heaven
  Are ringing me away."
For ah, ah !—I am so ill—ah !

THE THREE KNIGHTS. See p. 251.

From the second edition of Gilbert's *Ancient Christmas Carols*, &c. p. 68.

THERE did three Knights come from the **West**,
  With the high and the lily oh !
And these three Knights courted one Lady,
  As the rose was so sweetly blown.

The first Knight came was all in white,
  With the high and the lily oh !
And asked of her, if she'd be his delight,
  As the rose was so sweetly blown.

The next Knight came was all in green,
  With the high and the lily oh !
And asked of her, if she'd be his Queen,
  As the rose was so sweetly blown.

The third Knight came was all in red,
  With the high and the lily oh !
And asked of her, if she would wed,
  As the rose was so sweetly blown.

" Then have you asked of my Father **dear,**
With the high and the lily oh !
Likewise of her who did me bear ?
As the rose was so sweetly blown.

" And have you asked of my brother **John ?**
With the high and the lily oh !
And also of my sister Anne ? "
As the rose was so sweetly blown.

" Yes, I have asked of your Father **dear,**
With the high and the lily oh !
Likewise of her who did you bear,
As the rose was so sweetly blown.

" And I have asked of your sister Anne,
With the high and the lily oh !
But I've not asked of your brother **John,"**
As the rose was so sweetly blown.

[Here some verses seem to be wanting.]

For on the road as they rode along,
With the high and the lily oh !
There did they meet with her brother **John,**
As the rose was so sweetly blown.

She stooped low to kiss him sweet,
With the high and the lily oh !
He to her heart did a dagger meet,
As the rose was so sweetly blown.

" Ride on, ride on," cried the serving **man,**
With the high and the lily oh !

" Methinks your bride she looks wond'rous **wan**,"
As the rose was so sweetly **blown.**

" I wish I were on yonder stile,
With the high and the lily oh !
For there I would sit and bleed awhile,
As the rose was so sweetly blown.

" I wish I were on yonder hill,
With the high and the lily oh !
There I'd alight and make my **will**,"
As the rose was so sweetly blown.

" What would you give to your Father dear ? "
With the high and the lily oh !
" The gallant steed which doth **me bear**,"
As the rose was so sweetly blown.

" What would you give to your Mother **dear ? "**
With the high and the lily oh !
" My wedding shift which I do **wear**,
As the rose was so sweetly blown.

" But she must wash it very clean,
With the high and the lily oh !
For my heart's blood sticks in every **seam**,"
As the rose was so sweetly blown.

" What would you give to your sister Anne ? "
With the high and the lily oh !
" My gay gold ring, and my feathered **fan**,"
As the rose was so sweetly blown.

" What would you give to your brother John ? "
With the high and the lily oh !

" A rope and gallows to hang him on,"
As the rose was so sweetly blown.

" What would you give to your brother John's
wife ? "
With the high and the lily oh !
" A widow's weeds, and a quiet life,"
As the rose was so sweetly blown.

THE CRUEL MOTHER. See p. 262.

From Buchan's *Ballads of the North of Scotland*, ii. 222.

IT fell ance upon a day, *Edinbro', Edinbro',*
It fell ance upon a day, *Stirling for aye ;*
 It fell ance upon a day,
 The clerk and lady went to play,
So proper Saint Johnston stands fair upon Tay.

" If my baby be a son, *Edinbro', Edinbro',*
If my baby be a son, *Stirling for aye ;*
 If my baby be a son,
 I'll make him a lord o' high renown,"
So proper Saint Johnston stands fair upon Tay.

She's lean'd her back to the wa,' *Edinbro', Edinbro',*
She's lean'd her back to the wa', *Stirling for aye ;*
 She's lean'd her back to the wa',
 Pray'd that her pains might fa',
So proper Saint Johnston stands fair upon Tay.

She's lean'd her back to the thorn, *Edinbro'*, *Edin-*
 bro',
She's lean'd her back to the thorn, *Stirling for aye;*
 She's lean'd her back to the thorn,
 There has her baby born,
So proper Saint Johnston stands fair upon Tay.

" O bonny baby, if ye suck sair, *Edinbro'*, *Edinbro'*,
O bonny baby, if ye suck sair, *Stirling for aye;*
 O bonny baby, if ye suck sair,
 You'll never suck by my side mair,"
So proper Saint Johnston stands fair upon Tay.

She's riven the muslin frae her head, *Edinbro'*, *Ed-*
 inbro',
She's riven the muslin frae her head, *Stirling for aye;*
 She's riven the muslin frae her head,
 Tied the baby hand and feet,
So proper Saint Johnston stands fair upon Tay.

Out she took her little penknife, *Edinbro'*, *Edinbro'*,
Out she took her little penknife, *Stirling for aye;*
 Out she took her little penknife,
 Twin'd the young thing o' its life,
So proper Saint Johnston stands fair upon Tay.

She's howk'd a hole anent the meen, *Edinbro'*, *Edin-*
 bro',
She's howk'd a hole anent the meen, *Stirling for*
 aye;
 She's howk'd a hole anent the meen,
 There laid her sweet baby in,
So proper Saint Johnston stands fair upon Tay.

She had her to her father's ha', *Edinbro'*, *Edinbro'*,
She had her to her father's ha', *Stirling for aye*;
  She had her to her father's ha',
  She was the meekest maid amang them a',
So proper Saint Johnston stands fair upon Tay.

It fell ance upon a day, *Edinbro'*, *Edinbro'*,
It fell ance upon a day, *Stirling for aye*;
  It fell ance upon a day,
  She saw twa babies at their play,
So proper Saint Johnston stands fair upon Tay.

" O bonny babies, gin ye were mine, *Edinbro'*, *Edinbro'*,
O bonny babies, gin ye were mine, *Stirling for aye*,
  O bonny babies, gin ye were mine,
  I'd cleathe you in the silks sae fine,"
So proper Saint Johnston stands fair upon Tay.

" O wild mother, when we were thine, *Edinbro'*, *Edinbro'*,
O wild mother, when we were thine, *Stirling for aye*;
  O wild mother, when we were thine,
  You cleath'd us not in silks sae fine,
So proper Saint Johnston stands fair upon Tay.

" But now we're in the heavens high, *Edinbro'*, *Edinbro'*,
But now we're in the heavens high, *Stirling for aye*;
  But now we're in the heavens high,
  And you've the pains o' hell to try,"
So proper Saint Johnston stands fair upon Tay.

She threw hersell ower the castle-wa', *Edinbro'*, *Edin-*
    bro',
She threw hersell ower the castle-wa', *Stirling for*
    aye ;
  She threw hersell ower the castle-wa',
  There I wat she got a fa',
So proper Saint Johnston stands fair upon Tay.

THE MINISTER'S DOCHTER O' NEWARKE.

See p. 262.

FROM *Scottish Traditional Versions of Ancient Ballads*, Percy Society, vol. xvii. p. 51. This is the same ballad, with trifling variations, as *The Minister's Daughter of New York*, Buchan, ii. 217.

THE Minister's dochter o' Newarke,
   Hey wi' the rose and the lindie O,
Has fa'en in luve wi' her father's clerk,
   Alane by the green burn sidie O.

She courted him sax years and a day,
   Hey wi' the rose and the lindie O,
At length her fause-luve did her betray,
   Alane by the green burn sidie O.

She did her doun to the green woods gang,
   Hey wi' the rose and the lindie O,
To spend awa' a while o' her time,
   Alane by the green burn sidie O.

She lent her back unto a thorn,
Hey wi' the rose and the lindie O;
And she's got her twa bonnie boys born,
Alane by the green burn sidie O.

She's ta'en the ribbons frae her hair,
Hey wi' the rose and the lindie O,
Boun' their bodies fast and sair,
Alane by the green burn sidie O.

She's put them aneath a marble stane,
Hey wi' the rose and the lindie O,
Thinkin' a may to gae her hame,
Alane by the green burn sidie O.

Leukin' o'er her castel wa',
Hey wi' the rose and the lindie O,
She spied twa bonny boys at the ba',
Alane by the green burn sidie O.

" O bonny babies, if ye were mine,
Hey wi' the rose and the lindie O,
I woud feed ye wi' the white bread and wine,
Alane by the green burn sidie O.

" I wou'd feed ye with the ferra cow's milk,
Hey wi' the rose and the lindie O,
An' dress ye i' the finest silk,"
Alane by the green burn sidie O.

" O cruel mother, when we were thine,
Hey wi' the rose and the lindie O,
We saw nane o' your bread and wine,
Alane by the green burn sidie O.

" We saw nane o' your ferra cow's milk,
Hey wi' the rose and the lindie O,
Nor wore we o' your finest silk,"
*Alane by the green burn sidie **O**.*

" O bonny babies, can ye tell me,
Hey wi' the rose and the lindie O,
What sort o' death for ye I maun dee,"
*Alane by the green burn sidie **O**.*

" Yes, cruel mother, we'll tell to thee,
Hey wi' the rose and the lindie O,
What sort o' death for us ye maun dee,
*Alane by the green burn sidie **O**.*

" Seven years a fool i' the woods,
Hey wi' the rose and the lindie O,
" Seven years a fish i' the floods,
*Alane by the green burn sidie **O**.*

" Seven years to be a church bell,
Hey wi' the rose and the lindie O,
Seven years a porter i' hell,"
*Alane by the green burn sidie **O**.*

" Welcome, welcome, fool i' the wood,
*Hey **wi'** the rose and the lindie O,*
Welcome, welcome, fish i' the flood,
*Alane by the green burn sidie **O**.*

" Welcome, welcome, to be a church bell,
Hey wi' the rose and the lindie O,
But heavens keep me out o' hell,"
*Alane by the green burn sidie **O**.*

BONDSEY AND MAISRY. See p. 298.

From Buchan's *Ballads of the North of Scotland*, ii. 265.

" O COME along wi' me, brother,
 Now come along wi' me ;
And we'll gae seek our sister Maisry,
 Into the water o' Dee."

The eldest brother he stepped in,
 He stepped to the knee ;
Then out he jump'd upo' the bank,
 Says, " This water's nae for me."

The second brother he stepped in,
 He stepped to the quit ;
Then out he jump'd upo' the bank,
 Says, " This water's wond'rous deep."

When the third brother stepped in,
 He stepped to the chin ;
Out he got, and forward wade,
 For fear o' drowning him.

The youngest brother he stepped in,
  Took's sister by the hand ;
Said, " Here she is, my sister Maisry,
  Wi' the hinny draps on her chin.

" O if I were in some bonny ship,
  And in some strange countrie,
For to find out some conjurer,
  To gar Maisry speak to me ! "

Then out it speaks an auld woman,
  As she was passing by ;
" Ask of your sister what you want,
  And she will speak to thee."

" O sister, tell me who is the man,
  That did your body win ?
And who is the wretch, tell me, likewise,
  That threw you in the lin ? "

" O Bondsey was the only man
  That did my body win ;
And likewise Bondsey was the man
  That threw me in the lin."

" O will we Bondsey head, sister ?
  Or will we Bondsey hang ?
Or will we set him at our bow end,
  Lat arrows at him gang ? "

" Ye winna Bondsey head, brothers,
  Nor will ye Bondsey hang ;
But ye'll take out his twa grey e'en,
  Make Bondsey blind to gang.

" Ye'll put to the gate a chain o' gold,
   A rose garland gar make ;
And ye'll put that in Bondsey's head,
   A' for your sister's sake."

LADY DIAMOND.

From the Percy Society Publications, xvii. 71. The same in Buchan, ii. 206. The ballad is given in Sharpe's *Ballad Book*, under the title of *Dysmal*, and by Aytoun, *Ballads of Scotland*, 2d ed., ii. 173, under that of *Lady Daisy*. All these names are corruptions of Ghismonda, on whose well-known story (*Decamerone*, iv. 1, 9) the present is founded. — This piece and the next might better have been inserted at p. 347, as a part of the Appendix to Book III.

THERE was a king, an' a curious king,
    An' a king o' royal fame;
He had ae dochter, he had never mair,
    Ladye Diamond was her name.

She's fa'en into shame, an' lost her gude name,
    An' wrought her parents 'noy;
An' a' for her layen her luve so low,
    On her father's kitchen boy.

Ae nicht as she lay on her bed,
    Just thinkin' to get rest,
Up it came her old father,
    Just like a wanderin' ghaist.

" Rise up, rise up, ladye Diamond," he says,
    " Rise up, put on your goun;
Rise up, rise up, ladye Diamond," he says,
    " For I fear ye gae too roun'."

" Too roun I gae, yet blame me nae ;
   Ye'll cause me na to shame ;
For better luve I that bonnie boy
   Than a' your weel-bred men."

The king's ca'd up his wa'-wight men,
   That he paid meat an' fee :
" Bring here to me that bonnie boy,
   An' we'll smore him right quietlie."

Up hae they ta'en that bonnie boy,
   Put him 'tween twa feather beds ;
Naethin' was dane, nor naethin' said,
   Till that bonnie bonnie boy was dead.

The king's ta'en out a braid braid sword,
   An' streak'd it on a strae ;
An' thro' an' thro' that bonnie boy's heart
   He's gart cauld iron gae.

Out has he ta'en his poor bluidie heart,
   Set it in a tasse o' gowd,
And set it before ladye Diamonds face,
   Said " Fair ladye, behold ! "

Up has she ta'en this poor bludie heart,
   An' holden it in her han' ;
" Better luved I that bonnie bonnie boy
   Than a' my father's lan'."

Up has she ta'en his poor bludie heart,
   An' laid it at her head ;
The tears awa' frae her eyne did flee,
   An' ere midnicht she was dead.

THE WEST COUNTRY DAMOSELS COMPLAINT.

From Collier's *Book of Roxburghe Ballads*, p. 202.

After a broadside " printed by P. Brooksby, at the Golden Bull in Westsmith-field, neer the Hospitall Gate." The first ten or twelve stanzas seem to be ancient.

" WHEN will you marry me, William,
 And make me your wedded wife ?
Or take you your keen bright sword,
 And rid me out of my life."

" Say no more then so, lady, [1]
 Say you no more then so,
For you shall unto the wild forrest,
 And amongst the buck and doe.

" Where thou shalt eat of the hips and haws,
 And the roots that are so sweet,
And thou shalt drink of the cold water
 That runs underneath your feet."

[1] so then.

Now had she not been in the wild forrest
　　Passing three months and a day,
But with hunger and cold she had her fill,
　　Till she was quite worn away.

At last she saw a fair tyl'd house,
　　And there she swore by the rood,
That she would to that fair tyl'd house,
　　There for to get her some food.

But when she came unto the gates,
　　Aloud, aloud she cry'd,
" An alms, an alms, my own sister!
　　I ask you for no pride."

Her sister call'd up her merry men all,
　　By one, by two, and by three,
And bid them hunt away that wild doe,
　　As far as e'er they could see.

They hunted her o're hill and dale,
　　And they hunted her so sore,
That they hunted her into the forrest,
　　Where her sorrows grew more and more.

She laid a stone all at her head,
　　And another all at her feet,
And down she lay between these two,
　　Till death had lull'd her asleep.

When sweet Will came and stood at her head,
　　And likewise stood at her feet,
A thousand times he kiss'd her cold lips,
　　Her body being fast asleep.

Yea, seaven times he stood at her feet,
    And seaven times at her head ;
A thousand times he shook her hand,
    Although her body was dead.

" Ah wretched me ! " he loudly cry'd,
    " What is it that I have done ?
O wou'd to the powers above I'de dy'd,
    When thus I left her alone !

" Come, come, you gentle red-breast now,
    And prepare for us a tomb,
Whilst unto cruel Death I bow,
    And sing like a swan my doom.

" Why could I ever cruel be
    Unto so fair a creature ;
Alas ! she dy'd for love of me,
    The loveliest she in nature !

" For me she left her home so fair
    To wander in this wild grove,
And there with sighs and pensive care
    She ended her life for love.

" O constancy, in her thou'rt lost !
    Now let women boast no more ;
She's fled unto the Elizian coast,
    And with her carry'd the store.

" O break, my heart, with sorrow fill'd,
    Come, swell, you strong tides of grief !
You that my dear love have kill'd,
    Come, yield in death to me relief.

" Cruel her sister, was't for me
    That to her she was unkind ?
Her husband I will never be,
    But with this my love be joyn'd.

" Grim Death shall tye the marriage bands,
    Which jealousie shan't divide ;
Together shall tye our cold hands,
    Whilst here we lye side by side.

" Witness, ye groves, and chrystal streams,
    How faithless I late have been ;
But do repent with dying leaves
    Of that my ungrateful sin ;

" And wish a thousand times that I
    Had been but to her more kind,
And not have let a virgin dye,
    Whose equal there's none can find.

" Now heaps of sorrow press my soul ;
    Now, now 'tis she takes her way ;
I come, my love, without controule,
    Nor from thee will longer stay."

With that he fetch'd a heavy groan,
    Which rent his tender breast,
And then by her he laid him down,
    When as Death did give him rest :

Whilst mournful birds, with leavy bows,
    To them a kind burial gave,
And warbled out their love-sick vows,
    Whilst they both slept in their grave.

THE BRAVE EARL BRAND AND THE KING OF ENGLAND'S DAUGHTER. See p. 114.

From Bell's *Ballads of the Peasantry of England*, p. 122.

This ballad, which was printed by Bell from the recitation of an old Northumberland fiddler, is defective in the tenth and the last stanzas, and has suffered much from corruption in the course of transmission. The name of the hero, however, is uncommonly well preserved, and affords a link, rarely occurring in English, with the corresponding Danish and Swedish ballads, a good number of which have Hildebrand, though more have Ribold. It may be observed that in *Hildebrand og Hilde* (Grundtvig, No. 83), the knight has the rank here ascribed to the lady.

> " Hand heede hertug Hyldebraand,
> Kongens sönn aff Engeland."

The "old Carl Hood" who gives the alarm in this ballad, is called in most of the Danish ballads " a rich earl"; in one a treacherous man, in another a young Carl, and in a third an old man ; which together furnish the elements of his character here of a treacherous old Carl.

O DID you ever hear of the brave Earl Brand?
  Hey lillie, ho lillie lallie !
He's courted the king's daughter o' fair England,
  I' the brave nights so early.

She was scarcely fifteen years that tide,
When sae boldly she came to his bed-side

" O Earl Brand, how fain wad I see
A pack of hounds let loose on the lea."

" O lady fair, I have no steed but one,
But thou shalt ride and I will run."

" O Earl Brand, but my father has two,
And thou shalt have the best of tho."

Now they have ridden o'er moss and moor
And they have met neither rich nor poor.

Till at last they met with old Carl Hood,
He's aye for ill, and never for good.

" Now, Earl Brand, an ye love me,
Slay this old carl, and gar him dee."

" O lady fair, but that would be sair,
To slay an auld carl that wears grey hair·

" My own lady fair, I'll not do that,
I'll pay him his fee . . . ."

" O where have ye ridden this lee lang day,
And where have ye stown this fair lady away ?"

" I have not ridden this lee lang day,
Nor yet have I stown this lady away.

" For she is, I trow, my sick sister,
Whom I have been bringing fra Winchester."

" If she's been sick, and nigh to dead,
What makes her wear the ribbon so red ?

" If she's been sick, and like to die,
What makes her wear the gold sae high ? "

When came the carl to the lady's yett,
He rudely, rudely rapped thereat.

" Now where is the lady of this hall ? "
" She's out with her maids a-playing at the ball."

" Ha, ha, ha ! ye are all mista'en;
Ye may count your maidens owre again.

" I met her far beyond the lea,
With the young Earl Brand, his leman to be."

Her father of his best men armed fifteen,
And they're ridden after them bidene.

The lady looked owre her left shoulder then ;
Says, " O Earl Brand, we are both of us ta'en."

" If they come on me one by one,
You may stand by till the fights be done.

" But if they come on me one and all,
You may stand by and see me fall."

They came upon him one by one,
Till fourteen battles he has won.

And fourteen men he has them slain,
Each after each upon the plain.

But the fifteenth man behind stole round,
And dealt him a deep and deadly wound.

Though he was wounded to the deid,
He set his lady on her steed.

They rode till they came to the river Doune,
And there they lighted to wash his wound.

" O Earl Brand, I see your heart's biood ! "
" It's nothing but the glent and my scarlet hood."[1]

They rode till they came to his mother's yett,
So faint and feebly he rapped thereat.

" O my son's slain, he is falling to swoon,
And it's all for the sake of an English loon ! "

" O say not so, my dearest mother,
But marry her to my youngest brother.

" To a maiden true he'll give his hand,
To the king's daughter o' fair England.

" [To the king's daughter o' fair England,]
    Hey lillie, ho lillie lallie !
To a prize that was won by a slain brother's brand,*
    I' the brave nights so early.

[1] Qy. ? *of* my scarlet hood.

LA VENDICATRICE. See p. 273.

From *Canti Popolari Inediti Umbri, Piceni, Piemon-*
tesi, Latini, raccolti e illustrati da ORESTE MARCO-
ALDI. Genova, 1855. p. 167.— From Alessandria.

1 " OH varda ben, Munfrenna,
2   Oh varda qul castè :
3 I'è trentatrè fantenni
4   Ch' a j' ho menaji me.
5 I m' han negà l' amure,
6   La testa a j' ho tajè."

7 " Ch' u 'm digga lü, Sior Conte ;
8   Ch' u 'm lassa la so' spà."
9 " Oh dimì ti, Monfrenna,
10   Cosa ch' a 't na voi fa' ? "
11 " A voi tajè 'na frasca,
12   Per ombra al me' cavà."
13 Lesta con la spadenna
14   Al cor a j' ha passà.

15 " Va là, va là, Sior Conte,
16   Va là 'nte quei boscon ;
17 Le spenni e li serpenti
18   Saran toi compagnon."

1 guarda ben, Mon- 6 tagliato.   12 cavallo.
   ferina.   7 dica lei, sig ior. 13 spadina.
2 quel castello.   8 sua spada   16 (*boscon*) cespugli.
8 fanciulle.   10 vuoi fare   17 spine.
4 menate io.   11 tagliare.   18 tuoi.
5 negato.

NOTE. This ballad is undoubtedly the Italian representa-
tion of *May Colvin*. It is given more complete by Nigra, *Can-
eoni Popolari del Piemonte, Rivista Con.*, xxiv. 73, who also
furnishes these additional references: (Spanish) *Rico Franco*,
Wolf and Hoffmann's *Primavera*, ii. 22; (Portuguese) *A Ro-
meira*, Almeida-Garrett, *Romanceiro*, iii. 4; (French) Ampère,
Instructions relatives aux Poésies populaires de la France, p.
40; (Breton) Hersart de la Villemarqué, *Barzaz-Brei*, '. 354
(ed. 1846).

GLOSSARY.

☞ Figures placed after words denote the pages in which they occur.

---

aboon, *above, upon.*

abound, 335, *bound.*

abune a' thing, *above all things.*

a dee, 335, *to do.*

ae, *one.*

aft, *oft.*

aith, *oath.*

an, *if.*

ance, *once.*

anent, *opposite to.*

are, *early.*

assoile, *absolve.*

aucht, *owns;* wha is aucht that bairn? *who is it owns that child?*

ava, *of all.*

a-warslin, *a wrestling.*

ayont, *beyond.*

ba,' *ball.*

badena, *abode not.*

bairn, *child.*

baith, *both.*

ban, 89, *bond.*

beet, 340, *add fuel.*

bierdly, *large and well-made, stately.*

biggins, *buildings.*

ben, *in, within.*

bestan, *best.*

best young man, *bridesman.*

bidden, *bidding.* [(?)

bidene, *in a company, forthwith*

billie, *comrade, brother.*

binna, *beest not.*

birk, *birch.*

birling, *pouring out* [drink], *drinking.*

blan, *ceased, stopped.*

blate, *sheepish, ashamed.*

blear, [noun,] *dimness.*

blinkit, *blinked, winked.*

blinne, *cease.*

borrow, *ransom.*

bou erie, *chamber.*

boun, *ready.*

bour, bower, *chamber.*

bra', braw, *handsome.*

bracken, *female fern.*

brae, *hill-side.*
braid, *broad.*
brain, *mud.*
brent, *burnt;* 308, v. 31, *straight ?*
bridesteel, (Buchan,) 183, *bridal ?*
brigg, brigue, *bridge.*
broo, *broth.*
brook, *enjoy.*
brunt, *burnt.*
buird, *board.*
burd, *lady.*
burn, *brook.*
busking, *dressing, making ready.*
but, butt, *without.*
but and, *and also.*
byre, *cow-house.*

ca', *call.*
cannel, 327. Qy. a corrup tion?
canny, *knowing, expert, gentle, adroitly, carefully.*
cast, *trick, turn.*
channerin, *fretting.*
chap, *tap, rap;* chappit, 11, *tapped, rapped;* at the chin, *should probably be* at the pin, *or tongue of the latch.*
cheir, *cheer.*
claise, *clothes.*
clap, *fondle;* clappit, *patted, fondled.*
cleading, *clothing.*
clecked, *hatched.*
cleed, *clothe.*
cleiding, *clothing.*

clerks, *scholars.*
cliding, *clothing.*
close, *lane.*
cod, *pillow.*
coil, 324, *cock of hay.*
coost, *cast.*
could, *used with the infinitive as an auxiliary, to form a past tense.*
crap, *crop, top.*
croodlin doo, *cooing dove.*
crowse, *brisk.*
cuik, *cook.*
curches, *kerchiefs.* R. Jamieson. "*linen caps tying under the chin.*"
cuttit, *cut.*

dabs, *pricks.*
dang, 301, *overcome;* 361, *pushed.*
dapperby, 189, *dapper ?*
daut, *fondle, caress.*
daw, *dawn.*
dead, *death.*
dear-boucht, *dear-bought.*
deas, *sometimes a pew in a church.*
dee, *die.*
dee, do, *avail.*
deid, *death.*
deight, dight, *decked.*
den, *valley.*
depart, 124, *part.*
dight, 253, *skilfully, readily ?*
dighted, *dressed, wiped.*
dine, *dinner.*
ding, *strike.*

dinna, *do not.*

disna, *does not.*

dool, *sorrow.*

dout, *fear.*

dowie, *mournful, sad, gloomy.*

downa, *cannot.*

dows, *doves.*

dreaded, *doubted.*

dree, *suffer.*

drew up with, 94, *formed relations of love with.*

drie, *suffer.*

drumly, *troubled.*

dule, *grief, sorrow.*

dune, *done.*

dwines, *dwindles.*

e'e, *eye.*

een, *eye, eyes.*

eneuch, *enough.*

ezer, *azure.*

fadge, *clumsy woman.*

faem, *foam.*

fare, *go.*

farrow-cow, *a barren cow.*

fee, *property, wages.*

fell, *hill.*

fell, *strange.*

ferra cow, *farrow cow, a cow not with calf.*

ffree, *noble.*

firstan, firstand, *first.*

fit, *foot.*

fitches, 329, *flitches?*

flang'd, *flung.*

fleed, *flood.*

foremost man, *bridesman.*

forlorn, *lost.*

fou, fow, *full.*

frush, *brittle.*

fur, furrow, *a furrows length, furlong.*

gaed, *went.*

gair, 354, *gore, strip.* See gare.

gang, *go;* gangs, *goes.*

gar, *make.*

gare, 55, *gore;* apparently, here, *skirt.* So, hung low down by his gair, 296, *by the edge of his frock.* The word seems also to be used vaguely in romances for *clothing.*

garl, *gravel.*

gate, *way.*

gear, *goods, clothes.*

gin, *trick, wile.*

gleed, *a burning coal;* 97, *blaze.*

glent, *gleam, glimmer.*

gone, *go.*

gowd, *gold;* gowden, *golden.*

gowk, *fool.*

gravat, *cravat?*

greaf, *grave.*

greet, *cry, weep.*

gris, *a costly fur.*

grit, *big.*

groom, *man.*

gross, *heavy.*

gryte, *great, big.*

Gude, *God.*

ha', *hall.*

had her, *betook her.*

hallow-days, *holidays.*

haly, *holy.*
happit, *covered.*
hass, *neck.*
haud, *hold;* haud unthought
　lang, *keep from ennui.*
hause, *neck.*
head, *behead.*
healy, *slowly, softly.*
heght, *promised.*
her lane, *herself alone.*
herried, *robbed.*
hich, *high.*
hinny, *honey.*
hip, *the berry which contains
　the stones or seeds of the dog-
　rose.*
hooly, *slowly, gently.*
how, *ho!*
hows, *hollows, dells.*
howket, *dug.*
huggell, *huddle, cuddle.*
huly, *slowly.*

intill, *into, in.*
into, *on.*
iwis, *certainly.*

jaw, 233, *wave.*
jawing, *dashing.*
jimp, *slender.*
jo, *sweetheart.*
jollie, *handsome.*
jow, *stroke in tolling.*

kell, *caul, a species of cap, or
　net-work, worn by women as
　a head-dress.*
kembe, *comb;* kembing, *comb-
　ing.*

kenna, *know not;* kent na,
　knew not.
kens, *knows.*
kerches, *kerchiefs.*
kilted, *tucked up.*
kin, *kind;* a' kin, *all kind.*
kist, *chest.*
kitchey, *kitchen.*
know, *knoll.*
kye, *cows.*
kythe, *become, manifest.*

laigh, *low.*
lain, *alone;* ye're your lain,
　you are alone; hir lain, *her
　alone.*
lair, *learning.*
lane, *alone;* the same in com-
　bination with the pronouns
　my, his, her, its, &c.
lap, *leapt.*
latten, *let.*
lauch, *laugh.*
laumer, 327, *amber.*
lave, *rest.*
lealest, *truest, chastest.*
lear, *lore, lesson.*
lease, *leash.*
lee, *lonesome.*
lee-lang, *livelong.*
lei, 132, *lonesome.*
len, *lie.*
lent, *leaned.*
let, *stop, delay.*
leuch, leugh, *laughed.*
lichtly, *lightly.*
lig, *lie.*
lighter, *delivered.*
limmers, *strumpets.*

linn, *the pool under a cataract,*
   cataract.
lith, *joint.*
lither, *naughty, wicked.*
looten, *let.*
loup, *leap.*
lourd, *liefer, rather.*
louted, *bent.*
louze, *loosen.*
lykewake, *watching of a dead*
   body.

mae, *more.*
maene, moan, *lamentation.*
maist, 58, maistly, *almost.*
make, *mate.*
mane, *moan.*
maries, *maids.*
marrow, *mate.*
mat, *may.*
maun, *must.*
maunna, *may not.*
may, *maid.*
meen, *moan, lament.*
message, *messenger.*
micht, *might.*
mind, *remember.*
mirk, *murky.*
mith, *might.*
Moll Syms, 359, *a celebrated*
   dance tune of the 16th cen-
   tury.
mools, *the earth of the grave,*
   the dust of the dead.
mot, *may.*
my lane, *alone by myself.*

niest, *next.*
nourice, *nurse.*

oer, ower, *over, too.*
ohon, *alas.*
owsen, *oxen.*
Owsenford, *Oxford.*

pa', pall, *rich cloth.*
Parish, *Paris.*
part, 151, *separate from.*
pat, *pot.*
pearlin' gear, *pearl ornaments.*
pin, *door-latch.*
plat, *plaited.*
plea, *quarrel.*
pot, *a pool, or deep place, in a*
   river.
prin, *pin.*
propine, *gift.*
putten down, *hung.*

queet, quit, *ancle.*
quhair, quhat, quhy, &c.,
   where, what, why, &c.

rair'd, *roared.*
rave, *tore off.*
reavel'd, *tangled.*
rede, *advice, advise;* 263
   story.
reest, *roost.*
renown, [Buchan,] 169,
   haughtiness?
rigland shire, 331?
rin, *run.*
ritted, *routed, struck.*
riv't, *tear it.*
row, *roll.*
row'd, *rolled.*

sabelline, *sable.*

sanna, *shall not.*

sarbit, *an exclamation of sorrow.*

sark, *shirt.*

saugh, *willow.*

scheet, *school.*

schill, *shrill.*

scug, *expiate.*

see, (save and,) *protect.*

seen, sen, *then, since.*

send, 334, *the messengers sent for the bride at a wedding.*

sets, *suits.*

shed by, 77, *parted, put back.*

sheen, *shine.*

sheen, *shoes.*

sheet, *shoot.*

sheuch, *furrow, ditch.*

shimmerd, *shone.*

shot-window, *a projected window.*

sic, *such.*

sich, *sigh.*

sindle, *seldom*

sinsyne, *since.*

skinkled, *sparkled.*

slack, *a gap or pass between two hills.*

slait, *passed across, whetted.*

slap, *a narrow pass between two hills.*

smore, *smother.*

snood, *a fillet or ribbon for the hair.*

socht, *sought.*

sorray, *sorrow.*

soum, sowm, *swim.*

spakes, *spokes, bars.*

speer, speir, *ask.*

spreckl'd, *speckled.*

stap, *stuff.*

stean, *stone.*

steek'd, *fastened.*

stey, *steep.*

stint, *stop.*

stock, *the forepart of a bed.*

stout, 300, *haughty.*

strae, stray, *straw.*

straiked, streaked, stroked, *drew.*

streek, *stretch;* streekit, *stretched;* streikit, *laid out.*

striped, *thrust.*

suld, *should.*

syke, *marshy bottom.*

syne, *then, afterwards.*

tane, *one,* [after the.]

tasse, *cup.*

tate, *lock (of hair).*

tee, *too.*

teem, *empty.*

teen, *sorrow, suffering.*

tent, *heed.*

thae, *these.*

the, *thrive.*

thegither, *together.*

thir, tho, *these, those.*

thorn'd, 335, *eaten?*

thought lang, *felt ennui.*

thouth, *thought, seemed.*

thraw, 302, *writhe, twist;* thrawen, *crooked.*

thresel-cock, *throstle, thrush.*

threw, 130, *throve.*

thrild upon a pinn. See *tirled* below.

tilt, *puff* (*of wind*).

till, *to, on.*

tirled at the pin, *trilled or rattled, at the door-latch, to obtain entrance.*

tither, *other.*

tocher, *dowry.*

toomly, *empty.*

tow, *rope.*

triest, tryst, *make an assignation.*

true, *trow.*

twain, *part.*

twal, *twelve.*

twin, *part;* twinn'd, *deprived, parted.*

unco, *unknown, strange.*

virr, *strength.*

vow, *interjection of surprise.*

wad, *would.*

wadded, *wagered, staked.*

wadding, *wedding.*

wae, waeful', *sad, sorrowful.*

waked, *watched.*

walde, *would.*

wale, *choice.*

wambe, wame, *womb.*

wan, *reached.*

wand, wandie, *bough, wand, stick.*

wan na in, *got not in.*

wap, *throw.*

wappit, *beat, fluttered.*

warde, 35, *advise, forewarn.* Percy.

wark, *work.*

warlock, *wizzard.*

warstan, *worst.*

warstled, *wrestled.*

wat, *know.*

water-kelpy, *a malicious spirit thought to haunt fords and ferries, especially in storms, and to swell the waters beyond their ordinary limit, for the destruction of luckless travellers.*

wavers, 40, *wanders.*

wa'-wight, 383, *waled, picked, strong—men or warriors.* See vol. vi. 220, v. 15.

wean, *child.*

wee, *little.*

weed, *dress.*

weir-horse, *war-horse.*

werne, *were.*

wha is aught, *who is it owns.*

whang, *thong.*

whaten, *what.*

wicht, *strong, agile.*

widdershius, *the contrary way round about.*

wide, *wade.*

wight, *strong, agile.*

win. *arrive, reach, come, get.*

winna, *will not.*

winsome, *charming, attractive.*

woe, *sad.*

won up, *got up.*

wood, *mad;* wood-wroth, *mad with anger.*

worth, *be;* wae worth you *sorrow come upon you.*

wow, *alas.*

wraith, *wroth*.
wrongous, *wrong*.
wull, *will*.
wyte, *punish, blame*.

yae, *every*.
yare, *ready*.
yeats, yetts, *gates*.

yestreen, *yesterday*.
yird-fast, *fixed in the earth*.
yode, *went*.
yont, *beyond, further off*.
Yule, *Christmas*.

ze, zet, zour, &c., *ye, yet, your*.

END OF VOL. II.